BRANDON CASTILLO

JUDAS

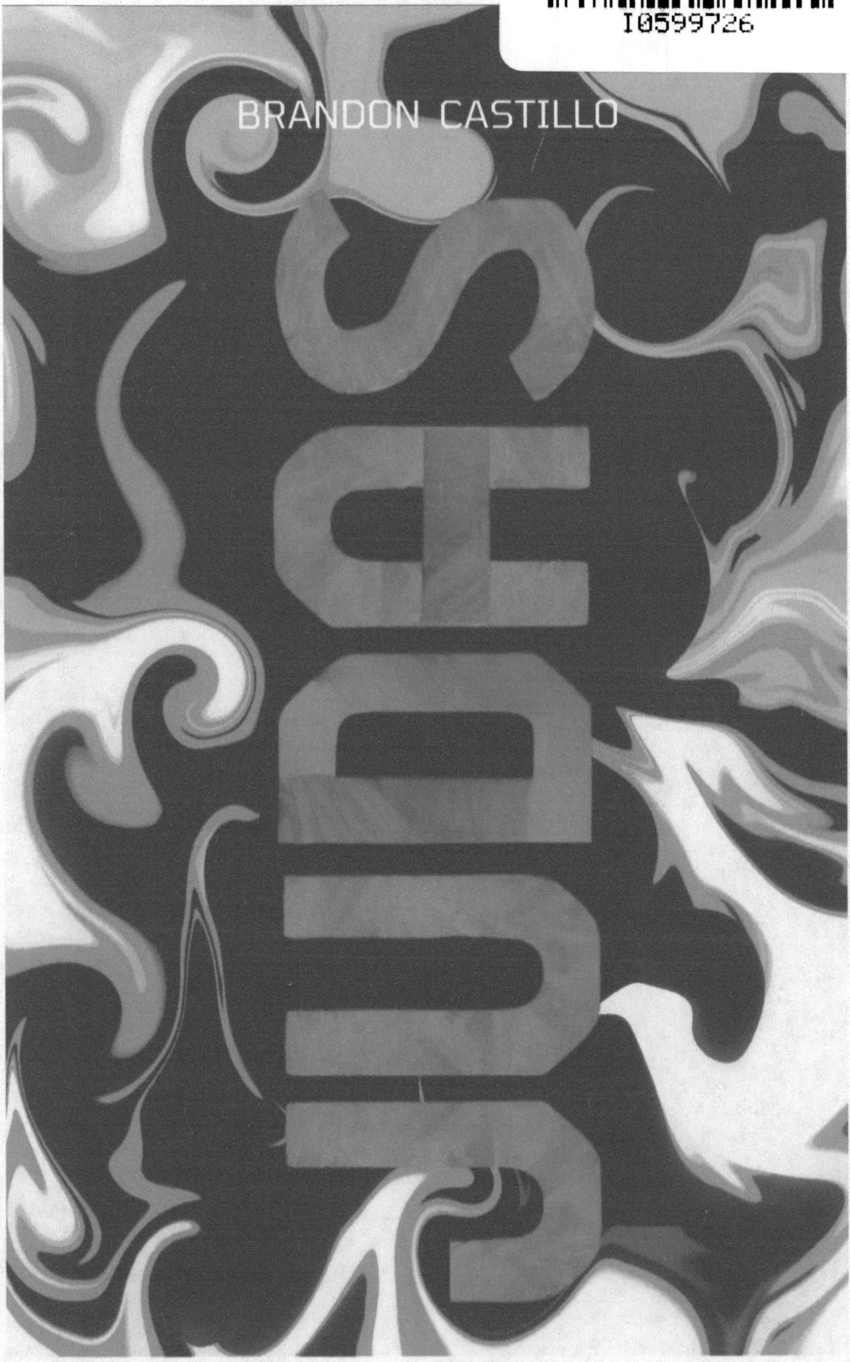

JUDAS

BRANDON CASTILLO

CASTILLO PRESS

ꞯ

Judas is a work of fiction. Names, characters, places, and incidents are the product of the author's imagination, or are used fictitiously. Any resemblance to actual events, locales, businesses, or persons, living or dead, is entirely coincidental.

Copyright © 2025 by Brandon Castillo

All rights reserved. No part of this book may be reproduced or transmitted in any form by any means, electronic or mechanical, including photocopying, recording, or by any information and retrieval systems, without the written permission of the copyright owner.

Published by Castillo Press

Book design by Brandon Castillo

ISBN: 979-8-9939784-0-6

First Edition

JUDAS

JUDAS PLAYLIST

For the oblivious heroes.

JUDAS

PART ONE : HABITUAL

This prolonged quarantine fails to grant me even a shard of hope cut with free will, revealing an end to where life mirrors what I once considered normal. That image is now intangible, lying adjacent to a form of happiness that lingered within life's expectancies. It was all a simple factor of what I managed to deem conventional, even if it was far from parallel to my desires.

The seasonal transition shows no remorse, nor does it play a pivotal role in our very few found moments of happiness. We neared ten degrees yesterday, and that alone was a celebratory number as we've failed to exceed anything over that in the past few months. The cold that persists through the bunker forces us to sleep in layers of clothing. I often lie in silence—reminiscing the heat I once took for granted. The daily privileges that I managed to belittle in lieu of my then situation. Yet this lifestyle contrasts my past as I once held the opportunity to rebel against my conditions, satisfied or not. Here I am, confined. For the better must I add, despite my arrogant desperations.

My skills have advanced in our five months here. Maddox has taught me how to fish, garden, and hunt the nearby animals—now a necessity for survival as our food suppliers declared their ties to the grounds more of a liability than it had been prior, forfeiting their relation to us. While the declaration at hand took place behind closed doors, it was evident that our trio had been the motive. Far from beneficiary to our notorious reputation, not that we shared a room with superiority. Yet it left no opportunity for improvement. Or rather, justification.

Maddox and I rose early enough to catch the morning's sunrise, which only briefly greets us with its inability to cut through the thick clouds. Lucky enough, no sign of rain or snow is present to disrupt our morning. Still, the crisp air pierces through my clothes, despite all my extra layers of clothing, making any movement uncomfortable to approach. Every step I initiate is greeted by the ache in my bones. Every breath I take is followed by a thin plume of smoke. I've noticed that my skin is much paler than usual in winter, leaving no room for my tan to express itself through the ash that accumulates in every crevasse of my body.

My hands tremble because of the cold, yet their posture fails to shift. A sheer reflection of the pain induced on my exposed knuckles. A broader reflection on the focus that lies behind my gaze. My eyes steady on the eyes of he who stands before me. His curiosity questions my firearm, and his presence to the unknown tells me that he does not recognize his fate. He doesn't draw concern to the threat I impose. Perhaps his innocence shines brighter than his intelligence, not a reflection of his own faults. Rather, a reminder that experiences live on a spectrum. And we just so happen to fall on opposite ends. For a moment, I desire his way of being. However, that doesn't steer away from my content. I can only assume that faulty experiences do that to people. Their bitter presence only results in a lack of compassion for some, if not all. That's the poison of comparison. You haven't gone through what I have gone through, so why should I care for you?

Much time doesn't pass by before I pull the trigger. In bygone times, I would have feared to follow through. This explicit moment would have brought me to tears with no sign of resignation. However, I near the body and show no remorse. The only shake in my body is a continuous fault of the cold's attraction to my lack of gloves. I push my foot against his rib to assure his demise, but a slow turn follows. Quickly, I take another shot of confirmation right between his innocent eyes. Now, any possible movement would be his soul's departure.

I don't reflect on whether or not he has a family back home, waiting for his steady return. I, too, have people who are expecting my immediate arrival. And amongst the few who are family to me, I have a job to fulfill for their livelihood.

I waste no time in tying his legs with loose cloth for an easy transfer. However, we are fairly one mile out from the bunker. Our awaited commute will not offer ease whatsoever. Perhaps we take this moment to convey gratitude towards the daylight who is a day's worth away from its repetitive slumber.

"Everything alright?" Maddox questions.

Confused, I flutter my eyebrows. He nods to my trembling hands. "It's cold," I assure, firm in my response to draw no assumptions of weakness.

Suddenly, he removes his winter gloves before handing them to me. I'm appreciative of his gesture, yet a sole second remarks my hesitation to accept it. Not for his lack of hand warmth. Neither for them being nonessential—my hands are begging for the comfort that lies inside those threads. I guess my ego just fails to recognize that he is the love of she who I once sought a life with.

"Take them," he insists, placing them into my bitter palms. I softly thank him, proving that once again my facade reigns as my greatest talent. Externally at the least, as I can't concur with what it has done to me internally. But I'll oblige with the tranquility it offers those around me.

We draw a countdown before making our first attempt in carrying the body. If I were to make an estimate, my exhaustion deems this deer to be around 350 pounds. Quite a jump from what we usually hunt, but enough to feed the bunker for the rest of the week.

I opt to take the front and lead our journey. A sheer sign of trust. And despite our lack of communication throughout, along with my crippled ego, Maddox and I managed to continue building a strong bond within my time here. He was one of few to understand my past. Long conversations led him to admit he would go lengths if his folks were still alive. Those same conversations drew us in continuous redirection of topic. We won't be able to erase our past. Admittedly, it's my daily struggle. But minimal attempts are valuable to our health, and I've learned my makeshift ignorance is beneficial to Maddox. As his is to me.

We begin dragging the deer only minutes into our journey. It's not long before Maddox requests a sudden break—his demeanor showing no sign of exhaustion, rather a gulp of excitement. He redirects himself towards some plants that reside beside a tree. I slowly approach behind him as he kneels down to observe the flowers, his enthusiasm palpable.

"This one I've seen before," he remarks, eyes still on the flower. "Lady slipper," he continues.

"What?" I question.

"It's the name," he reaffirms.

His eyes lie still with a glow before he begins to dig a few out, assuring they will be a great addition to the bunker's greenhouse. He has a garden plot dedicated to plants he finds within our perimeter. A healthy distraction to coincide with the surrounding misery. I dabble in the activity and can admit its ability to ease the mind. Not that it's a remedy, rather a temporary desensitizer. Our days align with the task at hand as the bunker's disconnection concluded with our reappointment to huntsmen and gardeners. A marked decision concealed behind a lack of staff to pick up the labor. However, Aria's reappointment to the kitchen assures that the decision lies behind the very few opinions garnered towards us. Pleasing the handful, even if the large sum does not oppose. Democracy didn't exist in our case, but I gracefully wish there was a way I can express my appreciation to Dr. Harrison for this settlement. My request for it would have felt like a burden. I can't fathom how self-centered I would have come off if I were to initiate a plea for my detachment from a nurse's role.

Soon enough, Maddox fastens the flowers, and we resume our journey. Yards in, we pierce through the chill and attempt to converse, but our unsteady breaths force it to be short lived. Besides, the only task our mouths are willing to partake in is a constant tremble, pleading for warmth. The weather is far from admirable, but I still hold these woods to high regards. Nature's offering is a gift that I wish I wasn't forced to take advantage of, but life led me here. And my life's handouts were no other than a Labyrinth compiled of un-circumstances and shadowed by catastrophes. I guess I learned some lessons. I must shamelessly admit that I still carry opposition towards accepting whether or not these said lessons were deserving. However, to an extent I am prepared to hold myself accountable towards any future expectancies' life throws my way, to which there would be little room for a victim shaped mentality. And despite my urge to neglect the past, there is not a day I rise to the thought that I am the same person I once was. Rather, I envy him. That person was stripped away from my hands at the sake of my own actions. My lack of control. I'd say no ounce of stability could have stitched the fragmented estate of my mind, but I fear that looms a circle of excuses. And while I make every attempt to deem my measures valuable to my morals, how indifferent does that make me than those who sit on the opposite end of my values. Evaluating the larger picture places us on the same pedestal. That is whether I like it or not. Perhaps a rush of reality has washed over me declaring me a stronger person, but that solely makes me no less of what I am made out to be: a wanted murderer.

The process of skinning a deer would be deemed inhumane if you were to explain the means to someone of little knowledge. It would sound even more cruel when explaining butchering. The more you continue to highlight the costs of hunting, the more you're left off with a price akin to survival.

I've become used to what would once cause my stomach to turn, and the smell no longer bothers me. Rather, I now only despise the cold that adheres to my job. My bones feel frail in this temperature, and I do not deem my layers enough to offer me the warmth I ever so desire in these long hours of labor.

My apron marks the blood of the deer, its crimson dye lingering within the threads no matter how many washes it goes through. Each stain welcomes the next, and I try not to ponder on the bloodline that lives on my uniform.

"This is going to last us a while," Maddox says, smiling at all the meat we've garnered.

It is nearly three buckets full, and I almost feel sorrow for the predator who likely had its eye on this deer. It is bound to last us a few weeks, but perhaps it would have been far more a prolonged feast for he who fell out of luck to outhunt our next meal.

"Well, we still got a lot of mouths to feed," I remind him. The bunker houses more people than we can count on both our hands combined. And I must admit, I wish more of them recognized how much work goes into assuring their next meal. More, when we are not so lucky to be embraced by the heat of the sun year round. Had the means of survival not lied on my shoulders, I would much rather starve than hunt my next meal in weather suitable for an arctic fox.

"We'll manage," he offers his promise, and I soon hope my response did not come off as rude. He is one of the last persons to deserve the matters of my frustration. He is kin, and walks these grounds with honest intentions.

"Sorry if I sounded rude," I apologize.

Quickly he shakes his head in opposition. "You weren't rude at all," he assures, before offering to be the one to take today's product over to Aria.

Every given chance he extends me the option to do so, and still I have never accepted his offer. I often stay back and clean up the mess we made. The terms between Aria and I are rather tense, and I hate that I fear to lock eyes with someone who I could never take my eyes off of. So much, that I rather cope with the cold I ever so detest, than embrace the warmth of the kitchen.

"I'll go," I say, his reaction rather shocked, but he makes an effort to conceal it.

He nods, the concern in his eyes falling behind his awareness between what divides Aria and I, rather than his intimidation of me. He is ignorant to what past her and I had; still, that would be no reason for me to avoid her. I could also benefit from the rush of warmth that the small commute has to offer.

This bucket weighs near 50 pounds, and surprisingly, it is minuscule to what I've since lifted in my time here. It is the trek that taunts the pace in my breath. Turning the corner greets me to Aria. Her early presence means she is operating today's breakfast. I wouldn't know her day-to-day schedule as we barely make formal contact. No harsh event between the two of us highlights our subtle detachment. Rather, we are two friends who drifted apart at the sake of a couple occurrences. And I can name the one and only thing that got in between us, but I'd be using the wrong form of noun. Not that any other person should carry the weight of our friendship on their shoulders. She and I are alike in our inability to vocally express what's on our minds. More so, in our inability to come to terms with what we self-proclaim as no bother. I assume I understand this much of her because we are so alike within our different ways. Still, I manage to make a swift reaction at her gaze, and no matter how prepared, or rather, unfazed I should be for our interactions, I fear what could quickly turn into an awkward confrontation. Reasonable to her emotions, yet inconsiderate to the intentions of others.

She's lost weight since our arrival, and I wouldn't put depression past the reason behind it. She was already so thin, so seeing her in this state draws a pang to my heart. Luckily, the brown in her eyes and the soft curly flow of her hair leaves no room to fixate on her nearly exposed collar bone.

I deliver a smile along with the venison, placing it onto the nearest steel counter. She acknowledges my presence before I assure her we have more venison in the root cellar.

"He weighed in at 342," I say, my smile embarrassingly forcing itself onto my messy attire. "About a week's worth of meat, but we got enough protein stored to last at least three."

"Thank you," she softly responds.

Silence suddenly floods the room, leaving us in a careless stance. The awkward tension that fills the gap between us would be easier to cut than the fresh venison that stares at us. Realizing our conversation has no room to reignite, I draw my attention back to where I came from and swiftly attempt my exit. That is until she stops me, presenting me with some courtesy tea she prepped. "I figured the cold outdoors is unbearable," she claims. "I used the mint leaves Maddox grew to brew it for the two of you." She hands me two large thermals, their heat traveling through my threaded gloves the moment I retrieve them. I accept her gratuity with a subtle thank you. These thermals are very warm, and will surely fulfill a double purpose.

She smiles before her eyes meet my blood stained jeans hiding below my apron. Butchering is not the cleanest of jobs, and far from beneficial to my appearance. And the look in her eyes do spell out her discomfort in my appearance, a probable response to how part of her remembers me and the trauma that continues to lie within her. "Don't worry. It's not Maddox's," I joke—her reaction quickly reflecting that my humorous attempt to ease her concern falls flat. I take her silent response as a sign to make my departure. At the minimum, I want to leave no room for judgment against my honest intention.

Obvious circumstances led me to pause my route for a small request from Dr. Harrison. I solely want a spare pair of winter gloves for Maddox. His generous act left him exposed to the cold, and a small part of me couldn't bare watching him try to conceal the tremble of his knuckles. The larger part appreciated his minor deed in lieu of my comfort.

I'd be deemed a liar if I were to deny the panic that increases my pulse upon approaching Harrison's office. Or from making any slight contact with her, whether intentional or against my will. The admiration our trio once held within these walls are still controversial. Her presence played an indicator as much as protector, and it's a shame that I find worry in our interactions. However, there is no memory worth storing that lies within the walls of her office. Every meeting came with faulty news. Luckily, my approach comes with a selfless request, minimal to anything I could desire.

I notify Harrison's guard that I wish to speak to her, to which he obliges, but assures I am aware of his stark stare prior to delivering my request. I first found trouble understanding what exactly is the pivotal reason behind her need for protection within these steel walls. I don't necessarily project an event where those who stand beside us turn on her. Nor am I completely familiar with the majority of them to draw that assumption. However, her trustful demeanor cancels out the need to fret. Or rather, to draw attention to what could possibly happen. I guess that's where she's managed to be successful in her operation. And where I would have failed had I been in her position.

Soon enough, I am allowed to enter her vicinity and my body language makes no attempt to design a facade—my eyes glued to the floor, my legs no desire to approach the seat. Luckily, her greeting cuts what could have been a long unwanted moment of silence.

"Sorry to bother you," I softly say, to which she assures is no concern.

"What brings you here today?" She draws to question, before shining a light on my abilities to avoid her. "You're like a mouse, and I hope you don't take that the wrong way."

I assure you, no offense was taken, though I do wonder if any snark lives hidden behind her remark.

"Is this about your father?" she questions.

I slowly shake my head, observing her ease. My response is dictated by my knowledge of my father's being. That awareness offers no fret, and while I nervously don't take this opportunity to properly thank her for what she has done thus far, I hope she's aware that I will always be indebted for her efforts. It's not long before I return her the same ease with my small request.

"Do we happen to have a pair of gloves?" I question, the look on her face preserves a wash of confusion. A reaction to which I comprehend—my hands are already snugged in thread. "For Maddox," I reassure.

It's no secret that necessities have been running low, but my request stands on the opposite end of my luxury. If it weren't, I would have never insisted on asking her for them. Instead, I would have dealt with the cold, as I have been for much of this winter. In that scenario, I saved myself the interaction I prefer to avoid.

"There should be a pair on the top shelf." She hands me keys to the bunker's storage, and I thank her for the accommodation.

She assures I make aware of a large bin filled with blankets living on the far end of the storage room. "Please relay to Maddox that I need him to pass out spare blankets to the patients," she says. "At his earliest convenience, but preferably mine."

I present my accessibility to do so, I truly do not mind the extra work. Besides, it would be nice to spare Maddox from more labor, he deserves some time. And despite my honest efforts, Harrison's quick reaction wastes no time in confirming my expectations.

"I don't think that would be necessary," she says, my generous embarrassment takes a stand, provoking my sanity for a reaction. However, I urge my patience to resist an irritable dispense. "I have other work for you," she continues.

When I re-offer her my attention, she instructs that I replace our heating tank.

"The current one is running low, and the weather is expected to drop much more than what we've been graced with," she says, her tone rather sarcastic. "It's the last of our propane, but I'm not too worried. Your friend has offered his time to work on solar heating."

Slowly, I nod.

"He's extremely smart, you know," she adds.

"I've learned a lot from him." My voice softens. The plush in my tone indicates that I don't want this interaction to overstay its welcome. Soon, the route of the conversation expedites my queue to leave.

"I will work on that right now," I assure her, as I make my exit.

I wouldn't say that I am the most familiar with changing the heating tanks, but my survival instinct insists that this shouldn't lie far from common sense. I would have accepted Maddox's offer of assistance, but I perceived Harrison's request for swiftness on both of our parts to be more of a subtle demand. Not contrary to her position, nor does it spell out an unwarranted ask. She wants to ensure the patients' needs are fulfilled. Thankfully, Maddox gave me a brief set of verbal instructions.

One thing's for certain, this 100-gallon tank is no heavier than most of the things I have been challenged to handle in my time here. That doesn't take away from the fact that I utilized a dolly to transport it. The journey the deer required left its footprint on my energy—a sheer indicator that I should savor the days I have off, rather than occupy them in spare labor. I accept my current ways as a reflection of my past. Inhabiting my days with tasks was a form of suppressing the turmoil that fueled my mind. And while I wouldn't classify my continuous efforts as a remedy, I still find worth in the few minutes of distraction made in those extra-long hours.

After finally reaching the heating room, I become wary of the atmosphere. Thickness strikes through the silence and the sensation travels through my ear drums. I do not intend to raise superstition, instead I accept it as a reflection of how much lower this room resides as opposed to the 50-foot depth already accumulated by the main bunker.

I turn off the heat before opening the propane chamber per Maddox's explanation. Luckily, no sign of leakage, though not to be expected, as the ease in movement of the tank makes the lack of gas evident.

Soon, I fail to pertain the sufficient amount of grip to loosen the valve on the tank and my strain quickly draws a reminder that Maddox insisted I utilize the wrench to do so. "There's a wrench close by," he said earlier. "You won't be able to get it open without it." I only giggled, as I thought it was a friendly testament to my strength. I can now see that I am proven wrong.

I look around in search of the wrench. The lack of artificial lighting only camouflages the tool—a singular lightbulb held by a string offers glow, and my squint only proves how useless it is. My fatigue fails to encourage the desire to even look for it. Still, I continue to look around the heating room, and despite its name, the temperature matches the cold ambiance of outside, only adding to my frustration.

I continue to make use of the lone bulb, until my attention makes a sudden shift. A few feet behind the chamber resides a square vault door. Enough to suffice a human's entry, but far from typical. And to retrace the swift mention of camouflage, its appearance makes a chameleon on a tree obvious. Its steel condition akin to the chamber, mimicking what could be an operating lever.

I turn the lever in hopes of a closet welcoming me to what I seek. It's slightly tight, but no opponent to the valve. It feels like a never-ending turn, and my apprehensive approach wakes my fret from its slumber. I ignore it, however, as neglecting my internal concern is a practice I've consumed a long time ago. Again, my emotional practices might lie on the opposite end of ideal, but my self consideration still fails to take the main stage. Perhaps it just doesn't feel welcomed. I can admit that I've never been so kind to it.

Soon enough, the latch's detachment is followed by a loud echo. To which does not bounce off the stone walls of this room, rather what lies on the opposite end. A quick recollection of thought reaffirms that I won't be introduced to a closet. The wave of mirrored clang that I just caused does not emerge from a small space. And if it could catch a glimpse of my heart, the rapid beating would travel alongside the echo with no end, each pulse louder than the other.

Slowly, I pull the door open, taking initiative to peek my head through. To my surprise there is no complete darkness. A wash of red lights illuminates a path with an end far from my already perfect vision's capabilities. The space closely imitates the entry to the bunker, yet its final destination is unclear.

I don't proceed any further. Rather, I close the door and assure its lever is completely sealed. I want to promise myself that I won't dwell on what I just saw, but promises to myself are often broken. Even then they are at risk of eruption—I speak from experience.

I look around, unsure if my eyes are following a need for understanding or the wrench. A few feet away from the door, my foot collides with something. I flinch at the sharp sound, but it is not driven by fear, rather the awakening from my state of mind. I look down and fortunately, I found what should be celebrated as treasure at this point.

My confirmation of it too lies on the subtle directions from Maddox. "Turn off the heat before you do anything. The wrench is beside the chamber." And beside the chamber it no longer is; I've unwillingly kicked it over a few feet. Still, it resides, and if I don't utilize this wrench soon, the cold will slowly start to invite itself into the halls of the bunker, ignorant to its unwelcome.

I grab the tool and continue what I was instructed to do. Each turn of the valve produces a shrieking sound which pierces its way to my ear drums. And while I wish this was music to ears, not even the fight to tune it out cancels my racing mind. Still pondering on what lies in the tunnel behind the door.

Oatmeal, canned peaches, and black coffee have been the recurring breakfast. Occasionally, we are offered a selection of preserved fruits. Still, I stick to the peaches or pears, as the mandarins are usually too tart for my liking. Again, this form of expression is far from an arrogant complaint—especially considering my past habits of skipping breakfast. Most meals to be frank. The knots that dictated my stomach made every swallow feel un-welcomed. And perhaps my nerves decided that I didn't occupy enough time to feed myself. When arms were open, however, the practice of consumption became unhealthy for the sake of distraction. My current routine is steady, and adjacent to the pace of my being. I'm okay. And as far as gaslighting myself into actually believing the accuracy of that statement—*things could be worse*—and I acknowledge that with a heavy heart.

Before I finish my oatmeal, little Amir has an empty plate. He often escapes from his mother and dines in the greenhouse with Maddox and I, as we frequently segregate ourselves in here for some peace of mind. Amir, for the sake of feeling included.

I pass him my peaches. "Have them," I say. The hunger on his face now masked by his gratitude, making any excess hunger that lingers within me worth it.

He is the only child in the bunker, to which I am unsure if that should be taken as a grace or a shame. However, he keeps himself occupied around us—never do we mind his presence. His spirit is evidently lifted when he hangs out with us. I could only guess it fills the void he's missing from a normal childhood.

"Thank you," he whispers.

For a mind so innocent, he wasn't manipulated into a vendetta against me. Never did he even bring my past to further interrogation. I'm in awe at his lack of arrogance, as not many kids his age would share the same mindset—their brain being a tool so easily shifted. And the idea of his feelings being a facade doesn't cross my mind, as there is no sensible reason for it.

"Dr. Harrison says I'm getting better." He looks down to hide his subtle smirk. I raise my brows and widen my glance to present a surprised mien, but I am already aware of the improvement of his well-being. I often check up on his status with Nova when I get the chance. Other times I seek an answer from the fellow nurses. However, I never inquire with Amir because the topic is too sensitive to be a direct exchange. Even now, and regardless of the news being positive, I am welcomed by a slight dawn to his words. I hate that a soul like his has to undergo what he has. Being on the confrontational end forces me to face the truth—he is fully aware that the strain on his life, while common for some, is not typically normal nor is it fancied after.

"Am I still getting that jump rope?" he asks.

I chuckle. "Of course," I assure. "So long as you fulfill your end of the promise," I continue, and soon Maddox's concerning eyes attempt to meet mine.

Again, Amir hides his smile. Behind it, so much hope—a common denominator between the two of us, but my mind repeatedly highlights our diminishing medical needs. I could only plea that it doesn't affect him. I do not wish for it to negatively impact a soul, but he is selfishly prioritized on my list. No one's status has an expected final date, it just slowly happens. And I wish I could say the opposite to one's demise, but evidently it would be sheer lies.

I don't want to meet the day a lack of needs strips his already extended finish line. In that unfortunate scenario, I wouldn't have to blame myself, because the blame is already premature.

A distant celebration from Maddox puts a sudden halt to our conversation. Swiftly, he props his head out from his garden plot, before calling us over. And from afar, I can already designate the lady slippers from earlier this morning.

"They look amazing," I claim with my approach in reference to the plants whose stems show no sign of exhaustion.

He shakes his head—not in disagreement, but at our faulty focus. "This," he points to a minuscule batch of stems who look as if they've hardly seen a day on earth. They live on a plot that hangs above the one below. "Some of the scientists helped me artificially create a Jade Vine." He pauses. "For Aria."

My cheeks flush out a color that resembles the Lady Slippers, but I try to mask it with a smile. "I've never seen one before," I admit. To which he assures he hasn't either.

He pulls out his sketchbook from the tool shelf and proudly reveals a sketch of the said flower. "Aria drew it," he ensures, before revealing that it is her favorite plant. "Well, her mother's at least. It reminds her of her younger days with her grandparents back in the Philippines."

I am not sure if the slow flow of my stomach attests to the sudden mention of Cynthia, or the fact that I failed to know her and Aria's favorite plant. Perhaps both remarks are assaulting me, but to avoid disappointment in myself, I'll blame it on the hunger that lingers.

Again, I put on my mother's famous smile, before Amir breaks the awkward silence. "When will they fully bloom?" he questions.

"I don't know." Maddox is quick to admit his ignorance. A normal response when considering the artifact that determines the livelihood of the vine. We can't guarantee that it will fulfill its expectations, nor that it will indeed be a Jade Vine. I do not doubt the experiment, nor do I doubt the intelligence of the scientists. But everything is as I labeled: an experiment, and the only driven factor behind all of them is hope. I guess hope truly is a common denominator. Many latch on to the idea of it, others quickly lose it.

I take a closer look at the stems, and from the corner of my eye I can see Maddox eager for my approval. His smile vibrant, to which I nod and return the same excitement. Except he doesn't seek my approval of the vine—I personally find myself unsure on the entirety of the creation, and my brain only produces a fog when I attempt to seek an answer. I've always veered more street smart than textbook savvy, my only fault in maneuvering that form of intelligence has been my heavy heart. Rather, he wants me to assure him that his efforts will enlighten Aria. I, in fact, know they will. Admittedly, there is no better person to be the courier of the happiness he gracefully provides her. Even from a distance, I can distinguish her shift of disposition.

"Can I ask you something?" Amir suddenly blurts out as he looks up at Maddox smiling ear to ear.

Maddox kneels down. "Go for it."

"Are you and Aria boyfriend-girlfriend?"

Maddox subtly laughs, looking around for an escape from the question, rather an answer. His awkward essence bounces off the stems before him. Perhaps he is unsure of their status, but the blind can determine that they are far more than friends, and while I might be just a bit jealous of it, I am happy for them.

"Something like that," he assures him.

The sound of the curtain rings brushing on its rod has become engrained in my head. Far from the ideal tune, but enough for me to mimic. It's quite often on repeat, as I find myself visiting my parent's cubical multiple times a day. Dad's body reacted quickly to the treatment. He does, however, have to continue it for some time for evident reasons. Despite the treatment eliminating much of his hair, Harrison would still classify the process an unfair fight. On his illnesses end at least, as it showed early signs of a white flag in only the first couple of months. Dad doesn't appear to ache when he is connected, but I believe we already shared the only moment in time where I was able to decipher how he feels behind his facade. His eyes are tired, the bags under carrying the weight of his exhaustion. Selfishly, I would rather see the bags living beneath his eyes force them open than be the reasoning for their infinite shut. I'd be a liar if I were to oppose the guilt that dawns on me throughout his recovery. A few cubicles down are patients who've endured the pain of treatment for years, yet their internal war laughs at their demise through a loop perceived as infinite. But if I let that guilt pioneer, I'd reclaim the same backbone I did many months ago.

All eyes shift when I step into their cubical, yet my eyes choose to lock with Nova's. She seems to be near the end of her task, to which I pause my entrance as I don't want to interrupt. "Sorry," I assure. "I'll return later." I attempt to initiate my departure, except Nova insists I stay. "No, please." She grins. Her smile is just as welcoming as her eyes. I accept her open arms and station myself beside Mom.

"Todo bien?" Mom asks, her tone soft.

I nod. "Yea, why wouldn't it be?" I counter out of genuine curiosity, before she draws attention to this being my third visit today. "I've seen you more here than I did back home," she continues.

I laugh, only because I intend to dismiss the concern behind her honest confrontation.

"We're under different circumstances—"

"We were when we first got here," she interrupts me, before further assuring my father health, confirming that I am aware of his improvement more than anyone else.

I look down, not only because I have nothing to say, but because I don't want her to see that I felt a strain from her words. Luckily, my cheeks don't wash in red from my own embarrassment, still, my efforts in concealing my interpretation is short lived as she reappoints the conversation to their appreciation for making myself present. "I just don't want you to over worry yourself," she says. I full heartily understand her approach. Perhaps, my way of secreting my worry requires more than a sole smile. I didn't consider my excessive visits a probable indicator, as much as I hate to do so now. Before I can dwell on this any longer, she insists I make an attempt to direct some of my attention towards Aria. "It seems like she can use your company."

"We spoke this morning," I reveal, recalling my delivery to the kitchen. Not much came out of it, but it played a purpose, one of which didn't highlight her need for my company. Or perhaps it did and I've actually lost my abilities to perceive her genuine feelings.

"Did you ask how she was feeling?" Mom questions.

The shift in my demeanor becomes an answer within itself. Fortunately, Nova announcing her completion puts any further conversation between Mom and I to rest. For now at least, but I currently refuse to feed the lingering tension any more than we had in that short span. And if there comes a time where we do nourish its undesired presence, let it be starving before we budge.

Despite my mother's previous concern, I still ask Dad if he's feeling okay. He smiles before assuring he feels great. Perhaps I already expected his answer to be a copy of what he had informed me earlier in the day, but I still felt the need to satisfy my initial intention in visiting. I look over at Mom, whose smile paints her appreciation for me, but still it is sketched in concern.

Nova accepting my helping hand makes for a swift departure from my parents' cubicle. My mother's concern didn't necessarily force me out, but it did create an awkward bubble that I needed to escape. Now I sit in the nurse's room while Nova fulfills her daily labor. The sight of her cleaning the medical equipment draws back memories. My position as a nurse was short lived, but in that long-felt time I learned that the job demands a heart of armor. I recall the moments where I continuously asked myself if helping others can cause so much strain, how do the coast's nurses aligned with Reign's agenda manage their sanity? And despite never having a satisfying answer, I repeatedly assumed a large sum fake it.

"Here," Nova extends her reach, as she offers a variety of supplements from the cupboard. "Take these."

I look at the mix of capsules out of curiosity. When she takes notice of my oddity, she assures me they are safe. "I've noticed your body isn't retaining the necessary vitamins, so I pulled a variety out for you," she says, before explaining the purpose of each. "These right here should help you manage stress." She points to the large white one in the center.

I smile, making no attempt to hide my admiration for her. I can't mask my value for her attention to my health. It is not something I even consider myself, as I solely live content and deem any uncertainties as a normal part of our lively transition. And while I appreciate every ounce of her approach and attention, I can't accept her selfless offer. Not when there are those who could benefit from them much more. I've taken enough from the people of the bunker, and don't see myself benefiting from these vitamins as much as they can.

When I reject them, Nova replies, "We have a year's supply. We might even have more if the scientists dedicate more time to their production."

I waver with hesitation, but embrace her concern and take the supplements. My initial disposition was led by my urge to spare as much as I can for the patients. Perhaps I am blinded to my needs, but if I don't take my own health into account, I will lead myself to be not just another patient, but one who long since chose his own fate.

6

My heavy breaths bounce off these steel walls failing to obtain a proper pattern. Still, I tend to make light of it, as it is the only form of symphony I can acquire to get me through my workout. I often lose count of how much exercise I complete within a set, usually resulting in late nights. Right now, I could estimate close to 40 bench presses, but the ache and vibration in my chest insists it's much more. And while I use every ounce of my energy to shake through another, my arms dictate an end to my set. The decision leaving its mark as my homespun dumbbells impact the ground. The cement that once lived inside the plastic molds now broken into pieces, and the pole I used to hold them together only stares at me. I sit up and take a moment to stare back at the destruction, still breathing, yet the new inhales draw a sense of frustration.

After catching my breath and playing eye tag with each broken piece of cement, I decide to ignore the demolition and work on my abs. I begin to drag myself on to cool floors, until a shadow joins me from the corner of my eye. I flinch at the figure—my demeanor relaxed the moment I realize it is Amir's mother, Elandra. She stands beside the door, and I am unsure of how long she has been standing there, but my awkward response would be no different had it been many minutes or just a few seconds.

I can't fathom a reason for her being here other than my growing connection with Amir. Perhaps I've taken another brotherly role, but I will never reject someone's silent hope for companionship. Especially the only young boy suffering within these walls. For him, having me is like having two Maddox's. There's to say it is evident that Maddox is extremely important to him. Akin to an older brother.

"Sorry," she says, at my body's reaction.

I quickly assure her it's okay, and before the new awkward silence can get any longer, I pick myself up from the floor. And quickly my suspicion towards her unexpected visit, finds a conscience. "Is Amir okay?" I worry.

Quickly, she puts an end to my fret and assures me that he is doing just fine. "Actually, I haven't seen him this happy in a long time," she continues, her graceful expression being the first smile she has ever given me. I nervously grin as I become aware of her perception of Amir's daily escapes to be around Maddox and I. My embrace is only a response to her carefree demeanor. I didn't expect her to be okay with our association, however, nor did I expect her to discipline me for it.

"I came here to ask you a favor," she says.

Slowly, I nod.

"I want you to teach Amir to do what you do."

My eyebrows ruffle, as I do not fully comprehend what she is asking me for. Clearly, I do not need to say that I am confused, it is apparent in my expression alone, and she is more than aware of it. While she struggles to explain, she urges that she wants her son to know how to defend himself. "Shoot. Fight. Everything that will keep him safe in case of-," she stops, and butterflies renounce their residence in my stomach. I still can't find the ability to respond, as her concern is quickly interlocking itself on to me. There is only so much time before our secrecy is exposed, and living in the delusion that we are completely safe is far from beneficial to us. It is unfair to those fighting for their lives.

"Ok," I agree, but it is solely for her peace of mind, as mine refuses to envision Amir shooting at anything, let alone anyone. I do not think he should have to defend himself in such a manner.

Her stare hugs the worry that lives within her, and I can only imagine that she, too, hates the idea. Equally, if not, more than I.

"Thank you," she says, before wishing me a goodnight, and when I believe that our encounter is over, she turns. "Please don't tell him I asked you," she pleads.

I nod, still lost for words, unsure if agreeing to it was good for the sanity I'm meant to uphold.

She tries to offer another smile, but only half of it greets me before she departs—bidding me goodbye.

Today's sun hides itself behind the large pool of clouds. Enough to light our hunt, yet it seemingly does not suffice to wake the animals we pursue. I don't know how far out we've come thus far, but it seems like we've spent more time seeking than we have spent shooting our next meal. The first deer in sight ran the moment it heard our feet shift through the crisp leaves. That lasted no more than a few minutes and we have been out since 6 am. It is currently quarter till noon.

"I think we should call it a day," I tell Maddox, who remains ambitious as I also tend to be under pressure.

He shakes his head, "I don't want to go back empty handed."

"It wouldn't be our first time doing so—"

"But it will be our first time after making it this far off the grounds," he explains.

I try to not let my desperation disrupt his goal, but who's to say that we'll become successful with livestock out in this proximity. We haven't studied it enough to learn the habitual patterns within, and today solely feels like a gamble with luck rather than an assessment.

My peace of mind remains civil despite Maddox's urge. I know we got the bunker covered until at least the end of this month. Just three weeks out like I told Aria, and my estimates have always veered more towards accuracy. I assume his demeanor is being driven by the need for distraction, or to solely prove his abilities. To himself I should add, as I can attest that his intentions are never to be pretentious around me. Luckily, we're far past that stage.

"What's going on?" I abruptly question him, as I am sure our long hunting route was veered by his anxious thoughts.

He lies still, his eyes focused on the prey that has yet to make an appearance. Seemingly, he is on the verge of ignoring my question, but his eyes swiftly brush mine as he assures that nothing is wrong. I want to nag him for an answer; however, I always assumed we've made an unspoken rule to support each other's form of distractions. Rather, I nod. If he wants to draw attention to the hidden concern, he can do so.

Seconds pass before a sudden crack of leaves garners both of our attention. This time we aren't the ones initiating the sound. Maddox's eyes glow, and I pull out my binoculars to observe the area. Except nothing greets me through the lens. I steer around the whole proximity, and still it's as empty as it's been this whole time.

"Do you see it?" he asks.

"No," I say, the confusion evident in my tone. Only the trees stand their ground.

I want to consider the outdated use of equipment, but it's yet to disappoint us. Instead, I separate it from my face and fog the lenses before wiping them with my sleeve. The moment I do so, I quickly realize we are not the only ones here, nor is it anything that we can consume. Behind a tree, I notice a black boot. It's still, but evidently occupied. I quickly look over to the far right after I hear the same sound of shuffled leaves. Only this time it's louder than the last. Using that trunk as a shield is another boot. In a state of shock, I begin losing balance to the internal earthquake initiated by the beat of my heart. We wear the same boots, and I did not retrieve this pair from the grounds. I came with them.

"Run," I whisper, my attempt to alert Maddox falling short.

"What?" he asks.

"Run!" I yell, before drawing myself up to my feet and pulling him up with me. He's confused, and pleads I tell him what I saw, but the first gunshot was enough of an answer for him to match my speed and anxiety.

Amid my trek, I swiftly look back and a pool of Forcemen follow me. Too many to count, but I know we are outnumbered. I reclaim my focus only to trip on a log who could have resided in any other part of the hundreds of acres that surround us. As my face plants onto the damp ground, my gun falls out of my pocket. I lock eyes with the weapon, yet the swarm that approaches me guides me to get up and keep running. When I do, Maddox is nowhere to be found. "Maddox!" I shout, and the only response I receive is a gunshot from one of the Forcemen. I shriek, as it grazes my arm—only thankful for the adrenaline it gives me to run faster.

At the rate I endure, my pace matches the palpable beat of my heart. I lost count of how far I've run, but the refuge I seek feels to be out of reach, and the gunshots headed towards me only seem to get closer with every step. I didn't expect turmoil so soon. Even with the subtle signs in my conversation with Amir's mother. I was blinded by the idea of time, and my self caused misapprehension believed it will slow down at my expense. I failed to consider that I'll never be so privileged, and the consequences will continue taunting my stupidity.

I look around for Maddox, but the amount of Forcemen that surround me make him hard to spot. I do not recall him parting ways; I was under the impression that he had waited for me upon falling to the ground. He could be dead for all I know, but to dwell on him only endangers my safety.

I run through the heavy rain that only just began to trickle through the trees. The puddles greet my ankles—water seeping through my untied boots. I hate this feeling. I am a lone man now, and perhaps it is for the best, as I won't conflict anyone else. That's considering I survive this, but the chances are low, and I am ready to accept that. Everything in life has led up to this moment. Perhaps all of my problems stemmed from my failure to accept the fate who's long attempted to dictate my demise. He's never concealed his hate for me, and I am ready to come to my senses.

I drop down to my knees, their imprint deep into the mud. I'd take a deep breath, but my loss for air challenges the thought of it. I close my eyes and remain surrendered. "I give up," I whisper to myself. I am vulnerable, and my ego has long made its departure. Seemingly, so has the rain that once ran by my side—now nowhere in sight. Light slowly pierces through my tightly shut lids, the sun urging I am aware of his sudden greetings. Slowly, I look up. The area now empty—no Forcemen around.

I am confused, yet my body defies any movement I attempt to take for an answer. The only feelings now present are the chills that rush down my spine as a gun presses on the back of my skull. In this moment, I no longer care to seek an answer—the benefits of doing so are too miniscule. The answer, however, defies my neglect, as a gun alongside the feet of a beholder is making themselves visible to me.

My eyes take their time when making their journey up to their face, and when they do they meet the snark stare of Justin. He smiles, enjoying every moment of my vulnerability. Our eyes lock in a staring competition, and the moment he looks at the scar beside my eye proves that shooting me will be the only time he will ever beat me in anything. Unfortunately, it will also be the last, and surely he will enjoy that much more than I will.

Suddenly, a distant shriek echoes around the trees that surround Justin and I. The painful cry draws our attention, and at any moment, I can grab the weapon from Justin. However, I don't as I've accepted my fate. And that is more than okay for someone who is exhausted from life's daily dose of pain.

Standing at the near end of the woods is Maddox, whose sole stare could punch through Justin's skull. He isn't alone. Gripped tightly in his raised palms is the firearm I dropped yards away. He is set on his decision, and Justin's fearless demeanor only deems him more of a stray. Slowly, Maddox looks at me. I attempt to urge him to stop, but my vocal cords are still held captive. The only will I am allowed is a slow shake of my head, that attempt flaunting a failure as Maddox shoots the gun.

I don't move, nor flinch. Not because I've become numb, but because I expected it. And while I see the savior in Maddox, I weep the burden that will now follow him in his remaining lifetime. A tear drop steadily races down my cheek, and when it finally jumps off of my chin, Justin's body simultaneously hits the ground. I take my time turning my head, and when my eyes finally meet the corpse, his eyes, yet to close, meet mine. Except they are not brown. Neither is his hair. My vocal cords finally escape the moment I recognize his blonde locks hugging the grounded leaves, and his blue soulless eyes staring back at mine.

"Steven!" I yell, as my body awakens into the dark of my bunker. The shriek gutting its way into the sane stare of reality.

I catch my breath, my heart making itself noticeable as it beats against my chest. I remove my bed sheets who drank up my sweat, and I make every attempt to elude the terror that was displayed to me against my will. Slowly, I bring my hand over to my right arm, no blood proves that the shot was real.

Over to my right, no figure lies in the shadows of the bed across the room. I have gotten used to the blank presence that surrounds me, however, and I do appreciate the recurring loneliness, because my nightmares are not becoming a strain on anyone else. That's not to say they don't have any of their own.

Alone in the dining hall, I watch the television. I crave the nights I've managed to obtain a full night's sleep, but I do not envision that being a dream come true. My brain will not allow me to give a cold shoulder to the wounds I've endured, and my exhaustion repels my extended wake. I've learned to confront what agony awaits my slumber. I accept those few hours with a heavy heart in return for a lackluster induced rest. Most nights, I stare at the ceiling. Other nights, like tonight, I sit alone and consume myself in the lies that are spread about me. One would assume this should be a mechanism to numb the trauma, but those odds will never be in my favor. The rage solely intensifies, and I often question myself if that rage is led by shame or desired karma. My vexation lies beside the reality that I've been painted as the most vile. I've accepted the danger I have done, yet I am far from shaking hands with the false narrative. Reign and Mason have made themselves clear—their hunt never ends, and it won't stop until our trio is captured. I find it comically appealing that they're censoring their urge to terminate us the moment we meet again. That is if they ever get a hold of that privilege. They seek to use us as an example, and I am unsure that is fair. Not to me, but to those who find themselves in a position where their livelihood is dictated because of their illness. Those like Cynthia. Those like my father. Those like Amir, and everyone who are confined within these steel walls with treatment submitting to their veins.

Suddenly, I hear footsteps approaching behind me. However, my eyes are too attached to the screen to investigate who it is. "Can't sleep?" Leander's familiar voice collides with the news anchor's. For once, I'd be okay if the subtle sounds coming from the television would fill the room. I wouldn't describe my relationship with Leander as anything other than forcefully cordial for the time being. There is an underlying tension that strains our improvement, and it wouldn't take a genius to designate it. Despite that, I personally do not wish ill against him. The patients adore him and his guardianship of the bunker. He is night security and assures safety when dawn arrives. I should've expected his appearance, I just prefer our paths to have no encounters. Especially when it is just the two of us. I hate the continuous tension that follows me throughout, but if I were to choose its variety, it'll be the one that offers an easy excuse for an escape. Getting up now would only feed it for future use.

I shake my head, hoping that the effort is enough of an answer to his question.

"Are you sure you should be watching that?" he questions.

"How else am I supposed to be up to date with myself," I say, before realizing that my approach was more sarcastic than humorous. "Sorry." I continue, further explaining that I am still unable to process the lengthens of the narrative. And as I do so out loud, I realize the idiocrasy that follows my words. I caused coastal turbulence. Aside from the moral of it, it makes sense that they'd want to go lengths. The video footage works against my favor, and this isolation doesn't grant me the option to defend my name beyond the bunker. I only wonder what I would believe if I were witnessing this all go down from a different lens. However, I'll never admit to that thought out loud, as it validates those skeptical of my truth.

"Well, you say you didn't do it, right?" he asks, his tone leaving me confused as to whether or not it holds interrogation.

"Most of it," I spew under my breath, my heart aching as I look at the photo of Steven and his grandpa displayed on the screen. Yes, I did steal government product, and can genuinely care less about that, as the motives were held with good intention. I do twitch at the reality of what we've done to the guards, but had we lost that fight, despite initiating it, we'd be the ones dead and they'd be deemed heroes by those in power. Above it all, I would have never contemplated murdering Steven and his old man, even in the unlikely scenario that they'd interfere with my flee. My heart only offers compassion for those I hold close to it. It is safe to admit that I know what it offers to those on the opposite end. They were nowhere close to it.

Leander follows my eyes and notices the pain in my stare. Suddenly, he asks me about Steven and my heart drops at the abrupt interest. "He was a good kid," I manage to admit. "We only knew each other for some months, but even he will tell you that we were like brothers." I continue, and if I didn't feel the need to detain the tears that try to escape my eyes, I'd happily tell him all about him. His ambition. The huge personality that lies behind those nervous eyes. Or his knowledge that attests much of mine.

8

Each chop of deer is accompanied by the throb in my skull. Lack of sleep has caught on to me through migraines, but I've become accustomed to the pain that I once considered unbearable. I like to think that the cold works as a medical agent to numb the strain. Or maybe I've just trained myself into thinking so like I've done everything else.

We in fact did have a successful hunt this morning. My nightmare did not manifest what it pertained, and I have held the story hostage from everyone. Word gets around in the bunker, and I don't want my hallucination to be mistaken as what could be. That would only lead to catastrophe and it is fair to assure that we do not need anymore of it. Not that anyone would think my mind holds prophecy, but I don't put twisting and assumption of words past those within. It is already an evident fear, Amir's mother the first indicator. I don't want to add any more fuel to the fire than I already have.

"How long before everyone gets tired of having deer everyday?" I ask Maddox, who chops away at the remaining thigh.

He lets out a subtle laugh and shakes his head. "Hopefully soon enough."

I ruffle my brows in confusion.

"We've been hunting most days for months now," he continues. "We have to allow the deers time to breed. If not, we'll erase their nearby species."

I nod, considering the fact that our current rewards in hunting fall flat in comparison to our early days. Finding deer was as easy as finding water in the lake. Now, we are lucky if we manage to find one within the first hour of our hunt, and considering their thick way of being, I doubt they hold the mental capacity to hide from us.

"What happens then?" I ask. However, I know what his answer will entail. I solely want to see if his demeanor sides on the idea of leaving the perimeter.

"We improvise," he says. "I won't allow us to kill rabbits, and going further out into the woods only puts us at risk. Maybe hope for an early spring, so we can easily fish down by the creek."

I find relief in his subtle objection to extending our hunting route. I hate to offer power to the turmoil my mind produces, yet I can not shy away from the fear it places in me. I know what lies beyond the perimeter, and I've only recently started to actually feel safe here. I guess I can say I feel as safe as the rabbits that surround us. The first time I spotted one through my weapons scope, I took fire. I was embarrassed to have missed the shot against the rabbit's speed, but Maddox's deranged reaction assured that failure was the best scenario. He was quick to apologize for his frustration, but assured to not kill the rabbits.

"We can do without them," he had said. And after a moment of awkward silence, he explained his attachment to the small animal.

"They were the only animal around to trust me as a child," he said, assuring that his conscience refuses to let him break that trust. The red wash on his face proved that he was shy to admit his vulnerability towards them, but it was the official beginning of a genuine connection between the two of us.

Maddox takes his bin of chopped meat and places it beside my remaining pile. "This is the last of today," he says, before I take my bunch and add it to the bin. The pile emerges, yet I know it's going to be short lived. I know alternative foods put ease on our concern for the patient's nourishment, but I find myself a bit surprised at his tranquility. At least a bit of worry should be explicit, more from him than me. Leaning on a backup plan that is the only remaining part of the duo leaves us out of another route.

I visit Cynthia more often now than when she was conscious. I try to not let the guilt inflict me, because I'd end up deteriorated from my own actions. I've accepted many things in life, a large sum revolving around my own being. Yet one thing I've failed to agree with is the universe's way of wrecking my loved ones. Good people who deserve no other than the best guidance. Transparency makes it clear that I am no savior—the barrier I steadily try to shape myself into gets continuously knocked down with ease. And the following guilt stems from my inability to accept that I did what I could to the best of my abilities. That is where I am most ashamed, because I hate to accept that I am so weak. Had I been more attentive to Cynthia, would she currently be in a frozen state? Or do I accept the fact that my effort was enough and I wouldn't have been able to steer her decision to trial.

Every time I walk down this hall to her designated room my stomach feels a bit heavy from the memory of Aria, now engrained in my mind. She was unaware if her mother was dead or alive, and the terror was painted on her face. I knew of her liveliness because I was quick to notice her heart rate being monitored. The evident worry on the surrounding scientists' faces who struggled to awaken her told me that she wasn't going to greet us for some time. And the gloom that mediated Liam touched me through the glass my eyes pierced through. He blamed himself, but I didn't. The bags that sat beneath his eyes from his days spent in the lab with no end only granted my pity towards him. Aria, on the other hand, doesn't share that same sentiment. And because of that, she despised my sympathy for quite some time. I do not blame her animosity towards me, nor do I blame her for the way she reacted that day—the room filled in chaos as she charged for Liam who held back tears. The thought of losing her mother already lingered in her mind, and now lying with the unknown only forms another layer of dread that I wish upon no one. She was quickly separated from Liam, before the scientists made every effort to explain the situation to her. But I wouldn't be surprised if, like me, every said word felt out of touch. The muffled murmurs exited an ear the moment it entered the other.

Liam later admitted to me that he emphasized the risks of undergoing human trials so soon, yet the fellow scientists were so eager to submit to it, that he budged. Amongst them, he lost the voice he once had in his past. His silent voice wasn't short lived, however, as Dr. Harrison appointed him head scientist. She was transparent in her lack of diligence when approving the trial. She was no stranger to his urge for more research. Despite all of their shared excitement for the knowledge and talent he offered, his idea of being close to creating the panacea had a much farther finish line than the one everyone else sought.

Aria cared for none of it, and I could tell that she felt betrayed. Liam didn't owe her anything, nor did she owe him. Their shared presence was so strained that I can not classify it a friendship. However, between the tension that stood between them, she didn't expect him to keep such a severe plan silent from us. I must admit, I didn't expect it either, but I appreciate that he held Cynthia's wishes in high regards. She knew we would intervene in her desperate nature and Liam respected her want for discretion. Maddox only found out hours before he casually told me, when he had happened to pass by the procedure room. He sought her as a hero for being one of two first in line. I do too. I just selfishly wish she would have put her heroic ways as our dearest loved one before her own desperate hopes for better health.

I look past my vague reflection on the window and see Aria beside Cynthia. I didn't expect her to be here at this time, yet I am not surprised by it. I miss the glow her eyes once continuously held—her newfound dead stare is an exact reflection of what she's feeling. Her prior gracious expressions slowly diminished alongside mine, yet it hurts more to witness hers to have lack of ignition.

She's just finished adding formula to the feeding tube inserted through her mother's nostril. The shake in her hands mirror her lack of sanity, but what other demeanor is there to sustain in a scenario like so. She's lost the trust she's never given the scientist, so she fulfills most of her mothers needs. It is as painful to watch, as I am sure it is to perform. And the pang in my heart makes it clear that it feels much more for Aria than it does myself.

I decide to offer her the space I've previously been so ashamed of giving her, and slowly step away from the window. Except when I begin to do so, her eyes lock with mine and her smile assures that I am welcomed to come in.

"How are you holding up?" I ask, slowly closing the door behind as if waking up Cynthia would be the worst miracle to happen right now.

She nods her head. "I guess I'm just happy we're safe," she says, as I take the seat beside her. "It's nice to wake up and know they won't find us here." I sense the tone in her voice unsure, as if she is trying to be rather convincing to herself. Still, I'll look past that and appreciate that she can at the least try to notice her own form of light amongst the turmoil.

"We spoke the night before the coma, her and I," she admits, her eyes glued to Cynthia's. "She wouldn't stop talking about you."

I try to smile, but my sorrow overshadows my attempt.

"She'd say how handsome you've become, and how much she adores you. If I didn't know any better, I would think you were her son."

My silence suddenly becomes louder than the medical equipment that occupies the room. And the thought that I actually might have let Aria down, beyond what I already have, only finds itself into my thoughts once more.

"She doesn't deserve this," I finally say. "I'm sorry."

"Don't be sorry," her eyes twitch. "I never blamed you," she assures, finally looking my way proving that she is being genuine, despite her not directly accepting my apology.

"You don't deserve any of this," I blurt out, maintaining my eye contact to offer her the same honesty. However, a few seconds pass by before she breaks the stare and I wish I could somehow regain my gift of reading her mind.

"I was here late yesterday, after wishing your parents a goodnight," she admits. "I sat here for hours and thought to myself that maybe it's better that the universe forced this on me." She re-submits to my eyes. "You wouldn't be able to experience this pain had your father volunteered. And if you're suffering now, I don't even want to think about how bad it would have been to see you suffer in that world."

Before entering this room, I would have believed that I no longer had any tears left to cry, yet the one that slowly streams down my cheeks seems to be the one of many left behind. "I care too much about you," she continues. "I don't ever want to see you go through that type of pain."

Her words grip what's left of my broken heart. I want to say that I share the same pain for her mother as she does, yet it would be unfair for me to compare my sadness for Cythia to the agony of a daughter. And to think that her pain would compare in a non-existing scenario only forces me to question my worth as a friend to her. I'd always thought that it was insane—the more confined we've become, the more separated we are—yet I never confronted the idea that I should have disobeyed her plea for distance. Because in that same said scenario, she stood by my side even when I despised her. Or at least that's what her demeanor is telling me, and if I know anything, it's that I trust hers more than my own.

"I'm sorry," I whisper. "I never meant to leave you at your lowest—"

"I wanted you too," she quickly intervenes.

She lies her head on my shoulder, and my body welcomes the warmth she is so kind to offer—slowly easing the guilt that rushes through my mind. Still, despite the efforts of my newfound conscience dressed in armor, I know I will never let myself forget about how I've let down the person most important to me.

"You're here now," she says before shifting her focus on to her mother, whose heart rate monitor continues to beep at a steady pace. "And you were always here for her." She adds.

I guess in terms of progressing and forgetting, that is all that matters to her. Yet when I look at it from that perspective, it only leaves me confined in regret. I hate confrontation, but I wish she would use up her bottled anger against me. Use her tears to invade my own pool of tears. My lack of direct consequences only excuses my prior distance, but who's to say she has enough energy to discipline my faults.

She no longer wants my apologetic offer, still I want to express how deeply pained I am. I am sorry that I did not nurture you at your worst. It continues to hurt me to see the pain you are going through, but I thought putting your spiteful wishes first was ideal. I now see they were only ideal to avoid how weak of a person I can become. You despised my continuous empathy for Liam. You felt betrayed, and I only countered your lack of understanding, yet I failed to put myself in your shoes. And despite still adhering to my compassion for the both of you, accepting your cold shoulder made me no better of a man, because sometimes we need to lean on the shoulder we turn on. Even if it means creating a facade for the sake of the person you care so dearly for. I wish I could say this all out loud, but you failed to pay any mind to my second attempt at an apology. I noticed, and I know you noticed as well, but for now I will seal my feelings for the sake of both of us. I refuse to salt the rose any more than I have. Its fragile petals are holding on, begging me to stop.

10

"You have to be kidding me," Maddox says, the minute Amir is out of sight. His anger is evident in both his eyes and face, his cheeks mirroring the shade of the Lady slippers that lie just feet away. No room was left for silence to fill the air, and I wish we had just a few seconds of it.

I do not condone the idea of Amir holding a weapon, nor learning how to defend himself in any way shape or form. However, the task feels more like something I must do, instead of an optional favor. I will admit that despite my lack of reaction, there was a pang in my heart. But if I want to be the medicine to his mother's worries, I need to get used to seeing him in a state of defense. I hate it, and maybe I'm letting down the person I once was for obliging, but he no longer exists, and I do not see myself ever sitting at a table with mistakes again.

"You're just going to leave your gun lying around near a child?" he yells so loud I'm unsure if waiting for Amir's departure made any difference. "What if he—"

"There's no ammo," I quickly interject him, knowing where his sentence was heading. And had it been a full chamber I'd agree with him. "I made sure the gun had no ammo."

"Made sure?" he says. His face now lies inches from mine, and he forces on an intimidating mien. However, I hope I know him enough to assure he won't put his hands on me. I look down and his fists are not even balled up from the anger. I'm upset that I've led him to this position, but I'm relieved at knowing he can't get himself to charge me.

"Elandra asked that I teach him how to defend himself," I responded to his anger with softness. "Hunt, fight, and shoot."

He takes a step back, and the silence I begged for a minute ago finally arrives. He is stunned, and I will not gaslight him into believing that he's wrong for being so.

"Why would she want that?" he says.

"She's scared, Maddox." I pause. "And I hate pretending like everyone in the bunker is fine because they are not. The coast wants me dead, and guess where I am hiding,"

"No one is worried—"

"Now you're lying," I interrupt.

The only thing I can properly think of at this moment is Dr. Harrison admitting to me that the people of the bunker only despise me for interrupting their peace. It plays like a broken record, and I wish I knew how to shut it off, but I long since noticed that the record seems to live up to what it's known for.

"I'm sorry," I say. "I promise it hurts me just as much to teach him the field at such a young age, but I don't want to let his mother down."

"Here," I say. "Have them." I offer Amir my cup of fruits for the fourth time this week.

Every time his expressive smile is contagious to the sight. Again, we dine in the greenhouse, away from what transpires in the dining hall. I did, however, take a quick peek into the dining hall and people barely touched their plates—their attention too occupied by the screen that continues to degrade us. The capture was utmost uncanny, until I remind myself that not a soul in this bunker has a device present to dedicate their span to. The television is now their only form of information. I only wish that I was not what is being broadcast across hundreds of coastal channels. It's uncomfortable, and despite the contrary to popular belief, I am unsure who does and does not feed into the propaganda built against me. Our explanation to it all was welcomed, our prior positions surprisingly playing a pivotal role. We had insight, and many wanted it. Days passed, and I was still garnering looks from some. And the day that I was reassigned a role in the bunker, Dr. Harrison assured me that my fret of their easy persuasion is self ignited. "You should know they do not despise you for your actions," she said. "They despise your interjection of their peace, which I hold most accountable for, but If I could identify those who malice what the three of you have done, I wouldn't be able to fill a hands worth of numbers. And I'd like you to know that I am not one of them." It's been months and still I wake up everyday with the worry that what they are mentally consuming is adding more of a count to Harrison's hand. At the time, I asked her to consider retracting the television, but she assured me that the bunker is supposed to be a safe space. "The moment I start to enforce more restrictions for the sake of you, I am abusing my role as a leader. I am not a tyrant. If they feel the need to indulge in what is occurring outside, then that is their right."

I solely sat in embarrassment, unsure if I felt defeated by her lack of favor towards me. That was the last I heard from her, prior to requesting the gloves for Maddox and I do not blame her surprise on my sudden approach. However, it would have never lived, had I not urged the threads for Maddox. I do not despise Harrison. Still, the tension that lingers in our encounters are worth avoiding.

I've noticed a pattern in the news, however, and I do not share my concern with a sole being in this bunker. The coast continues to cover the slightly fabricated story on what we've done, and the continuous search for us. Still, I've become aware of their storytelling. When they discuss the topic of our search, the footage timeframe does not seem to align with the present. Nor is it consistent. I am outside nearly everyday, so much that I find myself taking to the stars to pass time some sleepless nights. The moon phase tells me that they broadcast at least some days later, despite their live claims. Maddox can attest that I was excited about the full moon. Watching its bright complete cycle has been an admiration of mine since my younger days spent on the rooftop. One of the overnight live broadcasts failed to consider that one of the most wanted men of the coast holds that status because of how sharp-eyed he is. I didn't leave that trait behind, and I know that they, at the least, hope I am watching. And I am. Their latency is far from accidental. They don't want me to be aware of their current move, but I'll appreciate the notice of their past. They don't want me to expect their arrival, so they broadcast days later to tardy their trails. It is rather futile, but I will let them believe they're as clever as they think.

I hope they consider the struggle our search is forcing them to face, because it doesn't stop there. And if I can offer those beside me anything, it'll be my greatest effort to protect them.

Maddox observes the artificially fabricated Jade Vine from up close. They are yet to bloom, still he locks eyes with every stem that flows below. I slowly approach him; he's yet to touch his plate of food, and if anyone knows the meaning of neglecting a meal and accepting starvation, it's me. Luckily, I've gotten better at not skipping meals in lieu of stress, and the lack of ability to stuff my face in its honor only draws me towards an even middle.

"Do you see it?" Maddox says when he notices my swift approach.

I don't see a thing. However, I assure I do for the sake of his confidence.

"You're lying," he says, before adjusting my view and pointing at a sepal just rows down from the 5th stem. It is premature and has barely formed a sense of what it's meant to be. I try not to laugh at how familiar Maddox has become with my demeanor. I once prided myself in my ability to easily lie, yet I can only assume that being with someone on a daily basis forces you to study that person like the back of your hand.

"Wow," I say, my tone admitting he was right. "I guess being lab grown sped up their birth."

He nods. "Hopefully a few more days can determine if it's truly successful or not."

His commitment doesn't go unnoticed, and I wonder if being secluded from anyone his age other than Nova for so long leads him to be so attentive to Aria. I've always known that he and Nova's dynamic never hinted as romantic, and it only took Aria to wake his loving efforts.

"You haven't touched your plate," I say.

"I'm not so hungry," he admits, before offering me the meal. However, my intention in confronting his lack of dining is out of concern, not a desire for more food.

"What's going on?" I have a question. I've stopped introducing my concerns with "Is everything okay?" because everything somehow always seems to be, whenever that question is brought up. To me at least, and evidently I've studied my own traits to improve my way of interacting with those I care for.

"I'm worried for Aria," he says. "Losing my mother was hard, and I don't know how I'll be able to relive seeing someone go through that same pain."

His vulnerability doesn't catch me by surprise—I asked for it. However, this is the first time he has ever mentioned his mother. I knew he lost her as a child the day the underground clinic was raided. However, it was only briefly mentioned to me by Nova the day I arrived. His reaction that day led me to never consider asking about her, no matter how close we've gotten. The trauma doesn't disappear, yet there is no purpose in broaching a sensitive topic unless he is the initiator. Now I am all ears, and hope he knows that I will never disapprove of being his journal.

"Do you remember much about her?" I hesitate to ask.

He nods. "Of course I do." His eyebrows ruffle. "I just wish I had happier memories to remember her by. All my younger life was spent watching her fight to stay in it longer. And I hated seeing that, because I knew she was in pain."

Lost for words, I look away. Part of me almost wishes I never broached his vent, but to be there for someone means you have to accept the painful baggage that comes with hearing their experiences. Seeing him open up about his mother has brought out a gloss in his eyes. I've never seen this form of honesty from him, and never have I seen the emotional numbness that now presents itself. He's hurt, and I can see right through his war against his tears. For the first time ever, part of me feels guilty for having parents. More now that they are flaunted in the face of people who have lost theirs. I want to express how apologetic I am for my family's unity, but it only makes his hardship about my conscience. I am past being blind to considering others in despair. No matter how honest my intentions come fourth, it's unfair to respond to someone's tragedy with self infliction.

"She'd be really proud of you," I admit. "You've dedicated your life to helping people who were in her position."

He doesn't respond, rather his face drops farther into oblivion quickly forcing me to wonder if I've said something wrong.

"Put that down!" He rushes past me, charging for Amir who holds my unattended gun.

He takes the weapon away, demanding Amir never think about placing his hands on another weapon again.

I solely observe, yet I don't move a muscle. The chamber is empty, and I am assured of it. I was hoping I could introduce him to the weapon rather than his curiosity lead him to it, but I'd be deemed a liar if I were to deny that what just occurred is the better way of his easement into weapons. I made his mother a promise. A promise that is going to upset Maddox, but I can not go against his mother's plea for sake of his sanity.

"I'm sorry." Amir is evidently hurt, but less about what he's done and more about upsetting Maddox. Or at the least it's what I hope. I do not want him to be scared into never holding a weapon again. Especially when Maddox holds a broader influence on him. He looks up to him as a brother, and his opposition is bound to steer my objective.

"It's okay." Maddox assures him, darting his eyes at me. "It's not your fault."

Already I can feel the shift in the room, and when Maddox kindly dismisses Amir, I know what's not to favor me upon his absence.

"You have to be kidding me," Maddox says, the minute Amir is out of sight. His anger is evident in both his and face, his cheeks mirroring the shade of the Lady slippers that lie just feet away. No room was left for silence to fill the room, and I wish we had just a few seconds of it.

I do not condone the idea of Amir holding a weapon, nor learning how to defend himself in any way shape or form. However, the task feels more like something I must do, instead of an optional favor. I will admit that despite my lack of reaction, there was a pang in my heart. But if I want to be the medicine to his mother's worries, I need to get used to seeing him in a state of defense. I hate it, and maybe I'm letting down the person I once was for obliging, but he no longer exists, and I do not see myself ever sitting at a table with mistakes again.

"You're just going to leave your gun lying around near a child?" He yells so loud I'm unsure if waiting for Amir's departure to express himself made much of a difference. "What if he—"

"There's no ammo," I quickly interject him, knowing where his sentence was heading. And had it been a full chamber I'd agree with him. "I made sure the gun had no ammo."

"Made sure?" He challenges my claim. His face now lies inches from mine, and he forces on an intimidating mien. However, I hope I know him enough to assure he won't put his hands on me. I look down and his fist are not even balled up from the anger. I'm upset that I've led him to this position, but I'm relieved at knowing he can't get himself to charge me.

"Elandra asked that I teach him how to defend himself," I responded to his anger with softness. "Hunt, fight, and shoot."

He takes a step back, and the silence I begged for a minute ago finally arrives. He is stunned, and I will not gaslight him into believing that he's wrong for being so.

"Why would she want that?" He questions.

"She's scared, Maddox." I pause. "And I hate pretending like everyone in the bunker is fine because they are not. The coast wants me dead, and guess where we I am hiding,"

"No one is worried—"

"Now you're lying," I interrupt.

The only thing I can properly think of at this moment is Dr. Harrison admitting to me that the people of the bunker only despise me for interrupting their peace. It plays like a broken record, and I wish I knew how to shut it off, but I long since noticed that the record seems to live up to what it's known for.

"I'm sorry," I say. "I promise it hurts me just as much to teach him the field at such a young age, but I don't want to let his mother down."

He nods in understanding, yet it holds no genuine promise. Rather, I can see the rage behind his eyes but won't attempt to aggravate him further. The premise of what had just occurred makes it too soon to assure him that I will need his help, but the need is present and soon to be presented. I can teach defense, but the survival skills that I've learned in the past months have been from Maddox, and I hope the pain in this doesn't retire his reign as a teacher.

Drenched in sweat, I make every attempt possible to catch my breath before accepting what happened. I saw him again, and the terror that it entails every slumber assures that my mind is neglecting to accept his death. I hate that I have no control over what I reign, but perhaps this is the normality of losing someone. The same continuous dream, and I am unsure when I will be introduced to the next episode of this horrific show. I fear the answer is the grief of someone else, so I try not to confuse my curiosities as wishes. I'll appreciate the terror in the nightly recap for what it's worth.

"Are you okay?" A familiar voice glides through the dark room. The tone is concerned, and the kindness it offers calms me down far more than what a steady breathing pattern could. "Another nightmare?" he questions.

"You know about my nightmares?" I ask Liam, who's silhouette resides above his bed. It is a rare sight; he spends most of his time in the labs—so much that he often falls asleep there. I never had a roommate, and despite him technically being my first, his absence fails in allowing me to experience having one. However, how truly absent is he if he is able to notice the terror that follows me every night?

"I saw you shake in your sleep a couple months ago," he admits. "The few times I've returned, the shake never stopped."

"I was hoping no one would see me," I say. "I didn't want to worry anyone."

That is one fault Liam has. He cares too much for others. I noticed it quickly, which only led me to question his career path. The two didn't align, and I saw right through the facade he'd put on his face to style with his uniform. I wouldn't say it complimented his outfit—it mirrored a child whose parents forced him to wear the one shirt he hates. However, he put it on and smiled through the day. No one noticed the contempt he held for it, but I did. It hurt me to see, because I've grown close to him—so much that I consider him a brother. With that comes so much compassion that you hold dearly to your heart. I stopped questioning his reason for becoming a Forceman. It evidently stemmed from trauma, yet that is only evident to my observations. I know his traumatic past follows him like my short lived one does me. So does Cynthia's trial, and the burden of feeling the need to remain in the labs, and make up for what occurred. I know I will continue being on his list of worries, but if I can be last on his list, I will feel better about having him first on mine.

"It's inevitable," he says.

There goes his fault shining in the light that does not linger in this dark room. I must admit I thought it would have been buried with all I've caused him in fleeing. He turned his back on the life he once had, and despite hating it, I can't help but wonder if he hates his current one far more than he did his last. Like my curiosity of his past, I don't interrogate his thoughts on his current one. It has been punctured far too hard for a new beginning that was not his idea. I don't want to confront the turbulence I've initiated on his flight.

"Do you want to talk about it?" he finally asks, and pushing through the hesitation in front of me I relent.

"It's Steven," I admit. "Every night I see him die in my nightmare."

I purposely leave out the premises that reside within. Despite seeing it every night, it hurts to admit it out loud. And this is only my first attempt at doing so.

"None of that was your fault," he reminds me. The silence that follows is an answer in itself. I didn't have to blame myself for him to assure my innocence. He knows what I am thinking. I hate that my skull is made of glass from his lens, because I can never fake a brave face in his presence.

"I have them too." He soon cuts through the silence. "The nightmares"

I look at the sorrow that resides in his eyes. Unfortunately, his skull does not mirror the transparency of mine to determine what occurs within, but I have an idea of what terrorizes him. Still, I return his kindness and ask if he wants to talk about it. He shakes his head no, and provides me with the same silence I had just offered him.

"It wasn't your fault either, Liam," I assure him.

Still, he doesn't say a word, nor does he return my eye contact. I don't need to see his eyes to recognize the pain that they hold. It hurts me just as it does him. And it also hurts me to witness the infliction he forces on to himself. My words on it are only thin, they hold the same weight as the ones I use to try to convince Aria of his innocence. That's why Liam and I are so similar. No words can change the pressure and hate we force on ourselves, but we will look at each other's hate and try to convince each other that it genuinely has no place.

"I'm going to go back to the labs," he says.

"I'll come along."

His smile towards my support offers the same warmth as the smile Amir delivers upon my small gestures at lunch.

12

"Try not to touch anything," Liam introduces a strict demeanor that I've yet to see. He's protective of the space he's created within the lab, and being commander-in-chief only offers him the right to be so. I've never stepped foot in this laboratory, and I am unsure if it has to do with feeling out of place, or the idea of what it entails.

This room is as cold as the cellar. Uncomfortable for the average person, but who's to say Liam is normal—he who often resides here days at a time. After noticing my shivers, he apologizes for the temperature, insisting that it's the best climate for the treatment. However, I blame myself as the slumber attire I model is not the most layered.

The sound of muffled nibbles garner my attention, and a turn of my head reveals a sum of separately caged animals through the glass window in the divided room next door. They are injured, and while ignorance would lead me to question Liam on how they've reached that state, I am aware of it. They were found injured. In fact, Maddox and I happen to be the ones to find them. And instead of leaving them to die on their own out in the woods, they've been brought here. Of course, their wellbeing is not promised within the walls of the bunker, but unfortunately an expedited death assures Liam and the scientist that the treatment still has to undergo study. They've yet to utilize the animals. However, when they do, their possible demise will be easier on the heart than a human who resides with us. Some might call it heartless. The past me agrees, but the current me assures that it is survival.

A beaver lies quiet in his corner. I initially found him by the river. I had thought he had been attacked by a predator, but no signs of wounds proved that his pain was internal. His slow heart rate indicated he was still alive.

The chipmunk in the cage beside him was found in the same way, except I was quick to notice the rashes that surrounded her lower area. They were red and her continuous scratch was her cry for help.

We did eventually find a rabbit who was in higher need of assistance. He was limping, assumingly from a hard fall. He had a red lump that had formed on his cheek, only visible when one would separate his fur. Days had passed, and I noticed Maddox did not deliver him to the labs. Rather he kept him in the greenhouse and medicated the rabbit on his own. His limp took three weeks, however, it took his lump double the time to heal. Maddox utilized medicine from Nova to treat him throughout the whole process. When it came time to release him, he assured me that he could sleep peacefully knowing that the rabbit had the opportunity to heal, and he did not risk his livelihood for the sake of others.

I further slowly approach the window which isolates the caged animals from us, and notice the chipmunk who bites the metal bars of her cage. She is doing much better than the last time I saw her, and I look at Liam who joins me.

"You still haven't tested on the animals," I state the obvious. A panacea trial would either successfully treat the animals completely, or expedite their death upon failure. They're paced state deems that they are clearly being properly treated, and I am rather satisfied.

"The time for it has yet to arrive," he assures, but the moment he enters the room and caresses the chipmunk proves his fear of possibly harming them. Only because it retraces the tragedy of Cynthia. He fears failure, and while experiencing it is necessary to succeed, he rather not have to lock arms with it more than once.

In the far corner of the lab, large pieces of equipment garner my attention. They are not medical, and are as secluded as the chipmunk and beaver. Except, the equipment resembles a polar bear in the desert. It doesn't belong here.

I draw near to the corner, my curiosity soars through this unfamiliar room. I resemble a child in a museum for the first time. A large panel lies above the legs that hold it up. Inside the barrier, blue squares line up in columns, each row resembling the next.

"Solar panels," I hear Liam nearing my vicinity. "Harrison alerted me on the lack of propane to heat the bunker, so I've been working on solar powered heating." He kneels down and scans the panel with his hand. "It saves us the risk of a power outage if we were to connect heating to the electric."

I watch his eyes light up as he explains the project. Harrison was right, he is smart. However, I didn't need her assurance to know that. And slowly I remember why I am so appreciative of him being here. I can't name a person here who'd be able to take scraps and utilize it to create a heating system. Not Maddox, not Aria, not me.

"Actually," he says. "This is something ready to be tested. "I'd appreciate your help."

I nod assuring him that I offer my assistance. Hopefully, this opens a new avenue where we are not strangers in a bunker we fled to together. Losing Aria was hard on me. Losing him from his own isolation was another battle to confront. Maddox and my parents were my sanity, but no connection feels as strong as the one I hold with two of them.

13

"Why aren't you asleep?" I ask Amir who watches the television in the dining hall. He's alone, and I can attest that his mother would not be so fond of him sneaking out of his bed shy of 3 am. His eyes don't scream tired, and he doesn't look scared at my appearance. I wouldn't say that out loud, but I feel honored to be a person in his life who he doesn't fear when interrogated. He trusts me.

"I'm not tired," he admits.

"Why is that?"

He looks down trying to hide his guilty smile. "Aria snuck me some chocolate before bed."

I'm relieved to hear it's not derived from a situation as similar to mine, but a bit jealous that I've yet to be aware of this chocolate.

I sit beside him and watch the television. Despite our 24-hour coverage, luckily the news is not currently replaying our flee, but it wouldn't be anything new to his eyes. I explained everything to him. And in my explanation, I was transparent. Not that I owed it to him, rather I didn't want him to have a certain perception of who I am as a person. Of course, his mother's views at the time held no support for me, but as I've never failed to mention, Amir's innocence plays a pivotal role in being accepting towards others. Whether good or bad, he is curious to just know you as a person.

The coverage entails their hunt. They are currently searching in the lower range of the coast. Except the moon's first cycle reflecting in the background makes their live coverage yet again another false statement. That moon showed that side of his face last week.

I see only a few familiar faces within the crowd of Forcemen who star in tonight's coverage—Justin being the most familiar. For the sake of Amir, I attempt to conceal the rage that begins to flare within my body. This is the first time I've seen him outside my nightmare, but the reality of it ignites the same anger I felt in our last encounter. And in a perfect reality, I saw him one last time to assure he wouldn't be allowed the same privilege as me to see another day of life. He can deem himself lucky, for my bigoted response to his actions that led up to Stevens murder.

If I were to see him again, I'd ask him why. Any vendetta that tied us together was personal, reflecting the arrogance he's too egotistical to detest. If I could spend a night in his mind, I'd try to figure out if he even expected such a miserable outcome from a deed that seems miniscule. As if the raid of Aria's home wasn't enough, he lacks any social awareness to determine that exceeding your role as the government's puppet will never obtain you the respect they supposedly have for Forcemen. Because had that been the case, they wouldn't have latched on to the earliest moment possible to unlawfully terminate one. And if I were to be honorable to the life that was taken before our eyes at the Forcemen base, that would make two too many lives that were cut short out of insecurity. They are only two murders that are no stranger to me, yet I would not deny the possibility of more unlawful Forcemen deaths happening behind closed doors, at the hands of those who they should trust. Still, what trust should you truly offer those willing to kill innocent lives.

Perhaps Justin could deny my accusations, because the only proof I have against his actions is that he happened to be the only one listening in on the conversation between Steven and I on the train. And his current stance on the television proves he's offered something to be considered superior beside the Forcemen who wear the same exact uniform as him. He leads the pack, and a point of his finger shifts their route in seconds. Even the policemen who stride beside them look up to him, and it disgusts me to witness that he has gotten his way at the cost of my sanity and my livelihood. He is no saint, and I look at my knuckles every day wishing that the bruises from our altercation would have stayed just a bit longer, so I could reminisce about the triumph if even a single day longer. I might have thought I signed my life away the day I became one of them, but never did I officially kiss the ring of a leader who thrives off the chaos he so effortlessly purposes and delivers. I'd be far from surprised if he too has convinced himself that I actually committed the appointed arson.

"Do you know him?" Amir points to Justin who prepares himself for an interview.

I stare at him through the outdated screen. "I do," I admit. "I wouldn't say he is my favorite person."

"Why?"

"Some people don't have nice hearts," I answer as youthfully as possible.

The men storm a building. It is one of the few that stand on its feet, refusing to drown with the rest. Much of the lower region has begun to sink long before my time, and people slowly had to witness the steady loss of their homes, businesses, and immobile assets disappear into the ocean that marks its territory. All that was left to cherish were the memories, but how much weight do memories hold if their tragedy overshadows the many thoughts they want to revisit. I remember asking my mother if that had anything to do with the civil war, and she hinted at it being a contributor, but even then, I could sense the trauma she began to relive with my question. That's why I've avoided seeking an answer, because I don't want to chase an answer my parents worked so hard for me to avoid.

The building rests its thighs in the ocean, past just testing the water. Unfortunately, it will have no choice but to soon take an infinite swim, drowning in the demise of what was once a beautiful sum of cities. And I will accept that building's challenge on who will survive the longest, but he holds the advantage—she who hunts him takes her sweet time with decades of their teasing being taunted in my face. Hopefully we can one day sit together at sunset and call a truce, except I do not know how much time either of us has got left.

It would be a smart place to hide, and I'd be a liar if I were to deny that it intensifies my fears of being found. The men who jump off the boat swim towards the building, before rushing their way up the rusted stairs, and I am unsure if I feel bad for their time being wasted, or relieved that they are far from us. One thing's for sure, I fear that they've now exceeded the expectation of finding us. They utilize oxygen tanks, large waterproof flashlights, and a ton of equipment that portray millions of dollars lost to corruption. I wish such effort was put towards repurposing the distresses of the coast. The ones that don't involve me, Aria, or Liam.

"We're here tonight, still in search of the three criminals who are being accused for the alleged theft and arson of the innocent lives they took along the way in betraying our coast." She passes the attention over to Justin who doesn't look too fond of her statement. Neither do I, but I know our reasonings lie on opposite ends of the coast.

Evidently, he is struggling to maintain his composure, and I take these few seconds to contemplate if the anger I feel inside is worth sitting in front of this screen.

"Allegations hold the weight of being false," he says. "These crimes were never alleged. They were committed, and they were the ones to commit them."

The anchor looks embarrassed to say the least. She apologizes, as her cheeks slowly turn red—Justin's aggressive demeanor being no help. He assures to assert the dominance that he already has, because it is clear that he will not be belittled in that setting, and the need for it falls flat. Another sheer reflection that he will never be satisfied, even in a world where he receives the respect he doesn't deserve.

"You've had experiences with the three criminals," she finally continues. "Anything you want to share?"

He nods, his stare rather infuriating. "The girl, Aria," he says, "Brandon couldn't handle that she locked eyes with me one time at the cabaret. I never offered her my attention, but Brandon still attacked me for it."

Now I am the one who fails to hold their composure, and the tick in my knee is concerning Amir. The lies continue, and the effect it has on me proves that they are winning the game they so proudly play. The game in which they control, and I am no longer sure if I am still player number one. Aria rejected him. He couldn't handle her cold shoulder, so he scolded her—accusing her lack of valor for her mothers suspected death. I will boldly and proudly confess the overt, I did attack him, and I can still hear the sound of the glass crashing his skull. But to play victim in that scenario only adds fuel to the fire they keep ignited. Especially when the support of his pack led to my ultimate loss.

"I'll be sure to share more further down the road, but first I have to place our attention elsewhere." He continues, forcing me to get up from my seat and approach the television. I appreciate the topic being shifted, but butterflies emerge in my stomach from the unknown.

"President Reign has an announcement to make." Justin looks into the camera. "Mason and the Forcemen will celebrate his hard work come the 25th noon at the Capital House where he will have a speech prepared for us. We hope for the support of the coast, as these past few six have been difficult for all of us."

The anchor looks as confused as me, and despite still having more questions, Justin cut the interview short, leading the coverage to be shifted inside the building, where they do not find us.

Quickly, I turn off the television—my mind still focused on the said announcement to expect. Selfishly, I want to obtain this information in case I am part of the announcement, but Amir saw the same exact thing I did, and for the first time I see a bit of worry in his eyes.

"What do you think it is?" he asks.

"I don't know," I admit. "I couldn't tell you."

Whatever it is, I assure him that he should not worry. I ask that he don't let what happens outside of the bunker dictate his state of mind. And despite my attempt to ease his mind, my next approach is going to contradict me in my goal.

"Hey," I garner his undivided attention. "How do you feel about learning how to use a weapon?"

He looks hesitant, and I wouldn't place Maddox's prior reaction to his curiosity past blame. He doesn't want to go against his word—I do not plan to divide the two, but I will worry about any further opposition from Maddox later. When I notice the ruffle of his eyebrows, I assure that there will be more to it. "You can hang out with Maddox and I. Learn to hunt, fight, shoot."

"I don't want to upset Maddox," he says, but I quickly guarantee him that he should not fret.

"Maddox will be fine," I say. "I talked to him."

He smiles and nods, his interest evidently sparking from the curiosity he garners from what we do. I would assume it would be his ability to spend more time with us, but when he had grabbed the weapon in the greenhouse, it was ignited from a place of interest. Perhaps he was hoping reactions would be different then, but now I am opening a door to where it can be different now. And to say that opening the door is as easy as I am making it out to be, is far from true. I hate the idea that one day he might have to utilize the weapon in a way that I do not want to envision. However, if life leads him in that direction, I can be grateful for the precautionary measure his mother pleaded I take. For his safety above ours.

I do not mention that my offer is an extension of his mother's wishes. She asked that I not mention her involvement because if he becomes aware that it was his mother's idea, that subtle worry that I had just seen him experience, would branch out. In a place of sanity Elandra would never reside with—let alone plant—the concept of Amir learning the world of physical defense and survival.

Today, it is intriguing from his perspective, but another day it could be the only friend he has to keep him alive.

Nova smiles when I wish her good morning. Her energy is always welcoming, and I can't ever go without embracing it. She never fails to go without checking on my health, despite my reluctance to be a burden on what supply we have left. That's not to mention the many patients she so happily cares for on a daily basis. I sometimes feel bad for the person she's become, not because she is a foul soul, but because she is missing out on what beautiful life can await her elsewhere. I fear that is not an option, and who's to say a life outside of a bunker setting would have welcomed her as she would it, but I still wish for a future where her day-to-day life is not lost in taking care of others. She is the backbone of this bunker, and I say that with no caution. She assures to see every patient on her roster and more every day, fulfilling their needs, most of the time far beyond what they ask for just because that's how good of a person she is. If I am hopeful for a better future, I hope that she is able to put herself first, even if that selfless moment is short-lived.

Her shoulders deserve even just a second of a break from all the weight it carries.

I can attest that the tragic loss of her mother played a pivotal role in her demeanor. Why live a normal life, when you can wake up everyday with the task of bettering someone who shares the position that was once owned by your late mother? And why live a normal life obligated by the rules of the coast who took that away from you prematurely? That is where she and Madox are alike.

"How are you feeling?" Her vibrant smile embraces mine. "Is your body still sore from last week's hunt?"

There goes the genuine concern I ever so adore from her. I've become accustomed to the ache forced on to every movement of my muscle. So much that I forgot it was there, but she remembered.

"I'm feeling much better," I assure, before thanking her for insisting I rest my body.

Without having to ask, she is already separating my supplements for me. It wasn't my intention in paying her a visit. I came to confirm that Amir is healthy enough to start training. However, I decide to hold off for a few minutes, quickly realizing that the time I dedicate to such a kind soul shouldn't be solely for my necessities. She spends so much time checking up on me, that I've failed to return the favor. Not that she expects it—she does everything with a genuine approach.

"And you?" I ask.

She offers the same warm expression. "I'm good," she says, but to deliver her the same genuine concern, I can't accept such a basic answer. It's unfair to her, despite how oblivious she might be to it.

"No," I protest. "I want to know more. How is your week so far? Are you sleeping well?"

She turns, offering me her full attention. Her demeanor says that she is both appreciative and happy that I asked. And I only hope that it's not a reflection of the lack of compassion she is given from everyone else. When people look at a hero, they often forget that behind their powers there is a person who may just need a shoulder, and that shoulder is worth much more than any power can offer.

"My week is going well," She says. "I almost wish we didn't have access to the news, but I guess it's for the best."

I nod, agreeing with her, but I know our concerns for the news come from a different place. I tend to worry about what people think about me, but upon watching the news, she has to relive the trauma she once saw firsthand. No raids today consist of ill people, the underground hospitals that once lived within the cities of the coast no longer exist. That is why this far away grounds is a thing. However, broadcast about a month ago was innocent people being forced out of a location which is suspected to have our traces. It happened twice, yet twice too many to cause turbulence to the lives of those who have nothing to do with us. Unfortunately, Nova was present in the dining hall when both were broadcasted. And I hate that while no one was killed, at least on camera, she got a brush of the scenario that shifted her life forever. The aggressive handle of civilians was uncalled for, and I don't think any intellect expects an apology, let alone changes. I assumed that these instances were initiated with the hope that someone's fear would unveil our location, but we are nowhere near anyone who can do so. And that's what hurts, because it led me to wonder if those people will despise the government for what they've done, or despise us for being the fault cause. Two things can be true, and perhaps if I were to leave these grounds, people would have no issue announcing me to the Forcemen. They hate them just as much as me, but I interrupted their normal— forcing fear upon those who just want to get through life. Even if that normal was a society filled with devastation. Becoming accustomed to an unhealthy lifestyle is a dangerous thing, and perhaps they might force you to do unethical things.

"What really brings you here?" she soon asks, her tone sounding friendly rather than medical.

I ruffle my eyebrows, confused. Until she points out that she often has to hunt me down to take my supplements. "Your eyes also always have a soft squint when you really want to know something," she adds, identifying a trait I've yet to notice about myself. "I noticed a long time ago."

I blush at her attention to detail—her way of embracing me offers a feeling I haven't locked arms with since the last time I spoke to her. It's soft and compassionate, and she evidently pays attention to the things that I tend to self-neglect. She is too kind.

"Amir," I say. "I wanted to know your opinion on him becoming more physical."

She suddenly holds an expression of concern, but without judgment. It is obvious that she wants to know, and I don't plan on keeping it a secret from her. I'll allow her mixed opinions, but I only hope that if anyone else in the bunker becomes aware, they don't question the thought of Amir being introduced to aggression.

"Elandra asked that I teach him," I hesitate, "to fight and use weapons."

She looks taken aback, yet I don't blame her. And I know where she stands when it comes to weaponry, her opposition trying to fight through her lack of judgment.

"I know, it's stupid—"

"Amir's been showing some of the best signs of improvement among those in the bunker. I'd say he's even ready to get off from treatment, but that's not my call to make." She cuts my distress short. Quickly, she approaches me, supplements resting in her palm. "If that wasn't the case, it still wouldn't be the first reason why he shouldn't hold a gun."

Speaking no further, she hands me the pills. I can't digest what else is running in her mind, but it takes a stranger to see the resistance in her eyes. She evidently doesn't like the idea, and I wish I could tell her how much I agree with her. But I can tell she had a purpose in approaching me with my supplements, and I'll accept the distraction— turning my shoulder on the conversation.

In the lot of supplements, I see a blue capsule. It's new to me, making my familiar four a group of five.

"What's this one?" I point.

"I also noticed you haven't been sleeping," she admits. "Some mornings I wake up and you look like you've been awake for hours. Take these before you sleep later tonight. Your eyes are begging for it."

I accept the pills, my eyes meeting hers in appreciation. My cheeks begin to blush again, however, I'm unsure if they ever stopped after her previous charm.

"Thank you," I say, before losing myself in the green in her eyes. "For everything you do."

She smiles, her expression proving itself to be the best partner her eyes can ask for.

"Always," she says.

15

I don't understand the charts or blood tests in front of me, and despite the time I've been given to study them, I've refused out of the fear of understanding something opposite to my wishes. However, I appreciate the decrease in toxic detection. Even someone so ignorant to them as me can see progression, but Dr. Harrison continues to assure that the simplified tests run inside the bunker can only determine so much. However, from experience she can identify that the treatment cycle is soon to bid its goodbyes. She assures that she plans to keep Dad under treatment for months to come, hoping to reach a year before officially finalizing the decision. Mom's eyes tear, her glistening optics matching the gloss in Aria's. I value their relief for his wellbeing, but my mind is stuck inside the reality that despite Dad reaching the finish line, what life awaits after? Like everyone else, he is restricted from returning to his former reality until further notice—a reflection of my decisions. However, where he stands out, is that despite being given a new identity, his relation to me puts a target on his back that no haircut or physical alteration can cover. If we were to come to terms with a future, it would be inside this bunker. My subtle urge for their return to their life in the capital sounds hypocritical to the views I've once held reign, but my views centered more around me than my loved ones. I hated, and still hate the coast, but I would rather my parents go back chip- and illness-free and be able to live a life that is not confined with everyday desperation. I can accustom myself to a long life here for what it's worth. However, I hate that they too have to lie here in discretion, because I stripped those chances away from them. And perhaps their impulsive decisions were a reaction to my emotional manipulation—far from my intentions, but a reflection of my lack of control. Time is irreversible, and while most of the world wishes it was the opposite, all we can do is sit and dwell on the mistakes that led us all to sit there in the first place.

"There is still work to be completed," Harrison assures. "But the designated route is truly in our favor."

She smiles at our bunch, before letting herself out. The checkup failed to last fifteen minutes, but her busy schedule restricts her from appointing too much of her time to just one patient. The state of the news that awaits those next is unknown to me, and I can't imagine the feeling of welcoming a sum of hopeful patients with bad news.

My time as a bunker nurse showed me that the younger patients hold more hope than those elder to us. My heart broke when one of our older patients had admitted his regret to take the spot of someone who could benefit more. "My kids begged me to flee," he said. "But one day I am going to die regardless. I am okay with that." I allowed silence to fill the room, only because I didn't know how to respond. When he passed weeks later, the silence felt different, because his presence was not there to replace that void.

When a passing occurs inside the bunker, the body is cremated. The body is transported to a bunker miles out from ours. It is small and tight, only built for its purpose. Nasir and Leander are the two who partake in that process. A job built for hard personalities alike, and I'd say they're a reflection of each other. Ashes used to be delivered to the families, but my arrival halted that operation. I can only imagine the anxious state of the patients' families, but the more I dwell the more self-infliction I willingly carry.

"Gracias a Dios." Mom lets out a sigh of relief. However, I look at the shared smiles and realize their ignorance to the future.

"Is there much to be happy about?" I blurt, their faces quickly positioning mine. "I understand Dad is getting better, but what after?"

It's evident that they're not amused with my argument, but perhaps considering other opinions to my opposition is what adds to the pot that boils inside of me.

"We figure it out—" Aria says.

"Figuring things out is what got us here, Aria," I attest. "Are you guys okay spending the rest of your life here? Watching people fight for theirs?"

"Being back home is no different," Mom argues.

"Back home we can turn a blind eye," I admit. My reminiscent tendencies stem from once being able to wake up and choose ignorance towards what surrounds me. Here, I wake up and look at suffering faces, my only means for escape being the time I partake in hunting. Yet still I return to the same desperation.

"Some of us chose not to," Dad intervenes.

"Maybe that's where we went wrong," I say, my words kicking the rush of celebration out the room, but sometimes it's better a reality check makes its presence known much sooner than later.

The look on their faces proves that I've ruined their day, but I don't feel as if I need to apologize for it. Not when my cries are not being heard. Perhaps Aria understands my argument, but her lack of defense proves that like them, she believes it's an inappropriate time to give the topic attention. However, if not now, when? You refuse to turn a blind eye back home, but on these grounds it's your ritual.

I excuse myself out, realizing that the conversation has no more awakening. At least not momentarily.

16

"Steady hands," I softly say to Amir.

Watching him hold the gun bothers me, and evidently it doesn't amuse Maddox who stands a few feet away with his arms crossed. Yet I must admit, the young boy has a gift for utilizing a weapon.

We managed to get empty cans from the kitchen—they stand as targets on the log across from us. Amir has managed to hit every single target, except the one to his far right. And every time I organize the cans once more, he still fails to hit the same target.

We spent our earlier morning running through the basics of hunting. No animals were harmed due to Maddox's urge for their reproduction, and while Amir understood everything, an explanation with no proper presentation will always fall flat.

I was surprised at his lack of empathy towards the idea of harming an animal. He didn't ask the questions I expected, rather he sought the opportunity to ask when he could hunt his first animal.

I wasn't conflicted with his eagerness, just surprised. However, I can not argue that I am not relieved. I only hope our reasonings for lack of empathy lie on opposite ends of the spectrum.

"Aim the gun down," I urge, before heading to the target zone. I pick up all the cans, leaving the unharmed one in its position.

I walk back, and give him a nod of affirmation, assuring he can raise the weapon and try again. However, we are reaching his tenth round, and I can see the disappointment in his eyes every time he misses the same target. I make every attempt to show no emotion, as my priorities do not lie on whether or not he can shoot every can. They stand with teaching him what it means to survive. Shooting an empty can does not determine his abilities, and I wish he would realize that neither mine nor Maddox's validation should alter his confidence.

Amir lifts up the gun and begins shooting the already damaged cans. A perfect shot on the first. Then the second, and all the way up to the fourth. He shares a swift glare at Maddox and I before adjusting himself. He closes his left eye and tightens his grasp on the grip.

"Aim with your left eye," Maddox blurts. "And loosen your grip."

My eyes lock with his, surprised by his interaction. Maddox has been quiet all ten rounds, and now I'm scared to even say a word. His face looks like he accepted defeat, and I don't want to add to his gloom.

Amir looks at Maddox, who approaches him. Maddox adjusts his hands and releases the tightness from a few fingers.

"You're left-handed," he says. "You should always aim with your left eye."

Maddox resumes his position beside me, before I whisper him a thank you. Except he doesn't accept it. "I'm not doing this for you, Brandon," he admits. "And I'm definitely not doing it for myself. But I need to accept that while it is not what I want, I need to do what's best for Amir."

I look down, not allowing the conversation any further. Rather, I reflect on his acceptance. I don't take offense to his rejection towards my gratitude. Because I agree with him.

Amir takes his last attempt at the can, before turning around and celebrating his success. The empty metal fly's feet away, and in his face you can see the pride. I glance over at Maddox, and while his expression doesn't reflect the same amount of pride, his slight smirk spells out all I need to know.

It is cold. So much colder than usual. The clock strikes 1 a.m. and the sun allows the moon to take the main stage hours prior. I wish she were here to offer even a few more degrees—these gloves and layers offer nothing worth my sanity.

Liam finalized some panels, and the confidence that he radiates is something I've never seen him spew. Perhaps I've seen it in a different scenario, however, never did it stem from his confidence in a product he's created. The confidence that should have walked beside his first attempt at the panacea, before pressuring him to proceed the trail. It's the same confidence that I will seek at his second attempt, because without it, I won't trust anything that is manufactured inside the labs.

We spent yesterday afternoon connecting the solar panels to the bunker's heating source. The last time the electric heating was utilized, the sudden lack of power led the bunker to an unexpected chill after a few days, with weeks lingering in uncertainty towards what's next. Yesterday took hours of labor, but to fulfill the installment by noon was prevalent, so the panel gets its fair share of the sun's company. They've only mingled for shy of ten hours, but Liam's impatience led us for a midnight venture. He assured their spark should be enough to initiate a test.

"Everything looks correct," he states, as he briefly examines the panel. I don't know how I'd react had it not been correct. My sanity is teased by the cold, begging to take advantage of what little propane we have left indoors.

"We can finally give it a go," he smiles. "I'll stay back and make sure nothing malfunctions on this end. You can power the switch inside."

My feet almost initiate a rush back to the bunker on their own, but I insist I be the one to watch from the outdoors. The fridge wind is possessive, but I prefer to suffer just a few more minutes in his favor.

He nods, offering no debate, and as I stand here alone I observe what lies around me. White frost hugs the lifeless grass we walk on, and the trees parade their frail bones. A few white pines flash their needles, swinging left and right through the wind that offers no warmth, and I can't help but reflect on the generations it has sustained. Surprisingly unharmed, yet what blessing does that hold when forced to survey an abundance of lives. No neck to avoid the pain from torture, or the envy from happiness. If they could speak, the only question I'd ever ask would be what is the worst thing they've ever seen.

Moments linger, before a distant sound shuffles through the night. Too soon to be Liam, and too far to be the panel. I squint through the absence of light, yet the trees are the only beings that return my stare.

I focus on the bunker's camouflaged entry, considering that I have underestimated Liam's speed, yet my previous intuition is proven right.

Again, I am greeted by a shuffle, except this time it echoes behind me. I turn, matching the speed of the distant sound. Soon, I find myself frozen in position, staring at the eyes across from me. She stands in plain sight, parading her fur coat I ever so envy. I make no sudden movement, I do not want to disturb the coyote. I can not determine her intelligence from this game of eye tag, but if she had seen me previously use my gun, then she knows what I have to offer. I watch her closely, though my hands remain far from my weapon. Still, I pity her comeuppance if she dare challenges my patience.

She takes a few feet forward, initiating my few feet back. I do want to challenge her, still I do not want to be tender to her presence. I know her capabilities, and I do not want to befriend her. Her loyalty falls in question, and I would hate to be the pioneer of a failed assessment. Again, she takes a few feet forward. I can not determine if she fell victim to gentrification due to our settlement, but I can attest that the endless trails are hers to explore.

Suddenly, cheers pierce through the wind—the coyote quickly departing. I sigh in relief, the moment she becomes distant to my vision. I am highly strung from our encounter, yet proud at my restraint from weaponry. Her demise would have called for a pack, however, that was not what held me back. I figure if I want Amir to use a weapon wisely, I must start doing so as well—despite his absence.

I turn to Liam who lauds his accomplishment, the solar panel succeeding with no conflict to the bunker.

I offer a smile through the beat of my heart.

Reminiscent to last summer's end, we sit above the rocks that look over the waterfall. It is currently frozen in place, and I watch it everyday with the hopes of a few droplets insisting on a warm welcome. The rock is cool to the touch. So cool, that our venture up here was conflicted by the slip of the stone.

I gaze at the stars—so discernible that I can count each and every one if I ever so desire. Rather than prolong my endless night, I try to make shapes out of those stars who glow in the sky. My mind is so consumed that I quickly neglect the cold. I've solely accustomed myself like I do while hunting.

The moon is entering waxing gibbous. The last phase before he parades his full figure. It's been roughly a month since I've seen him in this state, meaning we are days shy of a new full moon. And despite the cold, I still sit outside the bunker to admire every full embrace. I often bring tea, and envy the confidence he radiates. As a child, I'd talk to the moon as much as I did the stars. I would often tell him about my day when Aria wasn't around. He'd stay and listen—some nights my tales adopting a full night's worth. I stopped the moment I began to judge myself for looking deranged, and I would argue that the start of self-judgment warranted the way I over analyze myself as an adult. It is exhausting, and despite my reflection of it, the flaw will never succeed in parting ways. Sometimes our flaws reside in our head, declaring itself an infinite member. Even when I've garnered the guts to evict him, he'd still stand. Untimely, I gave up.

"You're quiet," Liam points out.

I look over, offering a laugh. "I guess I'm at peace for once," I admit. "It's been a challenge to find any lately."

For a moment, he is silent, but I know he is finding the right words to say. It's an attribute I've since noticed in him. However, even if he were to remain mute, I'd appreciate the lack of judgment, and proceed to my state of silence.

"Your body's aware," he finally says.

My eyebrows naturally ruffle—trying to make sense of his claim.

"Your last moments of peace have always been on the rooftop back home. It was your escape," he explains. "You got the stars, the moon, and if you close your eyes a bit, those trees over there almost look like The Globe."

I laugh, yet it is short-lived at the realization of his words. Mine and Aria's rooftop—our escape from reality. I only mentioned that spot to him once, and I'm appreciative of his recollection. These trees act as the cities that reside in the capital, and this rock as the rooftop. It might lack the ambience, but I can treasure what value it has to offer. And the moon and stars who follow me no matter where in the coast I escape to. They have the same loyalty as Liam.

"I see you watch the news a lot." He draws concern. "Not watching it is the only reason why I've been able to not think about it."

I look down, following the truth in his words, yet I still wonder how often he does think about what occurred. Evidently, it consumes my mind, which only ties to the fear of being found. And my observation of the supposed live footage glues my eyes even more. I do not know what benefit it holds, but if my ideologies flirt with the truth, Liam would be the only one to confirm it.

"It's hard to avoid," I admit.

"Is it really?" He challenges, rather than draw a genuine question, and I do not oppose his confrontation of my self torture.

"You see the moon?" I ask.

He nods, his face evidently confused by what he believes to be a shift in conversation.

"It's a different phase on live news," I continue. "I watched the last full moon in person, and hours later it was just a full first quarter on television."

"It's not live," he says with a sense of understanding.

I nod, assuring that he is correct.

"They don't want us to know if they're close," he explains, only confirming my beliefs before questioning their last location.

"Last I watched, they were down by the drowning south," I say.

He looks down, drowning in his own thoughts. I take this silent opportunity to let Liam know about Reign's big announcement. So big that it needs its own celebration. "It can't be us if they're still searching the drowning south," Liam assures, adding that it is probably just another population announcement.

"No." I do not hesitate to oppose, because I doubt that the change in population has seen that much of a dent with us being the Forcemen's main priority. Even with the newfound association of coastal police, they've managed to misguide with their initial goal. "They wouldn't declare that with a big announcement, let alone allow it to share a stage with Reign's celebration."

Liam looks around, in search of an answer. "Then we watch," he finally says.

18

I can feel my body thaw the moment we enter the bunker. The warmth welcomes my body—he who urges me to take advantage of the next few liberated hours to rest. I wish I can convince Liam to do the same, yet he has already assured me that he must get back to the labs.

I never fail to express my concern, yet he insists that he is fine. The bags beneath his eyes oppose, and I wish he considered my worries. Yet when they revolve around him, he is quick to dismiss them— assuring that he is capable of long hours. I begin to sound like a broken record, and so does he in response.

The moment we enter the main bunker room, Leander causes a flinch in our journey. The lights are dim, and he sits beside the door as we step in. I didn't expect his unwarranted presence; he was not there as we exited—likely pursuing his daily overnight rounds around the whole bunker.

He is evidently frustrated with us, his deep breath shifting his entire demeanor. I choose to ignore it, however, never is he enlightened at my sight. Our encounters always met with his stale stares or eye rolls. Even when I taunt his insolence with a smile he remains uncivil.

I continue walking, paying no mind to him nor the panic in my reaction. Perhaps I'm too exhausted to interact, but even if I stroll with energy I do not find my urge to converse with him. Our last conversation was held when he interrupted my date with the television, and while I hate watching the news, I wouldn't say his subtle confrontation made our chat worthwhile.

"I'm sure you guys are well aware that there is a cut off time authorized staff are expected to be back in the bunker," he says, halting our return.

I look at Liam, who maintains his civil demeanor. "Busy night," he assures. "It won't happen again."

And while Liam is willing to dismiss the conversation at hand, I fail to let it diminish.

"Liam just saved the bunker from freezing to death," I attest against Leander's disrespect.

"It could've waited till morning," Leander argues.

"No," I stand firm. "It couldn't"

He shakes his head, frustrated at my challenge. "And what would have happened if we thought you were an intruder and shot you?"

"You'd be happier than one of our patients finding out they've been cured," I cut him off.

He lets out a chuckle, and I do not lack the knowledge to perceive that his amusement rose from harmony towards my claims. "I'll let Dr. Harrison deal with this issue come morning," he gives up, not bothering to disagree with the words that came out my mouth. Never have I personally affected him, and I do not see a reason I should attempt to reason with someone dense to the idea of acceptance. He will never be fond of me, and I do not ever plan to reconcile or befriend him.

"That's fine," Liam says, before pulling on my shoulder and initiating our departure.

I don't protest, because I know this confrontation frets Liam more than it does me. And while I know he doesn't fault me for my aggression, I know that had he been more exposed to what occurs outside of the laboratory, he'd be more understanding than he is now. Leander despises my presence—never did I contend his views on me, still I'll never appreciate a lack of a facade portraying anything but civil. Not when it is towards me. Even less when it is meant for those tied to me.

19

My venture to the greenroom is welcomed by a sweet smell. I've never proclaimed myself to have the greatest sense of smell, but I can tell the aroma is light, rather exotic. The closer I get, the more the scent asserts its dominance.

I've decided to start my morning early. My hopes to obtain a few hours of sleep soon failed, and I do not want to credit Leander for occupying my mind. Still, the frustration that lingered within me dictated my vital slumber. Time has passed, and that desire now lies in the queue till today's end. I am exhausted.

Upon entry, I am welcomed by Maddox who already resides in the greenroom. I did not expect him to be up so early, yet by the looks of the bright turquoise that wraps itself around the garden, I can sense that excitement was what interrupted his slumber. The Jade Vines are in full bloom. I knew its artificial contents dictated its growing pattern, however I did not expect it so soon. It has been roughly a month since Maddox obtained the seeds from the scientists, and only a couple of weeks since the vine presented itself leading Maddox to relocate them. Now it introduces its unique tone to every other resident plant in the room.

"Wow," I slowly approach the vines.

"They bloomed this morning." Maddox holds out a strip, proving my approach welcomed.

I extend my hand, accepting his offer. The petals are thick and leather like and the shade of blue radiates through the room. So much that it reflects off the sweat dripping from Maddox's forehead. His smile radiates the same way, his pride present.

"Has Aria seen them yet?" I ask.

"Not yet," he assures me, before sharing his plan to transfer some of the vines to Cynthia's room. "They should be able to survive a few weeks in the bunker's temperature."

I nod in awe of the plant, I can only imagine how much more artifacts are possible.

He slowly releases the vine, before offering me his full attention. "Why are you up so early?" he asks.

"I was out helping Liam set up the new heating system."

He slowly nods, the shift in his demeanor evident. We've never spoken in terms of Liam post-trial. It was always clear that he was solely concerned about Aria, and her well being. The idea of her sanity felt out of touch, and he made it his priority to reach. I do not assume he despises Liam for the trial, I want to believe he understands that the outcome was far from his dictatorship. However, I could always sense that it hurt him to see the state it put Aria in. Especially since he was the one to be there for her along with Mom and Dad. Or those were simply the three relationships she didn't force the need to push away. While never a topic of our discussion, I've accepted that in his mind, Aria was hurt by Liam, and despite his possible understanding of the contents, he rather not seek a bond he's never had. We just so happened to be forced together, and the friendship we've built always indicated that Aria never shed ill-intent on my name. I would never expect her to, no matter how hurt she felt.

"Does it work?" he asks.

I nod.

"That's awesome." He offers a smile, before quickly shifting the conversation. "Let's get to work."

The air is crisp, but I somehow do not despise it. The sunset garners my full attention, the sky mimics an artist's canvas. If one were to capture the sky in painting, you'd assume it is a warm summer day. Truly it's the contrary, but the beauty it pertains only sketches a smile on my face. The orange reflects off my skin, as the sun bids its goodbyes. It has been a long time since the sunset has been so prevalent, and I sit outside the bunker admiring what it has to offer before the clouds resume their position another day.

I take a deep breath and rest my head on the chilled rock behind me. Today was an odyssey of hours, these final moments seemingly having no encounter. And surprisingly I am able to cherish these next few. The sunset means a near curfew, but I'm not opposed to the idea of challenging Leander once more.

Maddox and I spent time with Amir today. We came across minor challenges while practicing physical defense, but those stemmed from his lack of strength. He is young, and I do foresee a future where his abilities improve. It will take time, and we are lucky enough to be granted with much of it. I can say that I am relieved he did not show any visual signs of frustration. Rather, he was enjoying his time.

Later, I did some planting with Maddox, before helping him transfer vines to Cynthia's room. It was during Aria's shift, so a surprise awaits her. I would return for her reaction, but I don't want any credit to latch itself on to me. Maddox did all of the work, all for the sake of seeing her smile. I am okay in accepting that any future smile I bring to her face will not hold the same meaning behind it. But for it to be given to Maddox warrants a smile of my own. She is deserving of the love I was not able to provide her.

A sudden creak of the Bunker's door interrupts my resting eyes. The moment I look over, Aria emerges from the bunker.

"You liked the surprise?" I smile. "It was all Maddox," I assure her.

"What surprise?" she laughs, before taking a seat next to me. She hands over a cupcake. It is chocolate, and dressed in vanilla frosting. The flavors are akin to what I'd enjoy annually back home. I smile in awe of her kindness the moment she rests her head on my shoulder. I myself failed to remember, and evidently so did everyone inside the bunker. However, I do not blame them, nor do I feel pity for myself. We hardly have a proper track of time, and with all that is going on, my birthday is the last of even my worries. Had Aria not remembered, this would have just been another day.

"Happy birthday." She looks up at me offering a smile.

"Did you make this?" I ask.

She nods. "I've learned a lot in this bunker."

"Thank you," I say, accepting the treat. "I didn't even remember."

"I didn't expect you to," she admits, before pulling out a match. "I couldn't find a candle, but a match should do."

She rubs the wooden match on a nearby rock before sticking it onto the cupcake. I can't help but laugh. The flame reflects itself off her large brown eyes—those that wait for me to make a wish. A mirror image of our time as kids, her anticipation never indifferent come a new year. The same excitement, and the same beautiful smile. It never changes, and I hope to never meet a day when it does.

I look at her, offering the same awe, and rather than make a wish, I extend my dedication. She'd never allow this as children, but at this point in our lives, I know she will appreciate it more than ever. "To Cynthia," I begin. "To my parents. To Maddox. To Nova." I look out at the sunset, the shade of copper blending into the impatient flame who waits to be put out. However, my mind dwells on he who I wish was here. "To Steven," I say, and I could feel Aria's hands pull my arm tighter. I look over at her, before placing my forehead on hers. Her head runs warm, and mine embraces all it has to offer. "To you." I give her the last dedication, appreciating this very moment. Never did I spend a birthday without Aria, and the warmth she's awoken in my heart conceals my cold exterior. She is perfect, and I fail to think of a better way to greet twenty-one than with her by my side.

I look at the flame one last time, allowing the next few seconds of silence to dwell in my thoughts. There is one more dedication, yet I will not disturb this moment between us. I want to remember it forever, and I don't want this memory to have a slight patch. "To Liam" I think to myself, before blowing out the flame, the air welcoming the smoke that emerges.

"Thank you," I say, embracing her smile more than the sunset that seeks all the attention. With no intention in doing so, I lose myself in her eyes, and she evidently does the same. Soon, she breaks the tension, and I appreciate her for it, because I wouldn't have had the guts to do so. The honey of her eyes is a maze to get lost in; I'd be happy to be considered missing.

"Try the cupcake," she urges, assuring that she was only able to make one, due to lack of ingredients. I try to not dwell on the subtle reminder of our emerging shortage, still it runs a lap in my mind. There is only so much Maddox and I can offer, and I don't know how we will bypass the discrepancies that await. Perhaps that is a fret for a later date, still I know it will linger until the moment I confront it.

I split the cupcake into two, giving her half of her creation. We both take a bite—the tough sponge requiring effort to chew. I laugh at her realization, her eyes upset. "This tastes awful," She complains, frosting lying on her lip. "No, it's amazing," I exclaim, wiping the frosting off her lip with the edge of jacket.

Again, we lose ourselves in each other's eyes, the tension she previously broke finding itself again. I allow it, however, because while a past me would want this to go further, I know those previous desires lie far from what would come from this. I've garnered a form of respect and admiration for Maddox, something worth more than my emotions. And by the look in her eyes, she too honors his worth much more than the tension that lingers in the lack of space between us. Perhaps I can awe her presence, still I will never take it a step further.

Distant steps emerge from inside the bunker, still we share a stare. I am unsure if the stare defines what could have been, but I can attest that it does not define what will be. She's found her other half, and I adore what I have with her. It is what we've always had—friendship. A friendship so strong that no being can mold a relationship like it.

"Aria," Maddox proceeds with caution, forcing us to break our eye contact. He takes a subtle pause, yet it reflects a swift apology for interrupting our honest interaction, because thankfully we did not present him with anything to despise.

When we offer Maddox our full attention, the sweat on his forehead is evident. He rushed here with purpose, the tremble in his hands a sole confirmation.

"Your mother is awake."

PART TWO : RISE

21

Everything feels distant, my pulse the only prominent sound. I can't make sense of what the nurses communicate to Dr. Harrison. I follow their lips for a sign of comprehension, still my focus fails to recollect. Her eyes are wide open and I can not determine her consciousness from where I stand behind the glass. Not because I am scared of her, but because I simply don't want to intrude. And perhaps the fear that does linger stems from possible future casualties. As much as I want to believe this is true, my brain programs this reality as another dream. It does not want to accept that something so relatively good could. Worse, it could be one more thing that gets taken away.

I never wanted to doubt that Cynthia would one day wake up from her coma. Still, my patience slowly began to fade—my hopes along with it. I'd sit beside Cynthia and look for the hope she had always retained, but that hope could only ever be found in her eyes—those who spent months concealed by slumber. Perhaps I did not want to be hopeful for something to then be disappointed. I rather lack that spirit and be proved wrong.

She sits up on her bed, no emotion behind her face. Not even her smile. Perhaps I noticed a subtle gloss in her eyes, as she observes the Jade vines that wrap her room. Maddox and I spent hours relocating them earlier. I look at her, and see no difference from the person I always looked up to. The mother who took upon herself to raise her daughter on her own after escaping an abusive partner. The woman who praised my family for their charm—blind to the fact that her maternal efforts were worth so much more because she did it on her own. She gave Aria a life worth living—far more than she realizes.

I reflect on being upset when she fled, and part of me wondered why she left us. I failed to realize that that had been the very first time she put herself first. Our inclusion was unfeasible, and when I first laid eyes on her after years of treatment, I could see why she would not want us anywhere near. I opposed her insecurities, because I did not want her to latch on to them. Still, my heart has never felt that much pity in its lifetime. I wished I could heal her illness, and perhaps I saw that same urge in Liam, which is why I cannot attest him. His motives are driven by the wishes of others, his only intention to accommodate them.

Aria's swollen eyes scan the room, assuring nothing affects her mother more than it already has. She watches the nurses check her vitals, and to my surprise none of them need to hamper her from Liam who quietly undergoes a study on Cynthia. Perhaps Harrison's presence hinders her reaction, or she is solely relieved from what is happening. Still the tension is palpable, and I do not know what benefits I provide.

Mom rubs my shoulder, noticing the strain in my expression. "She's going to be alright," she assures me.

I want to believe that she is, I really do. However, if I celebrate her life today, I will have trouble accepting the possibility of her demise tomorrow.

"What if she's not, Ma?" I ask, the crack in my voice pushing her concern.

"Cynthia is a strong woman. A woman stronger than I'll ever be," she admits. "If it doesn't turn out alright, then we can thank God that we were able to admire her one last time."

After a lot of effort, a tear begins to stream down my face. Quickly, Mom evicts the tear and grabs my face.

"I want you to be happy, hijo," she says. "You live your life in fear and the one thing that hurts me the most as a mother is not remembering the last time you were happy."

"It's hard," I admit.

"I know."

Silence lingers before I apologize for my frustration the other day. I admit it was uncalled for, a sheer reminder to myself as to why I always conceal my emotions. They are not worth being a burden to anyone else, and I allowed the frustration to break through my broken facade. I am okay allowing my feelings to consume me if that means exempting them from those I love. And even if they say that they understand me, I'll never believe them. I don't assume my problems are worse than others. Rather, they just know how to maneuver their conflicts far better than I can. I will always envy them for it, and I am comfortable enough to accept my wrongs.

"You don't have to apologize," Mom assures, before bidding her goodnight.

I can't sleep, and this time my dreams aren't what terrorizes my slumber. I am thinking about Cynthia. For the last few months, I held hands with the idea that she was far gone despite her beating heart. It was not pleasurable, and it terrorized me just as my nightmares do. I guess I was in denial that I would ever speak to her again—or at least, hear her speak again. These moments are close to watching a person's rare wake from death. And reminiscent of my past reactions, I do not know how to respond.   I sit on the floor beside my bed, staring at the blank wall ahead of me. I want to learn to appreciate the dark for what it has to offer. I do not need to close my eyes to conceal what lies around me, and the night it walks beside forms a sense of peace. I'm a victim of drowning in my own thoughts, no advantage available to take. Still, I count the long awoken hours for what it's worth.

I've yet to speak to Cynthia since she's woken up. I've offered her time out of respect, though if I wait any longer it will begin to mirror my old ways. I couldn't handle seeing her suffer, so I distanced myself for my sanity, not realizing that it only put a strain on her feelings. I guess all the credit I give myself for understanding others truly falls flat.

I hear soft distance steps approaching, and just a few seconds pass before Liam walks in.

"Are you okay?" he says with concern. "Another nightmare?"

The last time Liam stepped foot in this room was weeks prior when I was experiencing another nightmare. If he did happen to step foot in here after, it must have been amid me challenging those dreams—forcing myself to sleep.

"No," I assure, though I do consider the turmoil in my mind a nightmare in itself. I've long accepted that I do not dictate the continuous strain that occurs in my head. I am unsure who steers the ship—a sincere beg for mercy awaits them the day we meet. "I'm just thinking about Cynthia," I admit.

He takes a seat across from me. "I understand," he says. "I didn't think she'd wake so soon."

"I didn't think she'd wake up at all."

I admit my fear, still I refrain from going into further detail. I must be cautious with what I express, he already carries guilt from the catastrophe and I do not want my words to prove them right. I bet he's relieved, and I will be glad if the fault he continuously forced on to himself slowly glides off.

"Did the trial work?" I ask after moments of silence, only adding to the tension.

He stares at the wall, ignorance washed on his face.

"I don't know," he painfully admits. "But one of the other scientists is doing further tests."

My eyes join his stare at the wall across from me, observing the steel it pertains to. I stand corrected, Liam's guilt still remains. The tone in his voice determines it all, and it pains me to see.

"What now?" I ask, and after inviting a few seconds of silence once again, he assures me that we wait.

"I hope you're not still blaming yourself, Liam," I finally say.

Guilt is not what he deserves, and I can assure it is not what Cynthia would want from him.

"She's asleep," he says, dismissing my concern. "You should visit her before she wakes."

I slowly nod, and I let the silence fill the room as I wait for a reaction to my concern. However, no reaction comes and I realize that my mind might not be the only one running on turmoil. I think I failed to be there for Liam, but to contemplate on that fault only fuels my own pain. I might have failed, still that's not to say that I did not try.

My eyebrows flutter when I see him embrace his bed. His exhaustion had no room to hide itself, his eyes swollen from labor. He lacks the energy to talk, let alone to switch into sleepwear, and it doesn't take him long to fall into the slumber his eyes ever so begged for. His body drowns into the deep mattress—his tired relief evident.

Slowly, I rise, and although I know no distraction is enough to interrupt his sleep, I step cautiously. Steadily, I walk away, following his suggestion to go see Cynthia.

23

The beeping of the heart monitor bounces off the walls, complimenting the white noise that surrounds. I am surprised that the jade vines have yet to perish, they remain alive and teal—their shade being the only use of color in this room.

Cynthia is asleep, this time by choice. She's had a day much longer than mine, and I can't help but despise the endless poking and prodding she has to endure. She isn't some supernatural or extraterrestrial being. She isn't some peculiar case that warrants a new study every hour. She's a woman, and I wish she'd be left alone. She needs a rest, a break much longer than the coma she just woke up from. She is stuck in a predicament, and if she were to insist on another treatment, I would go lengths to disapprove. I know Liam doesn't plan on allowing it, and despite my trust in his craft, I don't want to see my loved one be the heroic subject. It is selfish, but I can name a few people who too would take the same opinion.

Once the noises begin to sound like a broken record, I rise from my seat, nearing the exit in hopes of returning at a later time. Cynthia is still in deep rest, and I don't want our encounters to be reminiscent of my visitations throughout her coma. Her heavy breaths tell me it is not so soon as Liam suspected. Still, I consider staying. I appreciate watching her sleep, especially knowing for certain that it ends with a rise. But ultimately, I decide against it. I shall return when she awakens.

I close the door softly behind me, shocked the moment I come across Maddox who stands behind the glass. I am unsure how long he's been standing there, though it's not a concern of mine. He doesn't say a word, still he smiles. I try to conceal my glossy eyes, before quickly realizing that he is no one I should hide them from.

"The vines look amazing," I say, as I stand beside him.

He nods, his grin proving his genuine pride.

"I don't think Aria noticed," he says. "But with all that has happened in the last day, I don't expect her to be aware of anything besides her mother."

I watch his grin slowly fade, and a rise of tension emerges. I don't say a word, rather I silently hope the tension finds its way out. Aria's mind is too consumed by the current circumstances to even focus on herself, and it is clear he knows that too. Still, he looks down upset.

"I didn't mean to ever get in between the two of you," he finally says, and my suspicions around the tension is proven true.

"I wish I had known—"

"No," I interrupt his honest remarks. "We were never more than friends."

I look down, reflecting on what Aria and I once had. To say we were never a thing makes me a liar, but I don't see the need for Maddox to be aware of what was. And besides, whatever our relationship, to deem it solely as our past contradicts the looks we shared yesterday. Maybe there were emotions lingering within our stare, but that's something that won't be explored further. Not again. To that, I can attest. It is not because of her previous rejection of me; I understood her reasoning. It was the moments after that that led me to realize our true journey in life. I admit, Aria and I are soulmates. However, what ties us together is how purely platonic we are. And had nothing ever happened between the two of us, the shift in our bond would have never existed. I can not speak for her, but I can willingly admit that I regret our night of intimacy. We are not meant to be anything more than what we are, and that alone is okay. Maddox does not need to know what can possibly hurt him. He looks as if his heart is torn by her innocent neglect of the vines, and to confirm our past will only add to his melancholy.

"You make her really happy, Maddox," I say, praising his efforts.

I've always drawn attention to the smiles he provides her, though what should truly be recognized is how sane he's kept her in these moments. I do not intend to compare our experiences—my father dodged his demise. Still, if I lack the means to be sane in my own story, I can't imagine being able to maintain it in hers. He was her shoulder to cry on for most of it. I can be her friend, her equal, someone to relate to. But he complements her. He brings her something more. In some way, as hard as it is to admit, he is the better man for her.

I rise from my bed in a sweat from the heat. The bunker's solar panels have done wonders—a reflection of Liam's hard work. To my honest surprise, I look over and there he is in deep sleep. My arms extend, embracing the stretch that reflects the slumber I just emerged from. Soon I appreciate my current circumstances. I did not have a nightmare, rare to my past months worth of sleep. Recent instances are uncanny to what I've deemed conventional—Cynthia is awake and Liam is asleep. I didn't expect those two rarities to dawn so abruptly. Everything is in our favor, and while it is nothing to despise, I must admit that I am never comfortable when good things align in my life. So much, that I still question if I am experiencing a dream.

The halls are empty as I head to the restroom for my morning shower. The only sound present is the brush of my slippers, and the moment I enter the restroom, it is joined by the slow drip of the faucet. Someone must have used this room prior, drawing me to wonder who rose so early. The fog on the mirror confirms my speculations, though I choose to ignore it and wipe away the moisture with my palm. I stand still, observing myself in the mirror. The scar above my cheek remains, however, it blends into my skin. I can not say the same for the one on my forearm; the defect is evident. I've come to accept it as it's the thing that connects me to every single person in this bunker. We rebelled, and are reminded of it with a lifelong stamp. Mine doesn't align straight, the rush of the moment did not allow me competence. I look back and forth at the scars I present and compare them. They are a sheer reminder of my battles, and I can not say that I despise my marks. My journey has not been easy, and I should take the duo scars and wear them with pride. How else would I be able to prove my hardship? Perhaps one day, the world will look at people with scars on their forearm, and cite their divergence. I contemplate on that future, and hope that their citations will be marked positively rather than shameful. However, I know the society we live in. And I fear what manipulation from the government can lead them to believe.

I walk out the bathroom, rubbing my towel across my wet curls. I have gotten used to the inconsistent flow of the shower, so much that I would start to be concerned if it flowed properly. The undulating pressure makes washing my hair a much more difficult task than need be. My hair is getting long, far more than I am used to. The tips tickle my neck, and the strands that shield my vision make me think I could use a trim.

Like usual mornings, I come across Nova who begins hers. She would be the reasoning for the steam filled restroom prior to my arrival—the silk in her locks says so. She smiles from a far, her wide expression summoning my approach.

"You haven't risen this early in—"

"Exactly seven days," I kindly finish her sentence. "It has been a rough week."

She nods, offering a look of sympathy. "I could imagine," she says.

She directs me to her medical room for my vitamins. I should admit, I am unsure if the supplements are having any affect on my body. Still, I assure her that they are so I do not make her efforts seem lacking. Also, I like the few daily minutes we spend together. With such a beautiful smile, why would I encourage her to focus her attention elsewhere. I continuously accept these few minutes to admire her beauty—often stopping myself from getting lost in her eyes. Her attentive nature, and the ambience that forms itself in her presence. It would be hard for anyone not to fall for someone with such grace. And like my last love, I will continue to conceal this one. I can not afford another broken heart in this moment of my life.

She passes me the same lot of pills, and before she can pass me a cup of water, I already feed the supplements down my throat.

"Thank you," I say, drinking every ounce of water she offers. And in the process, I notice steel scissors lying on the counter. "Are those any important?" I ask, signaling to the tool.

She shakes her head. "I don't use those for patient tasks," she assures.

I nod in understanding, my curls brushing the back of my neck at my gesture.

"Are you able to do me a favor?" I ask, and before I can present my ask, she already agrees to do so.

Strands hug the floor beneath me, and I could actually feel weight lifted off of my scalp. Nova assures me that she is no expert in cutting hair, however, I did not ask for skill. She offers me a mirror, to reveal my new style and I stare at myself. My vision is clear without the curls interrupting it. Instead, they rest above my thick eyebrows. More of my face and its shape is visible, and the scar beside my eye has no curtain to hide behind. I gaze into my eyes as they gaze back, wondering if they got bigger, or if it's just an illusion. I admire this haircut. "Is there anything you can't do?" I commend Nova's work. We share a smile, and these few seconds of silence prove that I am not alone in admiring my new appearance. Nova's eyes lose themselves in my stare, and perhaps the rose in her cheeks spell out much more than I want to admit. I break our eye contact and hope my sudden halt does not offend her. It is not that I oppose her feelings towards me. I was never blind to them, and I can not say that part of me doesn't feel the same way. It is just that the greater part of me knows that my heart will never be able to offer her my full attention when it is still trying to accept that it will never belong to a certain person. Hopefully the day I get over Aria will be the day I can offer Nova the same embrace.

Just a few seconds go by before we are interrupted. Except the butterflies in my stomach are not the ones to intrude. Dr. Harrison stands at the door, taken aback when she sees us. However, I can not determine if it is because of the mess created, or her feelings towards my new haircut. Perhaps both, but respectfully, her validation is not one I seek, good or bad.

"Brandon," she offers a swift nod. "I actually had hopes of speaking with you this morning. If you can be so kind as to get Liam and be in my office in ten."

I nod, offering no words. I also try to conceal the frustration that starts to paint itself on my face. Because I can already sense what our meeting will entail, and the thought of Leander only makes me upset.

"Nova," Harrison smiles, before raising her eyebrows at the fallen hair.

"I'll clean it up," Nova assures, prompting Harrison to make her departure.

I offer Nova a helping hand, though she quickly assures it is unnecessary. "You should go tell Liam about your meeting," she says, a drift of concern tied to her tone.

"Thanks," I say before obliging and leaving the room.

I pass Leander on the way to my room, though we do not exchange words or looks. It is likely for the best, because my patience for him is running low. I almost wish I did not understand his dislike for me, because then I would have further a reason to detest him more than I already do. When I turn into my room, Liam is still asleep. He has not moved an inch since earlier, still I can tell he is deep in his slumber. He has given in to the slumber his body ever so desired. So much, that I do not recall that there was ever a time he's spent this long on his bed. I offer him my back, walking away with no desire in interrupting his sleep. Perhaps the meeting can be adhered to just one of us, and if not, I would still choose to allow Liam these rare hours of doze.

Nervously, I near Dr. Harrison's office. A guard scolds me from a far, but his distance from her already open door assures me that he was expecting my appearance. And despite her request to arrive alongside Liam, I come solo. I've urged him to rest for quite a long time now, and I do not want to disturb his sleep when his next surrender to it is unknown.

I creep in the door, knocking as I peek inside. When our eyes lock, she welcomes me in, assuring I can take a seat.

"You've come alone," she states.

"Liam is asleep," I say.

"You couldn't wake him?"

"No," I say, hoping that I do not come off as rude. "He hasn't had a good night's sleep in months."

I can see the frustration in her face. However, whatever she has to express to me, I can simply relay to Liam. Besides, I take blame for our summon in the first place. I challenged Leander's scold, and had I not, we possibly would not be called in for a meeting. Liam deserves the break. I will accept this scolding on my own.

"Perhaps we should wait till he is awake."

"It might be hours," I assure. "And I know you're upset about us leaving past curfew, but it was with good reasoning, and we were sure to be careful."

"I am not concerned about that," she clarifies.

"Leander sure seems to be."

Evidently, my frustration makes her upset. She takes a deep breath and looks off to the side. Still, if that is not her purpose in requesting this meeting, then I can only ponder what brings me here.

"Leander's worry comes from a good place," she says.

"Leander would kill me if he had the chance." I challenge her reasoning, enough to make the room go silent.

She attempts to find the right words to say, but quickly fails at it. I do not mean to be a burden on her, my initial purposes in coming to the bunker were all honest. Never was there a time when I wanted to cause the strain that I have. Still, there is only so much I can do. Or rather, so much I can take.

"I have a mission for you and Liam," she finally says. "Perhaps others."

My demeanor shifts, I sit up and offer her my full attention. Perhaps my heart drops a bit, her sudden approach caught me by surprise, despite my urge for it.

"After years worth of effort, I was able to bypass the encrypted wall that prohibits our access to the west," she explains. My anxiety rises at her words; to bypass the wall means her work would have alerted government officials.

"Have we been spotted?" I anxiously ask, and quickly she shakes her head no.

"All messages are encrypted, and our location is set across the nation," she assures.

I look down at the realization of her words. I try to control the tremble in my hands, but the growing rage within me fails to allow stability. I want to find relief in our incognito, but it becomes much harder to accept when realizing that if it is not us in danger, those made to falsely parade our residence are soon to encounter punishment. "Innocent people are going to die," I say through my teeth, and as I wait for her dispute of my words, I realize that she is well aware. To falsely target our location elsewhere will lead the government to attack that area. Perhaps she expects gratitude for my own safety, but what thanks do I truly have to offer knowing more lives are at stake for it. This news inspires guilt, not grace.

"I set the coordinates to a meadow out in the eastern hemisphere. I can not assure you that there are people living there, but if Reign were smart, he would not dare start a war with those who hold greater power."

I let her words linger, because I have no choice but to listen to them. Reign is far from smart when it comes to the decisions he makes, and I see no world where he retracts from assuring we are dead. If that means attacking another country, he will do so willingly. I would bet my worthless life on it.

"We need Reign's attention drawn away from our coast, so we can escape to the west. We are stuck here until he finds us," she says. "And I do not know how much time we have left."

I stare in her eyes, the negative tension is thick between us. "So you hope for a war," I deduce.

She clears her throat. "It is not my wish, but it is a scenario that favors our escape."

My mind fails to process the words coming out of her mouth. Not rationally, but ethically. She is going against her morals and willingly turning a blind eye to the ill effects of her actions. We just survived a civil war against our own people, and to enter one with another country is unattainable. Our military is not powerful enough, not even with our Forcemen as allies. Perhaps we have all that it takes to defeat the west at any given moment, however, we do not have the means to fight outside our coast. And I do not want to risk the lives of people who have no say in what occurs. Somewhere out in the coast, there is a young boy whose parents will keep him segregated in his home—far from the trenches of the world. He will spend years begging to see the fireworks that emerge from afar, still his parents will object to his wishes. I spent years in that scenario, and who is there to say that that young boy will spend more or less, let alone come out alive.

"Is that what Reign's announcement is about?" I ask.

"I anticipate it," she admits. "Soon after, I need you, Liam, and some others to meet with the Western operative."

"Why can't he just meet us here?" I ask.

"No one should know our location, Brandon," she scolds. "We have too much to lose."

I can't help but chuckle at her concern for our safety, but lack thereof for those this is going to affect. However, I owe her much more than she does me, so I don't protest her request. And in doing so, I have to accept that I am no better of a person than she is. I suppose I was never a saint in my actions to begin with. Everything I've done for the grace of someone else only ever challenged the lives of others.

"The location must be public," she continues. "That way we know if something were to occur, the east would intervene."

"Something?" I ask.

She takes a few moments. "Betrayal," she says.

I sit back, staring at the steel wall behind her. She is asking a lot—she's asking I put my life on the line—but the favor she's asking is within reason given what she's done for me. She intends for us to escape through the east, a task so huge, yet still deemed necessary due to the obvious. I've put a target on the bunker larger than before. Apart from being suitable for the role, I am to blame for the role even existing. I assure her again of my willingness, and perhaps it is a sign of the lack of awareness I've grown for my life. I hate to admit it, but I would rather be the one blindly led to their demise over anyone else. I cannot speak for Liam or the bunch she has in mind, though I will assure I take the lead. I've never been a successful leader in life, and when I've attempted, the endeavor falls flat. I am a victim of bad luck. He latches on to me like grape does a vine. Despite this, I'll put myself in harm's way, and take a bullet if need be.

It seems most people who reside in the bunker like to wake up with the sun. Not Liam, though, at least not today. He is still deep in his slumber. I remain cautious when changing into my daily gear; despite his deep state of near hibernation, I was sure not to be the thing that woke him. Before exiting, I stood still and wondered if perhaps obtaining a full day's worth of sleep is best to extend what task awaits him. I feel as if I have complained way too much about our residence to be opposed to the mission, but Liam solely made it work—not once did he lay fault towards it. And had it been the opposite, I know that he would still accept this mission, not only because he's dedicated so much of himself to helping others, but because like me he can never find a way to oppose. I rather he obtains all this rest has to offer. And hopefully his later mind is not too occupied to conflict with the few rests we have left before our trek.

I thought I'd hold much more fear for what's to come, yet what lingered surprisingly stayed in the room with Harrison. I guess my only worry lies with those who she plans to recruit, I don't wish Liam the burden of returning to the capital that wants us dead. Our faces are plastered on buildings, and the news fails to offer a day silent to our story. Perhaps we will be walking into our own casket, still I trust what ball Harrison pitches. I hope I am not wrong in my intuition, and perhaps my desperation to seek more to life is what steers my acceptance. However, like Aria has stated before, trust is my greatest flaw, and I don't want to meet the day it becomes my final enemy.

Maddox too indulges in an early rise, he greets my entry to the greenroom. "I think we should probably head out to scope the animal population," he says. "Our month's absence should have allowed many to breed, and I wanna make sure we are set for summer."

I remain silent, my mind occupied with the thought of what this summer will offer. His hopes verify his ignorance to what Dr. Harrison has planned for us. Her end goal is to transport the bunker's residence out west. Perhaps the herds will be able to enjoy their life, no predator ready to feast on what they have to offer. Perhaps, I won't see it. And while the execution is still premature, I am unsure whether Harrison intends to make aware of it to those who reside with us. It may be that she does not want to offer alternative hope to those who seek a better future. And it may be that she does not want to go in depth of the consequences that can be produced. It is impulsive, and since I do not have the grit to tell her how stupid of a plan it ultimately is, someone will. I do not want to insult her intelligence by retaliating, because I do not fear what it holds, and perhaps my courage is where minds agree in this bunker. I'm lucky to count the amount of people my demise would affect on two hands, still I lose faith in filling my second set of fingers. I find myself accepting of that—I no longer seek to validate others. And if I truly wanted to obtain Liam's mindset, why would I put my life at risk in hopes of being glorified after. It takes away any genuine intention that I desire to gracefully offer.

"Too soon?" Maddox reacts to my silence, despite being well aware that it is not rushed. The animals are in mating season, and it's best to assure that they've partook in the signs of the times.

"Good idea," I say, before assuring him that Harrison might have different plans in mind for myself. "She wants to send me to the capital to meet with a rep from the west coast."

His eyebrows ruffle in confusion, mirroring what reaction I offered Harrison upon her approach. Still, considering the reality we are a part of, no one can attest that escaping to the West coast is our only solution to surviving.

"If things go right, then he'll assist in escaping our coast."

"And if things go wrong?" Maddox challenges my uncertainty. However, I offer him silence in return. And this time, it lingers for quite a while. I myself have accepted what burden comes with even revealing myself again to the cities of the coast. Still, I know it will be hard to accept for those close to me. And by the look on Maddox's face, my intuition of him being one of those people I can count on my hand is confirmed.

"No." He shakes his head in opposition. However, he and I know his appeal holds no weight. Harrison has long since been in contact with the west coast. It is only a matter of time before Reign is made aware.

"Who is to say the West coast is any better than here?" he asks.

I step back, lost for a response, because I myself do not know what the West holds. Reign's dictatorship cut our ties with the whole world, and to get in contact with anyone outside of our proximity in the slightest is rare. Perhaps I am too quick to dismiss the greater dangers that may lie beyond the wall because it is Harrison advocating we move. Even so, desperate times call for desperate measures. I just so happen to be the one made to find out.

"Who is a part of her plan?" Maddox asks.

"Me and Liam," I assure him from what knowledge I've been given. "I could assume Nasir will get us there, and a few others for safety."

Again, he becomes quiet, except this time I can read his mind through the silence he offers. He wants to partake, but I don't see any sensible reason for him to risk his life. Besides, in the likability of the worst case scenario, someone needs to be around to look over the bunker. And despite the lack of recognition, he is one of the many who keep this operation afloat. He has for many years, and to depart in my honor is a burden I don't want to be responsible for.

"No." I shake my head in opposition, though he quickly challenges my disapproval, proving that he has no interest to favor my pleas, as they will fall on deaf ears.

"You need to stay for Aria," I assure him, because I know that no other reason will shift his demeanor. He thinks with his heart, and is as persistent as the remaining jade vines that cling on to every shelf in this room. His experience with the coast has been nothing but trauma. He recognizes it for what he went through, still I do not think he is aware of how much worse it has become.

Maddox looks down, drowned in his thoughts. And by the look on his face, I can already tell that my efforts to change his mind have fallen flat.

"Aria is going," he chuckles. "She would never stay behind, and I definitely wouldn't be the reason for that."

There is a churn in my stomach at the fierceness in his words, the honesty and confidence his means portray. He is far from wrong, and he doesn't need to make me aware for me to confirm his words. The moment I entered Harrison's office, Aria became a sole part of the mission despite her lack of awareness. The moment I met Liam and enrolled to become a Forceman, Aria too enrolled despite her ignorance to it. She does not need to know what is next in my journey just for her to latch on to the decisions I am forced to make. In every single universe, Aria is by my side. And as much as I want to be her protector, she will continue to be the one to secure my journey in every world I am lost in.

As I make my way to my room, I am stopped early by who I intended to see. Liam is awake and he is just feet beside Cynthia who, too, parted ways with last night's slumber. I look through the glass, and for the first time since her before her coma, our eyes meet.

She offers the first smile, and I return the compassion. She is well, and it warms my heart to be able to share a smile together. So much, that I am able to turn a shoulder to the butterflies that rush the nerves in my stomach.

Soon, Liam's eyes also meet mine and he signals me that it is okay to come in.

I nod, accepting his offer, still I try to get a control of the rapid pace of my heart before entering.

"How are you feeling?" I ask Cynthia, who has yet to take her eyes off of me.

She nods her head and assures, "I'm doing good," and despite the rasp exhaustion in her voice, I can tell she is being honest.

"The labs came back," Liam says, drawing my attention away from Cynthia. He raises the documents gripped in his hands embracing the light above, and exposing an enlarged microscopic capture. "Some cells were successfully blocked throughout the coma."

Cynthia fails to react, and I watch her slow movements. I can notice she is a bit different, but I never expected her to be her standard self if she were ever to wake up. Her eyes peer, reflecting fatigue in the labor consumed to just maintain them open. The few months long rest was not enough to retire the bags beneath her eyes, and it is clear that neither was it beneficial for the exhaustion she feels. Still, the treatment seemingly began to work internally, and I should appreciate that for what it's now worth.

"This is good news, right?" I question Liam, whose eyes have yet to dissociate from the documents. Nor do his arms exhaust from being held up.

Frantically, he shakes his head. "Not necessarily," he says. "It means the inflicted cells reacted to some components in the treatment. Enough to block from further toxins, but too much to interrupt the cells that enter her brain."

Despite his lack of notice, I nod to assure him I acknowledge his words. And soon after, I look at Cynthia once again, to observe her reaction to them. I comprehended what Liam is explaining, I've studied enough of the notes left behind on his desk to make sense of his words. While there might have been an imbalance in the treatment, her body's reaction could've been a response to just one of the present components, imbalanced or not. To know which one, requires more research. And to deem if the coma was solely a human reaction or individual to her would have been a much easier task had Gregory and her been given the trial treatment simultaneously. She had the greater courage out of the pair, and soon after her outcome, it was decided for Gregory not to undergo trial. He didn't budge nor insist, however, I do not blame him for his elude from it all.

I keep my eyes on Cynthia, hoping that for once she is oblivious to the topic at hand. I do not want her courage to recover before she does, and even in that instance, I made Liam assure me that he will never fulfill her wishes to undergo another trial long before her wake. We are now living in that present, and I could only hope that Liam adheres to the loyalty he's always upheld.

"Did you walk today?" I steer Cynthia's attention away from Liam.

She smiles. "Some steps with Aria," she whispers, her voice rusty. "But I still have a lot more learning to do."

I offer her a smile, before Liam excuses himself out of the room. "I need Dr. Harrison's eyes on this," he explains, and just as I want to stop him and advise him of what's to come the moment he enters her office, I deem my efforts less of a burden if he hears it from Harrison herself.

When he begins to step out, Aria and him cross each other's paths. He apologizes and steps aside, allowing her room to walk in before exiting himself. Except the tension between them is dull enough to declare Liam still in this room through the energy alone. I suppose they've yet to converse despite Cynthia's wake. I never expected they would rekindle anyway. Nor do I want to arouse the sensitive topic any more than I have previously attempted to.

Aria holds a tray of food. I quickly notice it's distinct from what tonight's menu offered. She has mashed potatoes, apple sauce, and what I can determine is her best attempt at soft-serve ice cream. Perhaps the variety does not align, but it is considerate to the ache produced in Cynthia throat. Feeding tubes resided there for quite some time, and I hate to imagine the pain she is feeling.

"I got your dinner," Aria says, before I insist on taking the tray.

"I got it," I assure her, pleading that she go rest. Along with her shift in the kitchen, she's been fulfilling her mother's needs. Whether big or small, I've yet to see Aria neglect any task in relation to her. And perhaps I'm a hypocrite for imploring those around me to grasp on the rest Nova has been long petitioning me to do. However, I recognize that my needs do not run parallel with theirs. Their desperate needs are much more silent than mine, but I see their needs all the same.

"Thank you," she smiles, as she insists her mother notify her if she needs anything. And as she walks out, the short tension between her and Liam still lingers. So much that Cynthia inquires about it. "Are they okay?" she asks. And while I know the truth, I assure her they are just great. The moment those words come out my mouth, I realize I've lied to Cynthia for the first time. Never in my life have I been able to do so, but now here I am speaking in riddles for the sake of her sanity. Worrying is one thing, but to pin blame on yourself for the quarrel of others is a burden I do not want to risk she feel. And for that, I can only hope she does not see beyond my facade. Luckily, but still very unfortunate, her current state doesn't allow her to.

Cynthia attempts to scoop up her mashed potatoes with the spoon, however, her efforts are slow. And for Liam to brush over the idea of her illness recuperating only means that the coma left her with the burden of having to slowly re-learn the abilities we all take for granted. Perhaps not as stern as a toddler obtaining knowledge out of the womb, rather similar to having to find your lost item after you vow to have left it in a spot it no longer resides. As frustrating as it is, I try not to look at her differently.

I offer a hand, and she quickly denies my help. "I need to practice on my own," she says.

I look down, not only to try to mask the pity, but because I am embarrassed to have possibly made her feel less than with my efforts. "Sorry," I say.

"Don't be," she chuckles. "I've put you guys through enough, I don't want you to feel sorry for it."

While I do good in masking my reaction to her words, they put a churn in my stomach. Because all that we have been through has in no way shape or form been any subtle desire to hers. And what makes matters worse is her inability to steer away from the illness which inflicted her. Perhaps decisions along the way could have been avoided, but who am I to judge someone's impulsive settlements. Especially in a timeline we had no choice in.

"I didn't think you'd wake up," I admit, and to do so forces a ton of imaginary weight off my chest. So much that I do not notice the pair of tears streaming down my face until one falls on to my rested hand.

"I didn't either," she says, and when I ruffle my eyebrows she assures she could think throughout her coma. "I thought so much that I got tired of thinking."

"What did you think about?" I ask.

"You, Aria, your parents," she lists. "I thought about the life we shared, and what life we could all continue."

I offer her a smile in awe of her continuous hope. She's latched on to it her whole life, never a day she's departed, and I will always envy her ways.

"I even thought about Maddox," she reveals. "I remember Aria telling me about him before my coma, and while I love the boy, all I can think about is how he will never be you."

I look down in an attempt to conceal the red in my cheeks. I stopped comparing myself to him long ago and deemed it a sin for all the malicious thoughts that followed the comparison. Perhaps I didn't want to admit that I saw a flash of those same thoughts in Maddox's eyes the moment he came across Aria and I watching the sunset the night of her mother's wake. Or even when he admitted to not ever meaning to be what came between what she and I had. I do not wish he compares himself to me, because I am by no means better than he is.

"He had these vines made for you," I say, the tone in my voice silently challenging her innocent claim. "He knew they were your favorite and wanted them to be here the day you wake up."

She looks up at the vines that grasp on to the walls of this room. They've expanded quite a bit since we've placed them here, and I find relief in their managed livelihood.

"I was wondering where those came from," she says. "They're beautiful."

27

Upon leaving Cynthia's room, I came to realize that I spent near hours offering her my company. Or rather, honoring the company she now is able to give me. And contrary to our previous conversations, I was able to banter about much more than just a day's worth of gossip—though, I made sure to leave out anything that was cause for concern, as she could benefit from a cold shoulder to the unknown. She is oblivious to the distance that lingered between Aria and I far longer than it should have. And perhaps she is ignorant to the mission Harrison has at hand. She will find out eventually, and there is no harm in prolonging the news since it has nothing to offer her.

The moment I dropped Cynthia's dinner plate off at the kitchen, there was an evident shift in the energy. Perhaps the empty dining hall didn't offer much of it, still I can sense the unfamiliar vibration. Aria was not fulfilling her late night task, and upon reaching my bedroom, I could only assume Liam's absence is a sign of his speedy return to the labs.

Despite my long day, I found no desire for sleep. It didn't call me to bid a goodnight, nor did I attempt to seek it. Rather, I decided to check on Maddox. My heart ached a bit at the thought of Cynthia's subtle disappointment towards he and Aria's newfound love. Perhaps she doesn't dislike their unity, rather she is preoccupied with the idea of Aria and I choosing a romantic life together. I hate that she needs to learn that our love as friends is much stronger than our love as lovers could ever be. Perhaps Cynthia will see that one day on her own, but now I'd rather spare her the disappointment of knowing what we will never be.

I did not need to knock on Maddox's door. It was creaked open just enough to see that neither was he in his room. Assuming he was in the greenroom, I made my way there slightly frustrated at my unsuccessful scavenge. And as I did, I heard soft voices muffling through Harrison's office door. Ample enough to make out there is more than one voice, still insufficient to garner what they discuss. Slowly, I made my way to the door, her guards' lack of interrogation again proving that they were expecting me.

Slowly I knocked, and my heart dropped at the sight of Aria sitting across from Harrison. The door's creek filled the room's sudden silence, and my eyes failed to meet Liam, Maddox, Leander, and Nasir, who too filled up the room. Instead, my eyes chose to stare at Aria, and as I walked in slowly, my eyes neglected to dissociate. I did not retaliate, nor did I make any attempt to object to her presence. Still, I stand in the corner and watch her—the words that Harrison delivers just as far as they were behind the door. I knew her persistence would prevail, it is a trait that long held her hand in her lifetime. So much, that Maddox's previous warning on it was solely a necessary reminder rather new to my knowledge.

Aria avoids looking my way, this moment a mirror reflection of initiation day. She wanted to be there for me, still she did not want to confront the hurt it would force on to me. Perhaps that's much greater of a challenge for her than her initial decision could ever be.

"Are you with us, Brandon?" Harrison's question pierces through my blank stare. A necessary pull—her words bring me back to reality.

For the first time since my entry, my eyes depart from Aria. "Yes," I softly assure, nodding in case my whisper falls flat.

Aria briefly looks my way, but my eyes aren't quick enough to meet hers. And for the sake of her anxiety, I force myself to dismiss my attempt.

"Francis is set to meet you all where you deem appropriate. The more people there, the better," she explains.

"Who is Francis?" I ask.

The western government official," admits. "He will be expecting us."

"How do you know he's no fraud?" I challenge, and everyone's lack of question forces me to realize that they went over this long before my arrival. I wish they'd sought me sooner. Glancing around the room, I know why they're so willing to trust this Francis. That reason is sitting just a few feet ahead of me, her hair tied in a bun.

"I've been in the field a long time," Harrison says. "A lot longer than the war, and much longer than most of you have been alive. I've met many people along the way."

"And you're sure we can trust him?" I reiterate.

The lack of response after my question offers a new form of silence, one that suggests the matter wasn't already discussed. A common curiosity connects the room. Again, I do not mean to challenge Harrison's plans and motives, but lives are at stake. Aria's life is at stake. And her inclusion in this mission warrants me to question any plan and interrogate any motive if it means she'll be safe.

"I do not know," Harrison admits, forcing a long breath of anxiety on each and every one of us. "The west coast has their own opinions about us. If you are asking if I think he will deceive us amid our plan, no I do not. However, I can not guarantee you that he won't, for the sake of not breaking a promise. This explains the urge for a public area. If something were to happen, being in a public place accessible to authorities would not be the most ideal decision on their end."

I look around at the lot around us. Evidently, Nasir is our guide. If you were to offer me compensation to find my own way back to any region in the coast, I'd be no richer. Moreover, I do not have a big enough ego to deny the fact that Leander is great at observing an area. And if he were weak or relatively bad with a weapon, he wouldn't be the one who watches over our bunker. And of course Maddox has talents of his own. At least the three of them don't have their faces plastered on buildings decorating the coast. Aside from their connection to us, they are the safest in this mission—they are a new face to any person we come across. That includes the western official. And perhaps the rest of our roster is unknown to him. But soon after his arrival, he will be more than familiar with the three of us.

"This is the man in question," Harrison pulls out a photo. The sudden reveal leads me to believe that she has long been stocking this plan for when deemed necessary. Perhaps we are the reason for its expedition, still it is no secret that she prepared for it.

Slowly, I approach her desk. The photo is well kept, she evidently cared for its state. The man pictured wears brown pants, his white shirt tucked in its seam. He's slim–Lanky if you will. However, his eyes are what stick out to me. They are large and round, the shade so obscure I can not determine whether they are green or brown. Perhaps the darkness of his hair dissociates them from their natural hue, but that would not disclose the look on his face—his eyes dictating his very still expression.

"Francis was a pilot in his younger days—" she explains.

"So what," I interrupt. "The border security won't allow his entry."

Frustrated, Harrison clears her throat—the gesture quick to shed self-reflection on my tone.

"Reign doesn't have much air control," Liam blurts his first words since my arrival. I understand his motive in intervening, however, that doesn't take away the subtle feeling of ambush by their unity. Enough for me to embarrassingly sit back and avoid further interrogation. All in good motives, still I don't react to it lightly.

"Correct," Harrison agrees. "That explains the closure of airports. Air travel, even within our coast, allows higher risks of escape."

Harrison rises from her chair, her demeanor demanding more attention. "Nasir's knowledge on the coast allows us to know the few dead areas within. Perhaps they are not suitable for living, but that favors our plan. Francis will land his plan and meet you all at the capitol. This is when I leave the intuition in your hands." She turns to me, my heart noticeably beating at her persistence. I thought I was not going to fear this mission, but the fierceness in her words reminds me that I am not as courageous as I sought myself out to be. "I request you all have precautionary weapons prepared from a distance, and Brandon be the one to exchange first words with Francis. When and if deemed safe, you shall continue."

"No." Aria rapidly interrupts, however, I am quick to assure it is okay. I had already prepared myself to do so, and accepted that I am willing to take the risk over them.

"He will already be familiar with my face the moment he lands." I say, before turning to Liam and Aria. "He will notice the captures of you two as well, but please let me be the one to speak to him. You guys have done enough."

Suddenly, Aria and I have switched roles. She is disappointed in my courage, yet I do not have enough means to meet the eyes she heavily pierces my way, I could only wish she offered her stare a few minutes ago. I receive them without response, my eyes swiftly glancing at Liam who too seems distraught—he frowns at the floor, upset by my courage.

Harrison continues. "After, you will all be the first to escape the East, and will assist in gathering the rest of us in a few days' time."

I watch Maddox repeatedly tap his finger on the metal arm rest, his nerves rightfully having no shame to show itself. Despite his early upbringing with his mother in the regions, most of his life was lived within these steel walls. He's become accustomed to our little world here—he's made it conventional. So much, that I knew not to despise my transition in his presence—to complain about my current state only insults what he has learned to love. I don't think he wants to give it all away, more so, at the risk of our lives.

"How do we know we're safe in the West?" Maddox questions, failing at his attempt to hide the shake in his voice. "What makes you sure we won't get killed when we escape?"

Harrison turns to Maddox, her expression expecting a question like so. "The west has nothing to gain from killing us. Neither do they gain anything from helping us."

"And the Forcemen?" Maddox continues to challenge the reassurance of our livelihood.

Harrison looks my way at his question, her stare confirming the mutual understanding between us. I attempt to return the same assurance, still my eyes fail to meet hers for more than a second.

"I will offer you transparency in return for your service," she reveals, and I exhale the moment I feel her eyes just shy away from dissociating from my direction. Perhaps she feels pressured to admit what dark lies ahead, however I do not see where my demeanor suggested the obvious. "Reign and Mason's Forcemen should be occupied elsewhere. We were able to bypass the counter wall that blocks communication outside our coast's perimeter. That is the only way we've succeeded in reaching the West. We recently lifted that interference."

I slowly collect all of the reactions within the room. Leander and Nasir seem to obtain information they already know, their expressions offering no room for remorse. And I no longer want to judge them as people, still I can't help but perceive the difference in us as people. Aria, Maddox, and Liam look confused, their eyes reveal a sense of fear, and I myself do not blame them.

"No need to fret," Harrison assures, noticing their reactions. "I can assure our revealed location is far from our bunker."

Aria sits up, her eyes questioning what Harrison admits. I solely remain in the corner, as I try to avoid the realization on Aria's face. It is a mixture of distress and perhaps betrayal—it seems out of touch for Harrison to put other lives at risk for the sake of ours. However, I understand the irrationality the risk holds, and if Reign were to attack another country to assure our fatality, he'd solely do it to prove a point, because he has no power over those who are not our allies.

She continues to explain, "It is pinned out across the world in the eastern hemisphere, but I can assure that Reign will be stupid to attack another country." Her tone rises at the few frustrated reactions. "However, he should currently be offering the proxy his full attention. That offers us enough time to escape unnoticed."

"And what if he does attack?" Aria brings to question. I can still see the pain in her eyes.

"Then we should be thankful we will not be present for a war bound to be lost."

Abruptly, Maddox rises from his seat and storms out the room. I begin to wonder if he regrets his inclusion, still I do not question his repudiation from it. I know his new motive is to assure our safety, however, I can not brush past the fact that his mind is thinking about the lives that can be taken in the act of a war. It is what any sensible person would dwell on.

"He should have never volunteered," Leander hisses. He looks annoyed, and soon I match his expression—except mine are aimed at him rather than Maddox.

"I could guarantee you he is more of an asset to the team than you are," I confront his arrogance. Soon after, Harrison counters both of us, demanding we quit. Had she not done so, I can not be sure of where the altercation would have landed. However, by the look on Leander's face, he does not need more of a reason to strangle me. Soon, he is the next to storm out of the office, and I can feel Harrison's frustration frantically bounce off the walls.

She takes a deep breath. "I need you all to be prepared," she pleads. "You leave soon after Reign's announcement."

The energy in the room spells concern. And judging by the hearts that beat in the room, it is aimed towards the possible risk of mass lives above our own.

"You should all seek some rest as I finalize the means around the mission." Harrison dismisses us, offering me one final stare. "Thank you," she says.

Word about Reign's celebration got around quickly inside the bunker. So much that I can not recall a time where the dining hall has been this occupied. Everyone gathers around the television, except there was no intention of celebrating within these steel walls. Fortunately, what would unsettle the majority, still remains undisclosed outside the sum of us involved. It is safe to assume that those ignorant to the possibilities watch out of curiosity. Perhaps my trust in Harrison's instinct declares that my expectations should be as oblivious as the mass. However, I am no mutt to the knowledge Reign lacks. If I was, I'd be as blind as the others.

Aria sits beside me, offering a nod as she claims the last seat at the table. I did not expect her presence, yet I am relieved by it. As we left Harrison's office last night, she made no further efforts to look my way—her silence louder than the brush of her feet. I did not anticipate she would neglect me once more—doing so has always been sparked by her anger towards me. However, I knew from her previous stare that she was solely disappointed.

Nasir's eyes have yet to dissociate from the television. Not once did he make any attempt to even notice the crowd around us. We spoke last night. It was our first conversation in quite a long time, so long that I do not remember even interacting with him in the past few months. He stopped me as I ventured to my room, his eyes glossy. After a few stutters he apologized for what occurred out by the motel on our trek here. "I was only following orders, but I promise it didn't take the first explosion for me to realize that trying to steal the product and leave you all stranded was wrong," he said. "I thought you were gone the moment the cases exploded. I can't imagine what it would have been like to come back to the bunker and explain that to your parents." He continued, and for seconds to come, I was lost for words. I did not know how to respond, so I offered a slow nod, and seemingly that small affirmation healed what had been bothering him for some time. Amongst what ran through my mind, I contemplated apologizing to him for Liam leveling his weapon at him in response to his uncivil attempt. However, I didn't. If I had done so, it wouldn't have been genuine, because despite the state of my livelihood, no sudden movement of mine reflected the urge to stop Liam. Rather, my demeanor commended his reaction. And in that moment I felt a shift in the person I have become.

Forcemen parade the capitol house, and by the looks of their commitment, I worry that it is not against their will. I am no mind reader, nor can I perceive their willingness. However, if this celebration was programmed to force fear onto our trio, I wouldn't deny their endorsement of it. I know a greater sum of them feel betrayed by us, and even if few once despised their position as much as I did, to kill a member of their pack should have only forced a shift in the struggling dynamic. Perhaps I made them stronger. Or rather, Liam made them stronger—I couldn't get myself to gun down the Forcemen even when the means were necessary. I contemplated the evening Dad had asked me if I had killed anyone. By his honorable definition, I did. However, in truth, I never murdered a soul who homes a body. And when each moment called for it, I abandoned that effort. I sat in bed one sleepless and wondered about how much of a strain my accusations have caused him and Mom. I assume they hurt, but they never broached the topic in our conversations, so I can't be sure. That assumption will never be confirmed. Frankly, I rather they never ask and silently dread that their son is far from a saint. I do not see myself leaving this earth with my hands clean. To do so is foolish. I do not desire the act of murdering someone, I was not raised in that way. However, neither do I desire to be a peacemaker in a ring full of my enemies. I will not offer them the pleasure of my surrender—I will never parade a white flag so easily.

The Forcemen wave their armor as they make their laps around the capitol house, their demeanor emphasizing their urge to paint a threat rather than celebrate the man of the hour. I do not find the need to do so, their unified front has never been for the better of the coast. To deem themselves intimidating now comes with no effort, they've spent a line of years already doing that.

My stomach churns at their symphony, despite it being my choice to continue watching. I hate to admit it, but it hurts to see so many Forcemen continue to unify after our loud departure. We were solely the first three dominoes who failed to complete the domino run, and it is a shame.

"Top right," Liam whispers in my ear. "They're protesting."

I shift my focus and confirm his observation. There are protestors. There are also armed policemen tracing the skirts of the barrier around the capitol house and I fear for the safety of the protestors. As I've always said: Where there are Forcemen, there are protestors. And now the unpredicted unity between both forces only leads me to expect the worst. I do not now know how things have aged for protestors since our departure. Their motives were always to simply stop killing people, and we did nothing to better that. Unfortunately, my curiosities will remain unanswered as the broadcast makes every attempt to turn a blind eye to the cries outside the barricade. I wish we could hear what they roar, but the music tunes them out. Shamelessly, I must admit that I appreciate what they conceal. If one courageous man jumps over the barricade, they will not see another second of life. I do not want to be one of many witnesses.

Suddenly, the music comes to a halt. A few seconds linger, before Reign takes the stage, behind him Mason echoes his movements, before standing side-by-side embracing the cries of our coast. With that, our entire bunker goes silent. I see some grit their teeth, while others frown at his appearance. It is the first time I see either of them since the base, and the first time others see him in years. His appearances are now rare, and despite it being a few months since our last encounter, he's aged quite a lot. He looks exhausted, and I hide my grin at being the one to blame.

Reign stays back, as Mason reaches the podium center of the makeshift stage top of the steps. And to my surprise, he goes without introduction. He is first to talk, his confidence rather daunting, but I choose not to look too much into it, as my attention is quickly garnered by his tap of the mic—the screech echoing the fields of people.

"People of the East," he finally says, his voice sharp and firm, perhaps slower than usual. "I appreciate all of you who came out for this honorable day." He continues, and I can't help but chuckle at his spiteful sarcasm. "It seems we meet in spite, however, I hope for a future where we find ourselves in unison. This year is hopeful, and full of promises, but that shall not be fulfilled without recognition."

Slowly he turns to Reign, who grins at his arrogant words. Reign watches the crowds, and I wish I had his lens that flowers all the hate aimed towards him. Getting through life would be such an easier process if I were to acquire his confidence. I assume that is what got him to where he is.

"Our wonderful president continues to seek a better future for our coast," he says. "The population crisis can not go unnoticed, and I must assure you all we are defeating it one day at a time. What we do is not for us, it is for the people of our coast. We strive to make lives easier, more maintained, and suitable for those we care so much for."

The silence throughout the bunker is jarring. I get more chills from the quietude around me over what Mason delivers. I look at different faces amongst the crowd, his words piercing through all of their existences. Both Reign and Mason's motives in providing a life worth living came at the cost of similar lives alike. They had no choice in what demise their life's journey encountered, still he found their existence to be a burden. Our coast is made up of thousands of souls alike, and those who no longer home a body haunt the ground that took their life away from them.

"To be unified comes with prosperity. It comes with success by means of growth. Today we not only honor our president, but we honor our coast. And what a better way to do so, than to declare our official title."

Attached to the marble structure behind the stage, just below what would be the second floor of the building, a flag is unveiled. Its center is mustard yellow, quite the interesting choice of a color, still the black parallel borders level it out. Center, a black star lies below three circles who share the same hue with a cross piercing through the star, but its arms stand out in crimson. The accent positions are similar to me, but I would not blame those ignorant to it. It resembles the legs of the base, a clear homage to the Forcemen, and a star that I'd identify to honor the capitol. None worthy of honoring, and I wish I were there to inject in their minds the mirror shade of red to the blood of those they murdered. Still, I fear they'd find pleasure in that observation, and I wouldn't put it past their intentions.

"Yesterday, the east coast." He looks directly in the camera, forcing a spiral of chills down my spine. "Today, the country of Sudom."

There is a dark energy amongst us, and it is clearly a common thread along the whole coast. Or perhaps, across Sudom, as the ruckus once unavoidable is now mute through the television. The crowds are civil, and I fear they sense something that I don't.

"With a new title, comes new beginnings. And with new beginnings comes new leadership. He who will carry on the goal, and continue to seek and capture those who put a halt on it."

Slowly, I further approach the television. My eyebrows ruffle in confusion, a reflection of the reaction on Reign's face. He too is confused. His eyes wander around, and for the first time in his publicity, he looks vulnerable.

His sudden attempt to approach the podium falls flat the moment the surrounding masked Forcemen grip his shoulders, forcing him on to his knees. My eyes widen, and for once, I hate to admit that I feel pity for the man who's forced punishment onto those undeserving of maltreatment.

The concealed trio of Forcemen raise their weapons, painting an image I would have never thought I'd see. And before we have the opportunity to react, they shoot in synchronization.

Gasps echo in the bunker, fear sprinting in the room, as Reign's blood marks the new addition to the Capitol House's marble floors. My hands shake, and perhaps I am not enjoying this unforeseen moment as much as I anticipate, come the day President Martin Reign would meet his demise. And it is rather evident that the masks are used to conceal the identity of those who murdered our leader, but the broad shoulders of the center man assures that I am no stranger to he who hides behind the silk threads. And perhaps he will discard the mask if given the opportunity to see me once again, still I hope he is aware that I will put up another fight.

In the distance, I see Elandra forcing her hands over Amir's eyes, she is barely able to sustain the murder herself. And around the bunker not one reaction opposes fear. Surrounding crowds rumble, and I wish I could differentiate the reactions from the television, yet I am unsure if the majority found something to celebrate or oppose what just occurred. However, the distant gunshots force directly through the static and quickly put an end to my curiosity.

Mason offers another stare at the camera, his eyes uneasy to match. "I, your new President Daniel Mason, promise to continue the operation at hand and decrease the population." He's yet to look away, his lack of blinking convincing me he's challenging me to a staring contest. I lost seconds ago, my frantic twitch reflects the fear I fail to manage.

"It starts with him, and it carries on with you," he finally says, grinning at his last words.

My heart drops, the chills multiplying into the abyss of anxiety I carry on my shoulders.

He knows I am watching.

"It is not safe to go." Maddox rushes back and forth.

I stare at the floor, as the lot discusses what is next—their voices rather distant despite our close proximity. Reign is dead. Not only does he join the many lingering souls, but he was forced to the afterlife by his best friend. His partner in every venture he's undergone. I want to manipulate myself into believing that the population control was solely a venture too big to consume, yet they've managed for years, and Mason made clear his next intentions. An intention so firm, that I fear what power he has obtained to be able to successfully dethrone he who he spent all of his career under shadowing. His stare through the screen was vague, so much that it is ingrained in my already terrorized mind. Perhaps it pushed fear on to me, but what man am I to let his fear tactics be as successful as his murder.

I wonder what occurred behind closed doors—we are blind to even what they deem transparent. However, I believe nothing took place so big to provoke such a response.

I reflect on my times as a Forceman, my mind was always too consumed to mark every detail, still I never failed to notice the dynamic between both Reign and Mason. There was a power structure, still no mind could identify who had the upper hand up until an hour ago. Mason was the face of every fault Reign so quickly strayed away from. And from the beginning, he was the one who built the army of Forcemen. They veer more towards him due to his accessibility. He praises their sins, and in response they praise his.

I wish Reign were able to see that his greatest enemy smiled in his face and shook his hand everyday. This is not my confession to feeling sorry for his death. I am solely expressing that I do not believe Mason's dictatorship will be any better than what Reign had to offer.

"We have to continue the mission," Harrison says. "The sooner the better."

Maddox takes a deep breath, his pleas more fearful than frustrated. "We need to stay here—"

"Harrison's right," I interrupt. "You guys saw the riots. The coast is struggling. It's better to go now, instead of waiting until all of it diminishes."

The gunshots were alarming, still they assured that the coast is undergoing another riot. I am no prophet, but my intuition tells me this one is going to last a lot longer than the ones that occurred during our residency. Had I been a prophet, however, I would wish to see this coming so Harrison could spare the innocent lives currently at risk.

"We will be ready tomorrow morning," I assure Harrison, before letting myself out.

I seek no ally, and it is evident I stand alone with Harrison's persistence. So instead, I seek courage. I was once he who feared everything in life. If I become him once more, we will never make it past the barricade into the West. I do not want to forever be stuck in Sudom.

30

I stand ahead of my open closet, staring at the uniform that has long taunted my sanity. It still remains in its condition, each mark signifying my long journey. And the dried blood stains are so prevalent, that I doubt a proper cleanse could remove them. It resided in the bottom of my hamper for months—I never cared to wash it. The idea of using it even one more time never crossed my mind. And yet, despite the terror that came with wearing this uniform, some part of me chose to keep it.

"There's no point." Liam's sudden entry cuts my moment short. "If you wear it, you'll put a larger target on your back." He embraces his bed, sitting on what is likely to be his last moment on it.

I offer one final look at my uniform, before closing my closet and concealing once more the pain that comes with the attire. He is right. Honestly, I can not recall a moment where he was ever wrong.

Rather than mirror his approach, I sit on the floor beside my bed. I think to myself here often, and I wonder if I'll miss the peace it offers. However, if I can find tranquility right beside what bed terrorizes me in slumber, then I assume I can too find it elsewhere.

"Did you expect that to happen?" I ask Liam, still shocked about Reign's murder.

He looks around, seeking an answer. "No," he admits. "But I did know Mason never had the intention to be someone's second in command."

I take in his words, his past observations much wiser than mine, as he was a Head Forceman for quite some time. Some might say he was Reign's ideal example—for that, Mason never favored Liam. And perhaps Mason's stare through the television was more for Liam than it was for me.

"The population control plan was always Mason's idea," he reveals. "Reign just had all that it took to execute it. The fame, the money. The only reason he had Mason lead the Forcemen was to avoid a vendetta."

Despite the bond between Liam and I, he's never been this transparent. I wonder if he feels sorrow for what happened to Reign, but I do not ask, as I fear his answer will force me to view him through a different lens.

"If the population is the issue, why doesn't he just let us leave?" I finally ask the question I've always wondered, yet never had the means to seek. A fault of becoming accustomed to what is forced on to one's lifestyle, a lifestyle worthy of condemnation were it not the only lifestyle available.

"It was never about the population. It was about power," Liam admits. "If we're confined, he can control everything that happens inside with no interference from the West or any other country that desires to get involved. The border is a symbol of how far his power has taken him. And the Forcemen were just a way to expand the support he already had and give them armor."

I stare in his eyes, his words forcing a pang in my stomach.

"If you offer a desperate person an answer, they'll sacrifice everything just to have it, even if that means giving up everything to become a Forceman," he says, and finally, I look away. Not because of my opposition, but because I do not think he realized he described a past version of myself that I try so hard to forget. I was desperate for Dad's well-being. So desperate that it has led me to where I am today. And despite the troubled venture, I do not believe I regret it. Once more, I offer Liam my full attention. Perhaps he, too, was the desperate person in need of an answer. I can't say for sure; he's never revealed his purpose to me.

"Once you offer those in need a remedy, they'll love you for the gift you've given them, because it was once only a miracle. Now you've granted their only wish and have an army of people who choose to be blind to your faults because you've given them the number one thing they can ask for." His eyes pierce the wall, failing to blink. "I hate that it had to be at the sake of innocent people, but a man who seeks so much power has no heart to tell him right from wrong. I thought he found some compassion the day he took away the panacea. I assumed his next step was to stop the whole plan then and there, but it was clear he was just testing the waters to see how big his greatest possible threat can get. The one he created."

Liam's eyes do not form tears, still I can see the pain behind them. Perhaps he is hurt, or simply traumatized by what we all just witnessed. He didn't look away the moment Reign was shot. And despite having a few murders on his roster, Liam never made eye contact amid his crimes. Even when I reflect back to our time on duty, Liam looked away the moment every time a patient was injected with potassium. He could never bear watching someone's life being taken away from them, even when their demise was by his hands. Still, he chose not to look away from Reign's murder.

"I'll tell you one thing," he continues. "That threat is just as small as Mason hoped. Not even the forcemen with hearts like yours are enough to dismantle those with hearts like his. Mason is now the most powerful man of the coast and maybe one day he'll be the most powerful man of the world. It is what he desires. Of course when you have one of the most overpopulated nations to ever exist and chose to get rid of those who aren't on your side, even at their worst, you'll be left with a nation filled with a majority of folks who will do anything you ask. Maybe one day that will mean overtaking the west—who knows what else. He controls guns. He now controls the coast. And he won't stop until he controls every single one of us, and the world."

I allow silence to linger, as I digest his words—they are rather daunting, still I should not be surprised. Reign painted the plan as a sixteen-year mission, however, I had always sensed that his motive was to become dictator by the end of his run. And while I expected many things, I never anticipated that goal falling into the hands of Mason before his. He was betrayed by the man he created, I can only believe his soul looks up at him wondering why.

I look over at Liam, my tone strained. "Why did you become a Forceman if you knew?" I finally ask.

Again, he looks around. He is not bothered by the question. Instead, he looks as if he is tired of running away from it. "Because I am on your side, Brandon," he says. "I was always, always on your side. Sometimes we have to do things we don't want in order to find a solution."

31

The bunker's silence remains. What energy was torn at the capital has evidently seeped into this bunker and is yet to let itself out. Faces throughout share the same scared look. They're traumatized, and even if some saw such a sin in the past, this only revived what was forcefully forgotten. I fell into that minority, the murder mirrored what I saw happen to Steven's grandpa. Except I cannot truly compare the act, as Reign was far from having such a heart. I tried to erase that memory out of my mind, however, like my nightmares, this forced me to relive that moment.

I visit Cynthia, the only sound alive being the soft creek of the door. I attempt to seek my parents first, but their absence in their home and around the bunker forced me to look in less probable places, and my wandering led me to Cynthia. My sudden arrival proves my intuition right; they offer Cynthia company. They do not speak, and barely look my way upon entry. They, too, are visibly upset from what occurred early today. I find some relief in a bed-bound Cynthia being the only one to not witness the murder. However, her demeanor suggests she, too, is stunned—perhaps afraid of what comes next. I could assure they fear the safety of Aria and I much more than they do theirs. All that they've done in life was led with the intention of bettering our livelihood.

I swiftly study their faces, and I hate that I come with news that will only fuel their sorrow. Because even if all of my past efforts have been in their favor, I've managed to only ever make matters worse. Perhaps I was not placed on this earth with heroic tendencies. However, I never wanted to do anything outside of offering my family a better life. And despite them moving heaven and earth for the sake of their love for me, I can not help but believe that I've only failed to do the same in return. Because what bigger fear of a parent than losing their child. And with every attempt I've taken in their honor came my life at risk. Now they wake up every day to my face on the news, and many who desire my immediate death. I hope they know how sorry I am, because my decisions continue to haunt me. And what haunts me more is their unspoken judgment of me. However, nothing could haunt me as much as a life without them. Because I am still the little boy begging his parents to watch fireworks. And they are still the parents denying his request. For that, I will always adore them. And I hope they understand my next venture because I will not stop until I am assured of their safety over mine. I sincerely contemplated not discussing the mission with them—I expect no positive reaction. However, my sudden disappearance might spark a worse reaction yet. They deserve to know, even if I leave out a large sum of what even offers me fear.

"How are you guys feeling?" I ask, yet I receive no verbal response. They solely force a grin and nod their heads.

I take a seat in the far corner, my nerves unwilling to approach any further. Mom looks my way, perhaps she's noticed my odd demeanor. She smiles. "Are you doing okay, mi hijo?" she asks.

Her words seem distant, and it takes me a few seconds to deduce her concern. "Yes, I'm fine," I say, my response unconvincing. Luckily no one sheds light on it.

"Things are dangerous," she softly says. "Much more than before."

I nod, despite her lack of eye contact. She only ever avoids it when she wants to hide the pain in her eyes, when her makeshift smile is not enough of a facade.

"I've got some news for you," I admit, except my reveal falls flat, leading me to wonder if I wasn't loud enough.

"At least we're all safe here," Mom says, and I begin to believe she is talking to herself.

I look over at Dad, his eyes are glued to the floor despite it having nothing interesting to offer. And Cynthia rubs the edge of her blanket between her fingers, their lost minds forcing a strain on my heart.

I stare at their quiet agony, and once again ponder on whether I should leave without notice. I last saw them in this state prior to Cynthia's diagnosis. They always offered Aria and I a counterfeit smile for sake of our fragile minds, still I managed to see their misery from afar. Together they gathered in our living room. Not a proper sentence was delivered, yet the energy was present and dismantling what happiness we've previously obtained. I slowly walked away, assuring my soft feet didn't interrupt their sorrow, not because I was scared to break it, but because I knew they were not ready to reveal to me whatever had been inflicting their livelihood.

I slowly rise from my seat, my mind set on a silent departure. They do not deserve to suffer from fear, I am all they have, and I hate to reflect on all of the pain I've forced on them. Perhaps it is best I am not here to witness what pain I offer next.

"What is the news?" Cynthia asks as I reach the door.

However, I slowly shake my head. "Nothing," I lie, "I just wanted to wish you a goodnight." I say.

Cynthia smiles at me, her embrace igniting butterflies in my stomach. I thought I lost those butterflies, yet her smile proved them to still linger.

Swiftly, I leave before they question the gloss in my eyes.

32

My hunting gear has become pristine. One hour each day for many months now I've spent time polishing it—a small price to pay to honor the weapons I've come to cherish. I can see my reflection on the dagger, and my pistol is so shiny that it mirrors the light above. I make sure not to over buff the handle; I'd hate for it to slip on handling it.

Despite the fallen state of my bag, it makes quite the house for my tools. The largest pocket houses the pistol, and the knives fit snug in their allotted slots. Nova was kind enough to stitch the broken strap the day I accidentally tore it. I was going to resort carrying my weapons in my pockets and the side of my boot, but she was adamant the bag was worth fixing. Since then, I took it upon myself to be more cautious with the bag. It was a gift from Maddox. He told me it was his first bag, home to his early hunting gear. He insisted I have it weeks into our duo as hunters, and despite my refusal from guilt, he pleaded I have it.

I look at what necessities I have, realizing my departure means I will have to shed certain luxuries I've become accustomed to—even in the bunker. Harrison plans to provide us all with the proper equipment for safety, and while the possibilities with this trio are endless, it won't suffice. As I watch Amir from afar, he might appreciate these much more for the time being. I do not plan my departure to last more than a week, but Harrison knows what risks come with this and has arranged for Levi and Amir to take on the duties that typically belong to Maddox and I. However, he does not know what tomorrow holds, and for that I'll assure him to utilize these at the next hunt. Even if he is unaware that Maddox and I won't be present for it.

He sits alone, reading a novel, and from my observations, he's read the book multiple times since I've arrived at the bunker. I could only assume much more prior to. I picked it up once, and the story entails a young boy who left his life behind to be his brother's caregiver. Still, the younger brother embraced what life he had and found nothing wrong— a reflection of all his efforts to hide all the pain life threw their way. He was his shield, and I could not tell you what the ending pertained, my heart did not allow me the strength to finish such a tragic story. It is no children's book, and I always wondered if he understands the meaning of the book. If he doesn't understand it now, he will as he grows.

Amir looks up and smiles the moment he notices my presence. I smile back given that my intention was not to hide from him. Swiftly, I rushed up to him clutching onto my bag.

"What chapter are you on?" I ask.

"Thirty-two," he assures, before alluding his mother is restricting his access to the television.

I look down, slowly rubbing my palms. He shouldn't have seen that, and to be transparent, he should have not seen a majority of what the television had to offer. He is still young, and I wish he had not been in the room to witness the broadcast of Reign's murder. In all honesty, I wish I had not been present either. I had seen one too many deaths, and while this one hurt much less, it still forced a churn in my stomach against my will.

"Was he that bad of a guy?" Amir asks. The question is so sudden that I am taken aback. Part of me hopes he had asked his mother instead of me.

"Some people don't have good hearts," I mirror my response to his curiosity towards Justin. "That doesn't mean they should die, but sometimes they do."

He nods, and I sigh with relief when he doesn't question any further. I do not like lying to a soul so genuine, but sometimes I must for the sake of his innocence. Besides, I would rather not admit to him that I do not pity what happened to Reign. I wish it did not happen in that manner, and I do not celebrate his demise, but that is only because I do not have the heart to do so. He was an evil man, but his death does not work in my favor. Without Reign, Mason will continue the plan, and it is clear what awaits me in his leadership is far worse than anything Reign could conjure. Perhaps that is what conflicts me far more than his death, but I will not sit here and admit that to Amir. I do not want him to have that perspective of me.

"Are you hunting this late?" He points at my bag.

Slowly I shake my head. "I actually wanted to give it to you," I say. "You can use it on our next hunt."

He offers a big smile, pushing his book off the side. He grabs the bag in excitement, and I can't help but smile at his joy. He's always

180

wanted to be like Maddox and I. Now he can do so, and I must admit, it hurts to know that I won't be there to see his first official day hunting.

I urge him to be extremely careful, the moment he pulls out the dagger. "Keep it to yourself," I say. "Don't share it with anyone."

He looks up at me and smiles. And like my departure from Cynthia's room, I swiftly leave, before he questions the gloss in my eyes.

I had barely gotten any sleep last night, and I wear the lack of it on my face—the bags beneath my eyes are so heavy they are forced open. I spent late hours staring at the ceiling until the early rise. My mind was occupied on what this journey will entail. I pondered on whether or not I was built for such a task, I never sought myself to become the person I am today. So brave that his life no longer is his priority. I am sane enough to admit that to myself, because if I don't, someone else will, and unfortunately I've never escaped the stage in life where the words of others hurt more than my own. For a moment last night, I managed to put myself in a state of my younger self. And when I did, he feared who he saw. He vowed to never be like him, however, he is yet to know that life will lead him exactly to be he who he dreads. Perhaps he fears the man I am today. Still, I wish I could hug him and assure him that it will all be okay. That hug would mean much more to me than it would him. I need connection now more than ever in my life. I am led by terror, and that fear lives inside of me because I need to obtain a facade for those I love. For those too risking their lives for the sake of a reality I introduced them to. I have never been a good leader, and every day I wake up, I am reminded of my flaws.

I spent my final night in this bunker reminiscing on my younger days. Had I been the founder of time, I would utilize my strengths to freeze the measure of it. I'd put a halt on the little years I spent locked in my house, the only knowledge I had on the outside were led by my curiosities. I was able to create the world out of my imagination, only for that world to be shattered when I finally entered it. I can now recognize that I failed to appreciate how privileged I was.

I wear new clothes—new to me, anyway. Harrison provided us with outfits that do not garner unwanted attention from any crowd we join. I wear brown jeans, rather snug, and a loose black hoodie. She assured my hunting boots were just fine.

I leave behind my Forceman uniform, and perhaps this departure is just what I needed to finally solidify what separation I needed to initiate the moment I stepped foot in this bunker. Beneath my hoodie, I wear the shirt I arrived in—a shirt I do not plan to surrender. Its red stripes hug my body in a way no other can replicate. Maybe this shirt solely makes me feel far more protected than I do only with those by my side. Because if life was in my favor, its previous owner would have been walking this journey with us. Like my old uniform, I denied Nova's request to clean the shirt. Except my purpose in maintaining its state lies far deeper than what it meant to leave the cargos untouched. It means that I can conserve the only piece of Steven I have left. The way he left it.

Here, I stand in silence, far more silent than I've ever tried to remain. I am outside my parent's cote, separated by just the curtain between us. I won't be saying goodbye, because I plan to see them in a week's time. Still, I do not assure them I will see them later—I already can not control the flow of tears my eyes fail to delay. They deserve to know about our mission, I wish they had been those first aware. However, I fear their reaction would have led to my loathing. I've disappointed them far more than once, and I hope this will be the end of that trend. They deserve the peace I failed to provide them.

I feel a hand on my shoulder, and I do not need to look back to confirm her presence. What embrace she offers is always warm to the touch, and often not even her touch is necessary to meet her radiance.

"Are you ready to go?" Aria asks, resting her head on my shoulder.

It takes a moment, but I nod.

"Is it okay to admit I'm scared, Aria?" I question through the shake in my voice. I truly thought my prior bravery would manifest my ease, but I stand corrected.

"I know you are," she says. "That's why I'm here."

She extends her hand out, offering her lead. I glance over at my parents one last time, their breaths pacing steady in their sleep. And before I unwillingly welcome their wake, I take Aria's hand and accept her honest embrace.

Harrison assures we have everything we need. She granted all five of us weapons: modified pistols with silencers, and a quick access pocket knife for closer caution. I consider the duo an upgrade from what I used to hunt with. It is obviously designed to handle more than just an animal. It may even rival the power of the weapons the authorities use—not that the plan is to raise arms against another human being.

There will be threats. Exactly what those threats turn out to be, I can not know, but I won't give into fearing them. These threats may even walk the same journey as me. I do not know how much I trust Leander. His energy this morning is rather odd. If I were to call out his suspicious behavior, I'd spark more unwanted tension between the two of us without really accomplishing anything. But his behavior has caught my attention, and he may well be an unnamed threat.

I hold the weapon—it fits snug in my gloved hands. I wasn't even aware we had this much weaponry stored in the bunker, and judging by the curiosity on Maddox's face, neither did he. I can not deny that this raises concern, but what good is worrying about Harrison's secrets now?

"Here," Harrison pulls Liam aside, offering him a hacked cellphone. I watch from afar, hoping my prying eyes aren't noticeable. "Francis is the only contact. Message him only a time and address when you are ready."

Liam accepts the cellphone, nodding as he stares at what piece of equipment came close to becoming a memory from the months we've gone without it. Quickly, I look away, before they notice my eavesdropping. Not that they'd mind, but I fear what leverage the device offers. Perhaps knowing that someone other than I has it, is not appropriate to the courage I want to portray.

"There is a tunnel in the heating room," Harrison reveals to the five of us. I raise my head at her words, and as I do she is already looking at me. The alleyway illuminated by a wave of red lights, I do not question what I already know, her stare is enough of an answer, and it only forces me to assume she knew I'd come across that tunnel the day she sent me to change our last tank. I abruptly break our eye contact, my facial disappointment letting me down. This mission was always being designed, and while they might paint the picture of how honorable my courage is, I can't help but believe that I just lent her the final piece in this journey. I will accept it for what it is, because what I do is not for her. It is for those who I adore and those I've grown to love in this bunker. If this fails, and I am soon a dead man, I leave confident enough to know that my blood is in her hands. She's saved hundreds of them, still I know I was never worthy enough to be cared for to the extent she does every being in this bunker. "It will lead you ten miles out where a vehicle will be waiting for you. From there Nasir will be your guide to the capital, and you will all proceed with what we've discussed."

She takes a deep breath, one of which I can not decipher whether it is drawn from fear or frustration. Perhaps both.

"I wish you all the best of luck." She grants our exit. "I will see you on the other side."

I follow the lot who slowly exit, the tension evident. I am the last to exit, and before I can pass the door frame, Harrison swiftly assures her peace. "I hope you are aware that none of this comes easy," she says. "You are just as important as the rest."

Slowly, I nod. However, I do not offer her any more of an answer. I do not want to admit that I do not believe what she pleads. Because I gain nothing from it. I do not despise her. Still, I can't help but believe that from the moment she ordered Nasir to leave me for dead, she never intended to care for what I had to offer. I do not challenge her decisions, rather I pity them. I recognize the ordeal of being judged for your past.

We walk down the halls of the bunker one last time, the silence rather tense. Nova chaperones our exit, and her eyes paint the fear of all of us. I put on a facade, and assume the others do as well, but what we hide radiates off one another. We walk rather slowly, and I can't help but wonder if any one beside me regrets accepting the journey that awaits. I can not speak for them. I only recognize the energy that lies within us.

As we begin to pass the final room in the hall, I notice lights reflecting from the window that separates us from the woman I made an effort to avoid this morning. A few more steps and I see my reflection on the glass. Behind that reflection, Cynthia lies awake, her eyes following our trek. She doesn't seem confused. Rather, she looks at me and smiles, before placing her hand on her heart. I smile back, placing my hand on my heart. Among many reasons, what I do is in her honor. I beg for the future where she is cured. I continue walking—my eyes fluttering, before the end of the window cuts our interaction short.

The closer we get to the heating room, the colder it gets. I embrace the idea that this time I do not carry a one-hundred-pound tank, and I wonder how that weight compares to the burden I currently carry on my shoulders. Our footsteps echo through the steel steps, and the air gets thicker. So thick that I cut the smoke that pours out of my breath.

We enter the room, Nova wasting no time in opening the door to the alley. And when she does, the flush of red light meets our facade, and the echoing sound of the chains is reminiscent of my introduction to it.

"I can't believe I never knew about this," Maddox whispers to Nova.

"She just recently showed me," Nova admits, her voice a bit let down from the trust she thought she and Harrison shared. The lack of it only makes you wonder if this would have been her escape had she given up on all she's built. Perhaps others might belittle their feeling of betrayal, but I see right through their thoughts.

Leander and Nasir walk in first, my hesitation falling behind the rest who follow their lead. I watch the shade of red reflect off their faces—it only reaches my legs.

Swiftly, Nova grabs on my hand pulling me towards her. She hugs me tight, her racing heart winning mine in what relay they have. I hold her tighter, realizing that she needs this hug much more than I do.

"I'll see you on the other side." She echoes Harrison's words, before pressing her lips against my cheek. Her embrace quickly offers what warmth this room fails to give, but I try to now make this moment something she will later reflect and ponder on. Soon, I can't help but notice Aria's melancholy stare, her cheeks soon match the artificial light above. Her mien is rather envious, and like the sympathetic man I am for Aria, I try to not give in to Nova's embrace. Rather, I offer her my eyes, attempting to avoid the pain hers hold. I nod and assure her I will see her on the other side, before joining the others into the alley.

We have been walking for quite some time now, enough to remind me that I have long lost sense of it. I can not distinguish whether it has been a trek of one hour or 5. I do know, however, that if my parents aren't already questioning our disappearance, they will soon. I wish I had left them a letter, but to do so only sparks a greater fear for my life.

"I need to take a break," Aria pleads midway through our journey.

"Yea, of course," I comply. Leander huffs a breath of frustration.

I pierce a glare at him. Her evident exhaustion should offer him some form of compassion even if it is miniscule.

"A break is fine," Nasir assures, noticing my emerging snark.

Silently, I find relief in his interjection, I had far from kind words for Leander. I must remind myself to be civil for the sake of those too putting their lives at risk.

"Here's some water," Nasir offers Aria from his bag of nourishment Harrison prepared to get us through the journey.

"Thank you," she replies, taking a sip of the cool liquid.

"We don't have much water to spare," Leander says, taking a seat on the ground. "Make it last."

"It's okay," I interject. "She could have mine."

Liam rests on the rails, while the rest of us sit on the steel platform. I wish we had warmer attire; the crisp air perches through our threads. More Aria who's exhaustion is far from enough to provide her with body heat. Her hands shake, the cold bottle hard to handle.

I remove my gloves, handing the pair to her. Perhaps they can offer her some comfort in the slightest for what it's worth. "Thank you," she whispers, and as her chilled hands embrace the soft threads, our attention is forcefully interrupted by a distant quake. So present, that the steel beneath us vibrates into the end of this alley.

We quickly rush up, and the moment we do, a second quake follows—this time stronger than the first.

It stems from the direction of the bunker, and the distant shrieks and gunshots confirm my worries. "They're being raided," I cut through the shake in my voice, before I begin to rush in the direction of where my parents still reside.

"Hey!" Leander forcefully grabs my arm, putting a halt to my panic.

"Get off me!" I push him away, before he grabs my shoulders and forces me on to the ground.

"You go back and then what?" he yells.

I look around. Faces are still. Aria's body shakes much more than it did seconds ago, and I've never seen Maddox look so distraught. "We can't let them die," Maddox cries.

"I'll go back," Leander assures. "If you die, then there is no more escaping to the West."

"I have to go get my parents." I cry, before he stops my third attempt.

"You are going to continue what we planned." His eyes are terrorized by a fourth explosion. "You weren't satisfied with your life, so you came here to get away from it. The Forcemen didn't workout so you decided to come here and screw up everything we had going on. Now I'll go back and fix what's broken. Leave now!"

Taken aback by his words, I fail to form some of my own. I look around at everyone else, except they are too terrorized to speak. A tear streams down my eye, the cold nearly freezes its journey down my cheek. I look down the alley, humiliated that I know I will still walk down the direction I headed, rather than the one I came from. I do not feel the urge to charge at Leander, because perhaps he is right and I can not attest what truth is being exploited in my face.

"He wasn't the only one," Liam stands between us, and despite his interjection in my favor, I can't help but replay Leander's words in my head. The words he had long been waiting for the opportunity to say. Perhaps now is not the most appropriate time, still I do not blame what frustration he holds. "If you're going to go back, go now before it gets bad," Liam continues, before Leander pulls out his gun and rushes back to the bunker. He helps me collect myself, and I can't help but notice the slight shake in his hands. "Let's go," he says, before leading the way to the end of the tunnel.

We follow along, our tears leaving a trail of our existence. I look over at Aria who can barely follow the speed of her feet.

"My Mom," she cries as we lock eyes.

I catch her close fall into my arms. "She will be fine," I say. And while I had promised myself I'd never lie to Aria again, I do for the sake of our sanity. Swiftly, I lead her way, before the explosions are followed by the cries and shouts of patients.

35

The light at the end of the tunnel is not so welcoming when one has to abandon their loved ones to get there. I wish I had gone back, and while I still have the opportunity to, it is worth nothing. Still, I stop. I do not doubt what Leander says he will accomplish, but I can't get passed the lives at risk: My parents who were sound asleep when I last saw them, Cynthia who offered a smile, Amir who could not hide his excitement towards my gift, and Nova whose embrace awoke the butterflies in my stomach. I left them, and hate to continue walking in my own skin, I am ashamed of it.

The moment we reach the car, I embrace the crisp air that the day offers. It is cooler than usual, my tears still close to freezing upon departure. Still, the shake of my hands, steady to the quiver of my lips, fret at what lies miles back. I drop down onto the dead grass, my cries hitting the ground before my knees. I left my parents behind, and the only confidence I have in their livelihood lies in the hands of those within the bunker.

"I left them," I say to Liam who grips my shoulder. "I left them for dead."

"They are not dead."

"Then what are they?" I interrupt his honest attempt to console me. It is not that I don't appreciate his reassurance, but I do not expect the best. "You and I both know that the Forcemen will not spare any person in that bunker."

"You and I also know you'd be a dead man if you return,"

Soon, the only sound around is the whistle of the winds around us. I stand up, recollecting my emotions. And while I offer him a few seconds of understanding, I still do not agree.

"I'd rather die beside them, before dying anywhere else," I admit, my words piercing through his chest.

I look around, Maddox holds Aria who struggles to form a sentence through her cries. And a few feet away, Nasir unveils a vehicle beneath a tarp.

Suddenly, the distant sound of a helicopter's wings garnered our attention. I offer Liam my stare, the pain on his face evidently terrorizing him inside. Perhaps he is right, still I do not know how long I can force myself into believing that my story has a happy ending—one where my parents are by my side.

"Let's go," I say.

PART THREE : WEST

The moon shows we have been driving a full day, the car silent throughout the sun's slow set. We disappear into the darkness of the road, unsure what remains back at the bunker. In these last hours, I kept asking myself why it couldn't be raided a day prior. Liam made an attempt to assure that some things happen for a reason, and while I appreciated his approach, I did not choose to respond. No response of mine would have been so kind to his honest attempt. I did however take his words with a grain of salt, because I will not accept the meant-to-be's of life. I long since gave up on the idea that life offers purpose, and with that went the idea that I have one myself. If I did, it no longer subsisted with the livelihood of my parents up in the dull clouds.

I do not know how Mason managed to find the bunker. I wish the near decade worth of confinement came with an extension. Enough for us to escape what more drought Sudom has to offer. I am exhausted from it. So much, that I do not turn an eye at the sight of a street sign. Our trio was who they sought out to seek within those steel walls, yet here we are escaping what was our token of safety. We were not there upon their discovery, now here we are on route to be the probable devastation of what more lives we come across throughout our journey. I've learned a lot in the bunker, so much that I will cherish what it gave me. However, what I will honor above all, is what words Leander expressed just hours ago. I do not oppose his frustration. I hated my life as a Forceman. It was a life I chose in selfish honor, and when it no longer aligned in my favor, I fled. I had no business escaping the capitol, not when it was only beneficial to my parents. I should have accepted what separation we would have endured, because the goal was always to favor them. Still, I managed to prioritize mine above all. Now I have to live with the constant reminder that whatever occurred in the bunker lies in my fault. It will now reside in my consciousness for whatever time I have left on this earth. Perhaps in a different universe it was still raided despite my interrogation. However, we are far from that universe, because I chose to seek refuge from my own decisions. Now I must recognize what damage I've done. There is no sorry, nor going back—I am past being wishful for the reverse of time. I appreciate Leander exposing what I needed to hear. If he had not, I'd victimize what life continues to offer me. Slowly, I am accepting that perhaps I am deserving of what torture clouds my life.

The road comes to a sudden stop, but I do not make any effort to question the halt. I do admit, I am exhausted. Yet, contrast to my prior cries for sleep, my eyes are only wishful to release the tears they ever so lose the strength to imprison.

"I will be back," Nasir assures. The pressure of his door startles my exhaustions, still I offer the tree ahead of me my full attention. Lights reflect off its bark, their shades retro. Perhaps the hue is rather similar, but I am too deprived to offer it attention.

I look over, Aria is sound asleep on Maddox's shoulder, he rests his head on hers. I find relief in knowing they are getting sleep, still I worry what occurs in Aria's mind. I wish I were able to offer her an answer, she is more deserving of it than I am. However, I too worry about her mother as much as I do my own parents, and any maybe's I attempt to paint will only be colored in hope. I am hurt at the thought that she is feeling as guilty as me. I never limit her emotional capabilities, but I know her enough to see she must have been beyond exhausted to be able to sleep amidst drowning in a pool of tears.

Despite my motionless demeanor, I could feel the eyes of Liam staring at me through the rear view mirror. I know he hurts for me, but I hope he doesn't pity the outcome of my life's decisions. Rather, I hope he forgives the troubles I caused him, so much I did Aria. I inflict all that I come across, and I can not wait, for once, to be someone's medicine. I think I deserve the assurance.

"I hope you know this is not your fault—"

"We're clear" Nasir interrupts what words Liam felt the need to express. "Let's go." When I finally offer him my attention, I see the large sign behind him standing strong over the building. A sudden knot forms in my stomach, the colors now reflecting off my right cheek. I refuse to believe it even lives, and I lack the energy to confront the memory of its possessor—he who deserved a life past my interrogation.

Here we lie, behind the motel of the man who risked his life in our honor. I did not know much about him, but I know he woke up every day with good intentions. To help and serve, his self made purposes revolved around bettering the lives of others. And he died while fortifying mine.

Liam shares a quick look at the shake in my hands, quickly I make my best attempt to conceal what exposes my fear.

He nods, his expression waiting for my consent, and while it takes me a few heartbeats, I assure him it is fine.

I exit the vehicle, while Nasir wakes up the rest.

Slowly, I pace my footsteps as I approach the front of the lot. My reflection is accompanied by Liam's shadow, except one is shaded in caution while the other misery. He walks with his weapon raised, his protection evidently favoring me over himself.

After a few more feet, we are exposed to the hollow grounds— the wind playing its role and whispering the name of those forgotten. Except I never went a day where I neglected the memory of Steven's grandpa. He took a bullet in my honor, and the only grace I was able to offer him was my safety, because in that moment, he wanted that more than anything. Still, butterflies flutter in my stomach, reliving the day he was shot before my eyes.

I wish he were still here, as I do Steven, but those wishes are not bound to come true, I will never be so lucky. I guess I can only hope they have since met in what the afterlife has to offer.

My tan embraces the sign's blue hue, the orange only blending in. Not a being in sight, besides those of us who just arrived. The lobby is dark and empty, clearly untouched. I do not know how to feel, and it physically hurts to strain so much emotionally.

I continue walking, the bedroom doors are sealed shut. I didn't expect a place with little to no noise to have the possibility of becoming more silent. It is strange, and the shift in energy is tense.

A few more feet, and my eyes quickly gloss at the crimson painting that remains stained on the ground. I quickly look away, retching at the sight. I do not fathom at the thought of the coast being fed the lie of me murdering such an innocent man. Rather, I hold in the tears that cry for him.

"We don't have to rest here," Liam assures, but I quickly shake my head.

"It's fine," I say. "I'm fine."

The two of us continue, before I attempt to open a room door. "They're locked," I say, after failing to open one and a couple others. Liam assures we return to the lobby, and as we do, I give my best effort to not lock eyes with the blemish on the concrete. Just the thought of it alone aches me.

Before Liam enters the lobby, I take a step back. My legs halt, proving they have a mind of their own, and I know they want to protect what little peace I try to latch on to. "I will wait here," I assure Liam, who doesn't need to question my decision to understand my reasoning. Perhaps memories live forever, still there are just some I do not want to relive for the sake of my sanity. I've relived enough with solely being here, and I do not think I'd be able to confront the office where I failed to assure Steven's grandfather about his grandson's demise.

My arms tremble in cold as I observe what this ghost town has to offer. It is not so appealing in the winter, its lack of life indicating a lack of soul.

The remaining three turn the corner, and I lock eyes with Aria whose makeup consists of the dark circles beneath her eyes and the red blush on her nose, a kiss from the cold. I am saddened by what I see, still I try to not make notice of my pity. Her reaction to everything is far from strange, and I do not want my innocent judgement to make her feel indifferent.

"We all stay in the same room," Liam demands, his urge cautious of our safety. The lot of us nod—even Nasir believes it is for the best.

Luckily, Liam chose the key to room one. I know the decision might seem small, but I can't help but reflect on his expression to my reaction of the blood. I appreciate what attention he pays, because I do not want to walk over the dry blood of a saint once more.

When we reach the designated room, Liam opens the door. While expected, I still feel wary at everything functioning as it did the day we fled. It solely feels different without its possessor, and it is evident to all of us.

Liam walks in ahead of us, assuring safety. I envy what cautious approach he continues to maintain. Perhaps my open demeanor might reflect lack of fear, but it truly mirrors how little I now care about my own livelihood.

Suddenly, Liam's loud pant garners our quick attention. Nasir and I follow, and when we enter the room, he raises his gun at the bed, and the strange woman lying on it—a frail woman seeking rest, reprieve, and isolation. The sight of the gun alarms her, and perhaps me as well. I haven't seen Liam raise a gun since the day we fled.

It doesn't take long before Liam realizes the woman is harmless. Slowly, he lowers his weapon, embarrassed by his sudden approach.

"They left his body to rot," says the strange woman. Her southern accent proves she is not from my region of the coast. She introduced herself as Jolene, an old friend of Steven's grandfather. She typically played the role of room service, cleaning after the few guests they had. She was one of the unlucky folks to encounter what remained the day of his murder. She admits her residence is unaccompanied, still she gives her best effort to maintain what stands. Often, she powers on the motel sign to honor his name. It also works as a nightlight—the surrounding streets so dark she fears someone will get lost in the void. I ache at the shake in her voice, his death evidently hurt her.

"He was a good man," she admits. "Always looking out for others before himself."

I do not offer her eye contact, due to the shame that lingers. Rather, I look out the window, the 'M' on the sign slightly flickering. It matches the twitch in my eyes, her words feeling like a punishment with no liberty. I'd exit the room if it weren't an ill-gesture.

"Luckily, two men were driving by and helped me bury his remains out back, bless their hearts," she says. "Y'all are more than welcome to pay him a visit when you'd like."

I look down, my demeanor culpable or her pity. Her tone is rather shaky, yet she doesn't drop a tear. Instead she stares at the wall ahead of her, resenting the memory that replays in her head. However, I must admit I appreciate her offer, as it allows me to escape this tragic retelling.

"Excuse me," I say, before letting myself out.

I close the door behind me quickly regretting my decision—my hands begging for the gloves I gave Aria. It must have gotten colder in the past hour, and I begin to reflect if my frosted fingertips are punishment enough.

I look at the ground amid my walk out back, my cheeks have since lost the ability to express themselves. For the first time this season, the winter offers snow—steady flakes melting upon hitting the ground.

I expected inconvenience in locating the memorial, but the moon offers my guidance. The glow is subtle, yet it hugs the yellow carnations that lie above the distinct plot. The mint petals prove that Jolene often replaces the florets. They'd never be honored with a long life in this weather; perhaps their greatest hope for one is being frozen in time. I smile at the flowers, Maddox would take this opportunity to advise me that they are not in season, so she must have gotten them from a shop.

I kneel down, offering a few petals the kiss of my palm. They are crisp and rather sharp, their bones fragile. A few hit ground the moment I release them and sit them back to where they were. Slowly, they begin to be sheltered by the snowfall.

Distant footsteps grab my attention, but I quickly dismiss them. I'm among friends, and the memorial deserves my full focus. I am saddened by what lies across me, and my heart only strains more for he who resides six feet under. He did not deserve what happened to him, and the soul in me cries that no being deserves such terror.

"How long have you known him?" Jolene's voice breaks the flow of the wind.

"Not long," I admit, embracing her approach. "He lent us a stay and his car amid our flee."

Silence builds between us, and I could feel my tears begging for freedom. I pride myself in imprisoning them for as long as I have, I lost that talent quite a while ago. These last tear-free hours are a testament to what strength I ever so criticize.

"I knew his grandson," I admit, grasping the hem of my shirt. "We became really close back at the capitol."

"Steven," she says, my eyes quickly meeting hers.

I offer her a slow nod, with no answer. Perhaps my raspy cough is enough of a response, still I evoke my stare. I do not want her to take notice of the strength I endure. It is painful enough.

"He was a great kid," she admits. "Always thinking about the rest, just like his pa."

I look down, wishful for my prevail. He is far beyond a good kid, and if I could be deemed one wish, I'd wish for our places to be switched. He deserved to walk this earth much longer, and I hate to dread what every day has offered me. He would have appreciated the good in the bad, and I do not see a reality where I am granted such talent.

"I don't think y'all did it," Jolene reveals. "In fact, a lot of us don't."

Finally, I offer my glossy eyes.

She offers a smile, yet it doesn't reach her eyes. There is so much melancholy behind her stare, and I am now introduced to what she and I have in common.

"Thank you," I whisper through the dusk of dawn.

Jolene was so kind to accommodate us, she gave us all the necessities to get through the night. This room is warm, and I felt the pain in my body's change in temperature. I embrace the bed for what it offers, a comfort distinct from what I deemed contemporary at the bunker. And while I spent much of my time there complaining about what I was gracefully given, I miss what home I made in those walls. I had those I love beside me, in whole with no void. We do not appreciate what we have until it is gone.

Aria sits on the ground beside the bed where Maddox is sound asleep. I look her way, her freshly washed hair curling to her shoulders. Her fragile bones force a turn in my stomach, and I am wishful for the day I see her smile once more.

"We have to leave before the sunrise," Nasir states. "I'll make sure to wake you guys."

He begins to make himself comfortable on the couch, until I soon put a halt to his attempt. I get up offering him my spot on the bed.

I can tell he needs a better rest much more than I do and I do not see myself enjoying much of tonight's slumber. My mind runs on turmoil, and I fear the likability of the darkness offering a mirror image to our last rest here.

"Thank you," he smiles, his lack of opposition proving that the exhaustion his face paints is far from a facade.

I take a seat beside Aria, offering a shoulder. For a moment, we do not say a word to each other. She hurts, and I can feel what pain she is going through. Still, she accepts my embrace for what it's always meant.

"How is he holding up?" I inquire about Maddox. He has been much more silent than the rest of us, and I hate that his home was destroyed. Much of his life was spent in the bunker. Beside Nova. Beside Harrison. He doesn't know life outside of it, because he forced himself to forget what memories he has around his early life. He made a sibling out of Nova, and a parent out of some of the nurses.

"He's hurting, Brandon," she assures, wiping a tear off her cheek. He created a safe space for Aria, yet she cries at not being able to do the same in return. It is not that she can't, but right now she's hurting. It is hard to be someone's savior when you, too, are in need of comfort.

The bathroom door comes to a full open, the steam entering our room before Liam. He dries his wet locks with a hand towel, relief painted on his face. He looks our way, offering us a grin.

"You guys should get some sleep," he suggests.

I agree with his plea, but I know the attempt at rest won't pay off much. And while my eyes beg for it, I can not sleep unless my mind chooses to do so first. Right now, it is still busy focusing on what I left behind.

"I won't be able to sleep," I admit. He doesn't question further, as he knows what it pertains to. The lack of eye contact and subtle twitch in his are telling. He often looks away when he doesn't want to make his pity evident.

"Should we see the damage," Aria asks through the silence, her eyes meeting with the television remote.

I follow her stare, the television remote lies still on the side table. I knew watching the news was an option. However, I chose not to mention it. Perhaps fear is forcing me to run away from confronting what answer I do not want to foresee. Nothing assures me that my parents are dead, but I am not ready to come forth with what might be true. I fear that I am once again preparing myself for the idea that they are, so in the case that my greatest fear comes true, it hurts less. I am not done preparing, and perhaps I never will be, but now is not the time. If so, they might as well leave me for the wolves who seek prey in the woods. I'd be more beneficial as a dead man.

"We had another full moon yesterday," I say. "It should be a couple days before they broadcast the raid." However, I know my claims are likely to be false—they evidently know where the fleeing grounds reside, and they no longer care to fabricate what they transmit.

Aria looks down, the carpet below soaking in the sum of her tears. "I need to know if she's alive, Brandon," she cries.

I do not offer her an answer, and her eyes say she understands why. Unlike Liam, she holds an honest stare when she is aware of the means. It always feels like a challenge, and each time it becomes more difficult to meet her gaze.

I catch her tears in my palms, wiping away the slope. Aria lives for her mother, and I can see the distress in her eyes. They match mine, and I hate to see what pain I feel inflicted on her as well. Without our parents, we only have each other for guidance. It is not just what we desire, rather it is how we were raised. Aria and I against all—and here, we lie together. I adore her so much, and I hope that when my time comes, it is before hers.

I look at the remote, what I fear to confront is the answer to what Aria so desperately seeks. "Let's check," I say, the shake in my voice raspy.

My hands are as shaky as my voice the moment I grab the television remote. Liam offers his distance, standing in the corner. However, Aria latches on to my arm, her tight grasp proving what fear lingers inside her. I wish she knew how much more fearful I am, but I need to be here for her first before myself. I owe it to her.

I turn on the television, and unsurprisingly it is already on the news channel. We watch steady, my empty stomach ready for what meal I did not eat.

No moon in sight, but rather a distant sunrise. For once, my stomach unsettlingly drops at what sight should be captured by an artist. They do not fabricate a live broadcast, Instead they play back what occurred just as we were leaving.

They bombed the solar panels built by Liam. It was their first target, and just meters out they bombed the waterfall. The familiar sounds force me to flinch, Aria grasps me tighter.

The surrounding areas were searched, and by their attentive quest, I should consider myself lucky to even be alive, though I wonder what my luck truly amounts to after having to witness such a tragedy. Especially when all I could now reflect on is whether or not Leander made it back to the bunker in time. I was not so unfortunate to be around for the third bomb, but I doubt it being any more than ten minutes post our departure. Again, I could feel Aria's grip tighten. That bomb exposed the camouflage that conceals the entry point to the bunker. And while I could assume what tragedy awaits, the news broadcast cut off what follows. Soon after the bomb, right before a group of armed Forcemen entered the place we once made a home out of. The place that roofed those I love. The place that will always remind me of how big of a coward I was to return upon the first bomb.

The room door closes, the snap bouncing off these thick walls. I look over, Liam's shadow casting through the shades as he walks off, failing to conceal his exit.

39

Aria finally fell asleep, her curiosity remains unanswered, still I believe, like me, she prepares for the worst. I watch her slow breaths, and despite her slumber, her eyes still beg for sleep. Perhaps it is a beg for mercy, she has yet to be granted a break from life.

Liam remains outside, and I fret he will meet his frozen demise before ever returning. He's always been the leader in our trio, now quintet. However, I can't help but notice how difficult creating a facade is becoming for him. He is losing what strength I ever so looked up to, and I plead he does not lose his greatest trait. It is part of what keeps me motivated.

I clothe myself in layers, before heading to search for him outside, except when I slowly open the door, he sits on the steps just feet away.

He watches the snow fall, thousands of flakes coloring the dark night with white. I hesitate in my approach, as I do not want to interrupt what little peace he's managed to find amidst the chaos. Gently, I take the spot beside him, offering the same embrace I do Aria. We all need a shoulder, and I'll never forgive myself if I dare neglect his cry for it.

Despite the silence between us, the snowfall sings throughout the darkness. It keeps it company, and so happens to offer it the same embrace. So much, that I convince myself that it is not as cold in our appreciation. The streets embrace the snow for the moment. I can tell their intimacy will be short lived, and the snow will be gone come sunrise.

"It hurt me seeing them raid," Liam finally says.

I look down. "Me too."

Again, I let the silence linger, only because I'm here to be his shoulder. I no longer care how I feel, I cry he doesn't break apart.

"It reminded me of my early days as a Forceman," he soon admits. "We were ordered to raid an underground clinic, and I watched so many innocent lives be taken."

I offer him my eye contact, and I soon regret the decision, the tears on his face quickly saddens me. I've only seen him cry after Cynthia's failed trial, and even then it felt like an expression of his that I should not be exposed to. It upsets me that I hate his vulnerability, but it is only because his tears are enough to trigger mine.

"It was the first time I met Nasir," he continues. "He was one of the few left in the clinic, and I went after him. He turned and looked at me, but I never thought to raise my gun. I only followed to make sure he got out okay."

The tone of his voice proves that he's long been holding this in. It is shaky, and it follows the flow of his tears. And evidently so, the pressure inflicted on my heart validates his reason.

"I didn't shoot a soul that day, and still Reign praised me for what he thought I did. So much that he made me a head forceman." He takes a deep breath before continuing. "I didn't know what felt worse. Having to accept the position in fear of my life, or people believing that I killed the final human in that clinic." He wipes a few tears, but the flow is so strong that he fails to clear his face. His glare fears my reaction, but I offer no judgment. Rather, I pity him for what I've put him through. I didn't expect he and Nasir to have such a history, and had I known so, I would have never raised my gun at him the night he attempted to leave us stranded. My heart only sinks at the thought that I painted a picture he never thought to sketch. "It is why Harrison allowed us to stay in the bunker." He continues, and soon my mind replays the dead stare Liam had on his face the day we had arrived. I had never seen him so ashamed, my curiosity on it died the moment he pushed away my second inquiry. "In all honesty, I've never shot anyone until the day we fled," he soon reveals. Those words being what forces me to break my stare.

Liam and I were always alike in ways I didn't consider. He never killed a being before that day, but still I fear I previously expected he had. However, what forces my face to drop is not our similarities. Liam first killed a man in my defense. Now he lives with that tragedy, and I pout at the thought that I believed shooting that man was much easier for him than it would have been me. I know his intentions in revealing so only followed my embrace. Still, I fear the day that this news stops haunting me will never come.

"I'm sorry," I finally say through tears that found their way out of captivity.

The outside light greeted us a good morning through the window shades. The sun hides behind the dull clouds—the day lit up, still not as bright as it could be. We've been on the road for quite a while. So long that I think I mangled to obtain a few minutes of rest against my will.

Prior to our departure from the motel, I thanked Jolene for all she has done. However, I did not seek the opportunity to assure her that I will be back. Not only did she seem content where she is, but she found peace at the motel. And even if that were far from the truth, I do not have the capabilities to make such a promise. Whether my return were to signify bringing her to the west or simply seeing her once more, I do not know what tomorrow holds. I long since assured myself that I am done making promises I can not keep, and in doing so, I don't have to risk another life for my unintentional benefit.

She was so kind in refilling our bag of nourishment, and while doing so she conversed with us. She spent an hour's worth telling stories, and I spent that same hour tuning out what might lead to a story about Steven. I do not have the strength to sit through his past memories, and I am ok with avoiding them for now.

The closer we get to the capitol, the deeper the pit in my stomach feels. The ride is silent, and the only symphony we are given is the car's engine. I am ashamed to even be given a distant glimpse of the regions we pass. The stress I've punctured into those people's entities lives on, and I fear they despise me for it.

Seeing these roads again brings back memories of the day I fled. Retracing these neglected roads feels like the closest I'll get to turning back time. I feel wary, and my eyes betray me as I falsely perceive a person from afar. It feels weirdly distinct from what life I made conventional, and despite not being seen, it still feels like people are watching me—not just through the wanted signs that decorate the far buildings.

We've been on an empty road for some time now. I recognize this avenue. It is not far from the mid region, and the gut wrenching sensation that fails to leave me alone proves that we are getting closer. The only time we spent parked since Jolene's goodbyes was at a gas station. Since then, we've been one with the roads, the sun watches our journey, and as it sets, the clouds still hide its hue. Once again, taking away the attention from the sun as it bid goodbye.

I almost begin to miss what portrait the sun would paint upon its departure, the set often casting a glow. That glow usually offers me another seat on mine and Aria's rooftop, and I do not recall the last time I was able to accept its kind gesture.

After a moment, Liam shares words with Nasir, his intention concerning. I, however, am too focused on the road to offer them any more worry. That is until a sudden glare pieces through the tint of the windows. The two colors switch out, allowing one to have just half a second center of attention, before the other takes the stage. Perhaps rival tones on a color chart, but often complimentary to each other beyond those tones that keep them separate. My stomach drops at the red and blue police lights that flicker behind us.

It is blinding, and I find myself blinking along with it in hopes of hallucination.

Maddox tries his best to compose Aria's panic, but fails, as her worry only bounces off the windows. Nasir prepares himself to speed our way to safety, but Liam hovers his hand over his who tightly grips the gear stick. He shakes his head slowly, implying he pulls over. "You'll only make this worse," Liam says, and I could nearly see his heart beating through his chest.

Nasir hesitates, but obliges—his shaking hands reflecting his control of the wheel. "Put your hoods on, and stay quiet," Liam urges the three of us as we quiver in the back seats.

I look down, my hood already suffocating my curls. As the cop approaches our vehicle, the only thing I am able to be grateful for are the tints on the window. Still, my mind convinces me that they are not enough to conceal us. Perhaps this is what the universe wanted: my demise to be at the hands of an officer who pulls us over, while his lights blind me.

"Good evening, officer," Nasir greets him with his window midway.

The officer shines his flashlight in his face. "What brings you near these roads?" he asks aggressively, ignoring Nasir's greeting.

Nasir looks around for an answer. "Just enjoying a drive," he explains, and it clearly is not enough to subside the officer.

He leans forward, his flashlight blaring through the crack in the window. Liam looks away, and the rest of us follow suit. The beat of my heart is strong enough to rattle the drum in my ear. I hold Aria's hand to offer her solace, still the shake only vibrates through my embrace. "We're okay," I whisper.

"May I have you put down your back window?" the officer requests.

It takes Nasir a few heart beats to answer. "I'm afraid not," he finally answers, and I bite my tongue at his risky response. The cops eyebrows furrow, confused at his lack of compliance. "Old car," Nasir finally chuckles, implying that the windows do not function.

The officer takes a slow step back. My eyes pierce at his hand placement as it hovers his radio, and I fear that he suspects who we are. Regardless, he doesn't seem like the type to make accusations before he's confident in his suspicion.

"I am going to have you all step out of the vehicle," he commands.

Nasir looks at the lot of us, his face washed in fear. With no response ready, he slowly grabs onto the door handle and steps out of the vehicle. The rest of us, however, are too shaken to get out in fear of what will occur upon stepping out of this vehicle.

"I asked for all of you to exit the vehicle," the officer repeats his demand, and we all share a look of defeat. And rather than make matters worse, we accept that same defeat, and slowly exit the car.

I keep my head down, eyes glued onto the pavement that seemingly has no end. I make every attempt to avoid letting our eyes meet each other, and as I get a glimpse of the others, they too elude from his stare.

I do not know what led me to think that my efforts were enough to direct this situation. The shake of Aria's hands only makes us appear more suspicious. Still, I do pay close attention to her fear, rather I offer my eyes to the officer's demeanor whose movements only add to my fret. His hands hover his belt, home to his array of gear—radio, gun, taser, and cuffs. Just one of each, and judging from his demeanor, he knows who we are. He knew the moment we hesitated to get out of the vehicle, and I am only waiting for him to express that, to do anything that might trigger a response from me.

Soon, he stands ahead of Aria, his ruffled brows only question her fear. He glares the flashlight at her face, blinding her stare. His reaction is telling of his knowledge. Aria, so famous amongst the coast she might as well be deemed the lady of Sudom.

He reaches for his radio, but I shout a plea as if he's reaching for his gun. "They're not on your side," I blurt, causing him to retract. Finally, I reveal my face and he's taken aback, his eyes wide. "They never were, and they never will be," I affirm. What vendetta lingered between the Police Unit and Forcemen only came to a halt upon our flee. Had we been civil, the silent rage amongst the two would have lived on, and still they'd be belittled by what force affects them just as they do us. They will never be in honest conjunction, and if he harms us now, he will see the end of their unity, because they will no longer serve purpose.

We stare at each other through a long moment of silence. Perhaps the shake of my breath is louder than the tension. His hands steer away from his radio, and I begin to find relief in his cooperation. However, his quick movements only draw him to his gun, and I am not quick enough to reach mine.

I blink, and the kiss between my lids is not quick enough to capture what suddenly occurs. The officer meets the ground, the gunshot echoing the empty streets.

I look over, and Maddox is standing feet firm, holding his gun out, aiming at where the officer was standing. Slowly, he lowers his weapon, looking at the rest of us. His soft eyes flicker, and I can faintly see a tear twinkle in the blaring lights.

Suddenly, his gun hits the ground, and his steady hands begin to lose control. "You're fine," I assure him, his eyes proving he needs to hear those words, but perhaps they are not enough, so I offer him a hug.

"Get in the car," I say. "We'll take care of it," I assure, and beyond his blank stare, he manages to embrace my plea, following his shaky feet to the car.

41

These hours feel prolonged. We've since been greeted by the sun's rise once more. We had a silent journey all through its slumber, not a word was exchanged between the lot of us. I slowly watched Maddox's demeanor throughout, hoping what lingers in his mind is not dictated by guilt. We were dead had he not come to our defense. Me beyond the rest; I was the one who shared glances with the barrel of the policeman's gun. I kissed the sight of death. Like Liam, Maddox came to my defense. I once more stand in between what will offer someone nightmares, but there is a distinction between the two who've come to my defense. Maddox has always been used to killing animals. We are just not able to feed off this one.

Finally, we reach the capitol. We drive slow, remaining hidden in the vehicle. I've always recognized that this coast never sleeps, but as I watch the crowds of people, it proves that it hasn't even rested since our flee. People carry signs, they chant, and flood the streets. A reflection of what I've seen before presents itself, but never have I been at the forefront of their efforts. I see my face, no mirror before me, rather the signs embrace my facial. They protest in my honor. In favor of my livelihood, and I wonder what had I done to deserve such reverence. I never expected my actions to be deemed forgivable, yet here I watch an array of strangers honor my name.

The people of the coast have labeled me a hero. They've deemed me the face of a new found revelation. Perhaps they've excused my actions as a necessary measure, but the weight balanced on my shoulders is speedily losing itself, fighting the urge to stay a float. My heart races, its pace bolting at the scene. And while my anxiety has let me down in the past, it doesn't fail to continue to occupy my thoughts with the possibility of being the first stem to fall off my family tree. Humor greets me as I am a hero with no cape. No suit, nor powers. Rather, one who carries a facade of courage behind his scars, all for the sake of assuring hope to those around him. Even more for the fear of living in a reality where I let them down. But maybe I've long since departed from what drowns my thoughts. The first stem to touch the ground doesn't have to carry all of the weight. It doesn't have to carry the transition into the trunk. And even if I took on that role prematurely, failure in resisting my status draws a conclusion to the sum of it all. If I give those in control what they want, I might find awe in what lies beyond our universe. Most of all, he who awaits me with his large blue eyes, no form of sadness lingering behind them. And his sweet grandpa whose welcome mirrors my introduction to his motel. Both their smiles don't mask the sadness underneath as happiness is all she now knows. Oh how true I wish for that to be, but who says it has to be made to believe. This is far beyond what I ever expected, and perhaps I am not ready to confront the idea that people actually favor me. I guess I am so used to being ashamed, that I would deem their opposition to me a chore.

"They love you," Nasir chuckles. I do not respond, nor do I even crack a smile. I solely do not know how to confide in such a gesture. Especially when any embrace should equally include the two much more courageous than me. I watch their reaction, and seemingly they are not fazed by their lack of acknowledgment, just a couple signs favor Liam and Aria. I could only assume that, like me, they do not want to carry the burden of being praised for what we've done. "How are we going to keep hiding now?" Nasir continues.

Maneuvering through these streets is much more difficult than what it was getting here. Some buildings lost the facade they once maintained. It was stripped from them, and I remember watching them be raided back at the bunker. People abandoned what they called home, because they had no choice after being invaded.

"Keep driving," I say, reflecting on the vacant building by The Globe. I pitied what horror was inflicted on those who once resided, there was never any shame in what was broadcasted. I never thought I'd see the day I would be embraced by those doors.

This alleyway is decorated in unattended clothes and furniture. I yearn for the people it once belonged to. Even more at the thought that it was stripped away from them in hopes of finding me. I appreciate their sacrifice, still I can not erase the thought that it was all against their will. This was one of the first locations to be suspected of where we were hiding. Perhaps the idea of hiding in plain sight would have been smart, but had the fleeing grounds been centered in the capitol, I would have met my demise the day they stripped this building.

Nasir drives into the alleyway as far as he can, before we're forced to park our car and trek the rest. The moment I step foot on the ground, I am relieved at being the only presence. Still, walking through the clutter, I can almost see the cries for help from those who once called this home. I wish shame were more common.

The chants echo through the thick winds. I never thought I'd hear so many people celebrate me. Never was a glimpse of our support ever broadcasted, and I can't help but ponder on how livid it must make

Mason. I was the one who was framed for Steven and his grandpa's death. I was the face of accusations, and I did not expect such an outcome. Even after Jolene assured that no one believed what story was fabricated, I continuously feared that a greater sum seethed for my death as much as Mason and his unit.

Nasir breaks open the side door effortlessly. The door had been previously damaged by the Forcemen. He holds his weapon up as a precautionary measure, and we follow suit, except I know that if there is any being left in this building, they offer no threat.

It is cold. So cold, that the fog of my breath leaves a trail of my presence as we trail up the stairs. This building is empty and the only sound is our echoing footsteps. Each echo rings a memory in my mind, memories from this very building long ago, memories that I have to brush aside in order to keep my focus.

We settle in the first vacant apartment on the final floor. It is an open concept unit, and it almost reminds me of the loft I once called home. The patio door was left wide open, and from the bite marks on the couch, I figure it must have been raided by squirrels.

I walk over to close the door—I despise the cold that lingers. However, as I do, I am drawn to the sight beneath me. The crowds have gotten larger, and so have the chants. No distance between us is enough to mute the voices of the people. I stand above, watching as the crowds honor my name, and Liam and Aria stand by my side. We listen to the chants. For once, the instincts that haunted me are proven wrong. The people of Sudom are on our side.

I shut the door tightly to gain some privacy, but the glass center of the door doesn't do us any favors. Noting my discouragement,

Maddox hands me a couple of t-shirts he's found in the closet. "We can cover it with this," he says, assuring I be cautious of the shattered edges.

"Now is probably a good time to reach out to Francis," I overhear Nasir suggest to Liam who sits on the soiled couch.

Maddox looks down at the scratched wooden floors, the distraught on his face hard to miss. "There's too many people," he loudly admits, and I see a pang of regret in his face—not the first time in this venture either. "If this doesn't go as planned," he continues. "Those people are going to suffer the consequences."

"What did you expect?" Nasir challenges his concerns. "We knew the risks that came with this."

I hate to say that I do not blame Nasir for his frustration. We knew from the moment Harrison proposed this venture that lives were at risk. So much the people Sudom, as the people who were planted as our supposed location. That intention fell flat, and while I find relief in knowing that innocent people across the globe are likely no longer at risk of being targeted, I can't help but wonder if the bunker's raid was a moral punishment. I have confidence in Harrison, and I do believe she would not have reached out to the West had she not been confident in her formulations. Had it not been successful, the Forcemen would have located the five of us the day we left the grounds. Our contact with the West is not what caused the raid, but perhaps the intention within just so happened to be the universe's ledger. If there were a time to hesitate, it is not now.

"Those people are on our side—" Maddox says.

"And if they weren't it wouldn't be any more of a burden," Nasir interrupts his concern, evidently frustrated. "But our goal was never to kill people."

"If Francis is not who he says he is, no matter who is hurt, it is going to create a chain reaction."

I watch the fear on Maddox's face, he doesn't blink an eye.

"Then you don't fight back," I say. The room suddenly quiet, and I can feel the disagreeing eyes piercing my way, but while I do want to accomplish what we initially came to do, I agree with Maddox that more people do not deserve to die for our sake. "If Francis is a foe and decides to shoot me," I explain. "I give you all permission to save yourself and run away."

My words arm tension, and I hope I have firm enough of a say to get them to agree with me. I owe them my life, and the final position I want to possibly be in is witnessing them get killed upon taking my last breath. I rather they run, because Maddox is right in this case. If one shot is taken, it calls for investigation. If shots are taken back, it calls for war. And the moment Forcemen get involved, they will shoot every being in sight until they get every last one of us.

"That's not happening," Aria counters, but I quickly plead she just agree with my request. I do not want to hurt them more than I have, and her disapproval will only make matters worse.

"You guys are expecting the worst," Nasir attempts to ease our concern. "If Harrison says we can trust Francis, then we take her word for it. There is no need to fret."

"We should only ever expect the worst when our lives are at risk," Aria shouts, her words bouncing off the walls.

There is a tense, silent ambiance that emerges in the room upon her aggression. I have actually seen Aria get this defensive, and it is always met with the same reaction. I do oppose her anger. Had I done so, I'd be a hypocrite, because in a world where the roles are reversed, I too am cautious and defensive over her safety.

"Then we meet at The Globe," Liam says, and we all offer him the same blank stare. I make an attempt to analyze his tone, I can not distinguish whether or not he is being genuine or trying to joke in lieu of the tension.

"You want us to walk into the lion's den?" Nasir asks, seemingly more frustrated with him than he was with Maddox. He offers Liam an intimidating stare, and I fear he wants to strangle him the moment he suggests The Globe.

Ideally, I'd step between the two, but I myself fail to wrap an understanding around such a suggestion. And while I will always be a confidant to Liam's intentions, I do not want to offer such leniency before his reasoning.

"Are you sure you were ever on our side?" Nasir asks, just inches away from Liam.

"I hate that you doubt me?" Liam pierces his lips, offering me a look of sorrow. I solely stare, my eyes questioning his intentions. I fear that he senses my hesitation, but no means offer me the strength to hide them. "Had you been more attentive, you would have noticed that many of those of high profile purposely choose to attend the cabaret in masquerade attire. Now, I don't expect a seductive mask to conceal our cover, but it will do the job around those intoxicated."

He slowly walks over to the window, his eyes scanning the crowds of people.

"And Brandon is correct. If Francis happens to be an enemy you do not retaliate." He continues, "Instead, you run."

I can sense the rage from Aria's side of the room, she makes no effort to hide how she feels, and again, I do not oppose her.

"But Brandon will not be speaking to Francis," he assures. "I will handle the risk,"

"Liam," I put a halt to his saving grace. "I don't want you to do that."

He turns to me, his eyes washed in betrayal. "I saw the way you reacted to my suggestion," he admits, his tone is soft enough for my ears only. "You doubt my trust, and that's okay. I will do it."

I take a step back, now insecure of my intention, never were they aimed to hurt him.

"If Francis is as smart as Harrison claims, then he will find a way to get into The Globe." He turns to Maddox and Nasir. "Since your faces are unknown to the coast, I kindly ask that you go shop for our clothing."

They slowly nod, their faces shocked by his courage, but I do not share that same surprise. I know Liam, and part of me even expected such an act to emerge. I hate that it was at the cost of feeling strain in my faith in him, because those intentions never resided in me. Rather, I needed to hear him out, as it will never truly reside in me. His interrogation is the only proof I needed, and if Liam is faithful in my acceptance of him taking another possible bullet for me, then he has learned nothing about me in our time together.

I do not have the strength to oppose him right this moment. I would rather not argue. But this is my mission, and I will be the one to greet Francis.

Hours linger, and the chants only grow throughout the day. We've made shelter out of what little these enclosed walls have to offer. The cries and echoes are beginning to wear me down—my hands quiver on their own, and I attempt to conceal the strain, but frustration and fatigue get the best of me. There was a time when our oath betrayed the people of Sudom. They despised us in uniform and feared us in action. Here lie those same people honoring our name. Their chants are not solely a ploy for justice, but a cry for help. They need us, and I am unsure what leaving them behind will look like. Perhaps I am feeding into the praise, thus accepting what cape they offer me in grace. I can't help but taunt myself; just hours ago I wanted to run away from such a commitment. Now, here I retract my thoughts. They deserve peace as much as those I love do.

While the others went to retrieve the night's attire, Liam set out to heat the rundown apartment. After some thought, he took a large pot and filled it with timber—once the spine to a love seat. Then he found coconut oil in the kitchen and added it to the pot to fuel the flames. He dropped a match in and the timber went ablaze, filling the room with a strong, pleasant aroma.

He, Aria, and I sit around the pot, embracing what heat it proffers. "Do you think we're doing the right thing?" I ask Liam.

"I don't think we have any other choice.," he admits, his eyes fixed on the flames, cautious of its blaze.

"We can't just let those people fight for our name and abandon them," I say.

"Do you suggest we board hundreds of millions of people onto a plane to the west," he responds, his tone rather distraught and I fear he is still hurt by my previous hesitation. There is never a scenario where Liam is wounded by what Nasir assumes, but if my beliefs begin to align with the assumption in question, he is evidently hurt. Perhaps it is one of the first times I feel his animosity towards me, and I must admit the strain it is forcing on me. Still, it is necessary, because with it, I know Liam is always to be trusted. I never doubted his honesty, and I hope he soon realizes that. But even with my faith in his hands, it is good to be proven right.

I walk over to the window, once more embracing the view. Each time I take a look, I can see the crowds grow in size. It is a shame that I can not join them—assure them that I am alive, and for the most part, safe. The chants flow through the buildings of the capital creating a venturi effect, and they soon retire their previous war cry. My name now takes no part of their shouts. "Mason's next!" they repeat, chills rushing down my spine, as the forcemen retaliate their cries with bullets.

I look over at Liam and Aria, they too make notice of the chants. They rise from the ground and join me, engaging in the punishment of seeing what occurs in the city below.

I offer Liam my stare, his eyes concerned over what I am thinking—my thoughts only proving that this time logic will not prevail over emotion, because for once my logic and emotions shake hands in unison.

"We honor what the people request," I say, offering Liam's sarcasm an answer.

My proposal is so perilous that neither responds. They solely watch the crowds, perhaps awaiting my evocation. However, I do not demand an echo to reassure my words. I thank Mason for one thing; he managed to do the hard part and get rid of one of the most vile beings to walk this earth. I admit, Reign will not be missed, and I want to extend my appreciation to Mason for his service. However, one still lingers, and no shame is enough to stop him from embracing his reflection in the mirror.

Like the people of Sudom cry in vain, Daniel Mason must be next.

More hours pass, enough for the sun to announce yet another daily slumber. The distant uproar continues, and Liam has added more than half the jar of coconut oil to the makeshift pit. Maddox and Nasir have yet to return. It has been a few hours since their departure, and Aria's concern has long since instilled my demeanor.

I sit still and stare at the photo of Francis—his eyes stare back. Liam has notified him of the designated location. No response, and while Liam assured me that we should not expect a reply, his silence makes me worry that we will be walking into the depth of danger with no purpose. I urge that not be our fate, I do not want to utilize this night as a scape to a final dance at The Globe. I never should have accepted the first dance. My celebration only mirrored the shames of life, and I do not believe anyone is ever worthy of dancing the night away, while others pray that same night's moon watches over their back in slumber and cry it's not their last. Tonight, I must dance with a motive.

"We should probably save the rest for later." Liam puts aside the coconut oil, as the pit comes to a close end.

Aria's demeanor makes a subtle shift to his words, her bones traumatized by the idea of cold. The windows lack proper sealant, and the outside air is bound to invade what little warmth we've managed to obtain.

Liam stutters at her reaction. "It's ok," he assures. "We'll find more."

He pours what is left of the oil into the dying flame, bringing it back to life for a while longer.

The tension between both Aria and Liam was never resolved. It still lingers, and I continue to be caught in the crossfire of their awkward stares and exchanges. I was never able to discuss their relationship post-Cynthia's wake. Still, I believe it is no longer my role to be a peace maker. I continue to fear that my attempt will burn bridges, and at this point in life I do not have the energy to give outside what I put towards the livelihood of those who resided in the bunker.

The creek of the front echoes into our corner, Liam and I quickly grab for our gun. Despite our instinctive reactions, Aria does not reach for hers, her guard down in solace. I watch her speed herself up off the floor. She seeks the awaited arrival of Maddox and Nasir, and I do not let go of my grip until I watch her wrap her arms around Maddox who holds large bags—Nasir closing the door behind him.

"Sorry we took so long," Nasir apologizes after noticing the wash of relief on our faces. "The crowds delayed us more than expected."

"Is it as bad as it looks," I ask from the window. The crowds only doubled in size since our arrival this morning.

"Worse," he blatantly admits, tossing me a gold mask. It's thick, and I don't anticipate a tragic fall enough to shatter it. I follow my fingers along the sequence, I would assume it would look best on a Greek gladiator by the Pegasus on its forefront. It is enough to cover all but my mouth, and I almost feel it would be an honor to display such a mask. Never have I seen such a piece.

"I think you'll like the dress I picked out for you," I overhear Maddox tell Aria, her arms yet to unwrap him.

I hope they can one day look back at these moments and appreciate that all that they've gone through has at least been endured together. Still, I hope when Aria reflects on her hardships, she does not forget about me. Again, I do not rue their relationship, however, I do not want to grow into a future where we drift apart. I do not anticipate it, however, I do not know a life where Aria does not hug me the way she does Maddox. I noticed the way he reacted to our intimacy back at the bunker. And if he had attempted to hide it, he would have never apologized for what he thought me and Aria once had. I do not strike him as someone who will learn to grow envious of the dynamic between her and I. However, his lack of a facade will only force her to create a facade of her own. One where she pretends to be okay in letting go of what she and I have. I understand that we no longer strive for anything romantic, but it will always be a challenge to ignore the way she looked at me while embracing Nova's kiss. Perhaps that is the same way I look at her now as she still rests her arms around Maddox's shoulders.

I look at myself in the mirror. This outfit is so snug, one would assume it was tailored to fit my body. The guys chose all black attire for me. Black pants to compliment my button up shirt of the same shade. And my shoes are so glossy, I can actually see my reflection. I do not find use of my belt, other than to complete the outfit. However, my satin vest makes for the perfect addition to conceal my gun inside its brim.

I offer myself a few more stares in the bathroom mirror, worried that my weapon might enter a room before I do. Perhaps my mind convinces me that it is noticeable, but I no longer choose to oppose what delusion my mind makes up. There is a chance of that concern being what saves my life.

"It's not noticeable," I hear with Aria's sudden approach.

I look back, and there she stands at the door. She wears a short red dress, her eyes matching the sparkle in the crimson diamond chains that embellish one end of the satin fabric to the other. Maddox was right about one thing: she would love the dress he picked out for her. However, I do not know if he expected me to love it on her so much more than he would.

She walks up to me, before closing the last button on my vest. "And the only reason I know it's there, is because you've hesitated for the last two minutes." She says, finally patting my chest right where the weapon resides. Her lace gloves cover her scar, and they only add to the exotic look of the outfit.

I fail to respond, because I know I will stutter from her beauty. Her ruby lips match the dress, and I fear I stare at them much longer than I should.

"You look beautiful," I finally manage to say.

She offers me a smile embracing my compliment, before grabbing my mask up off the sink and putting it on me. She ties it a bit tight, still I do not interrupt her favor. I am too immersed in a beauty I thought I could let go of.

"If it makes you feel any better," she stands behind me, and stares at me through the mirror. "I can't even tell it's you."

I look at myself once more, and while I do not agree with her, I still trust her. Perhaps I am so familiar with myself that I see right through this mask. And perhaps my fear is what steers what I choose to see, but at times like these, I will honor her word over mine.

"We're ready to go," Liam comes to say. He takes a step back, and I can not decipher whether or not he believes he interrupted a moment between Aria and I.

He wears his mask. It compliments the gold in mine and conceals his entire face. The sharp ends reflect a wolverine, and the sequenced patterns are so pristine that it's safe to assume they were hand carved by he who honors art above all.

I offer Aria a nod, embracing her nod in return. I offer Liam the same assurance, and the nod he returns promises much more than solely being ready. It assures our safety, and no mask is enough to shelter what embrace Liam continues to proffer.

The bass from inside vibrates the balls of my feet. My heart beats faster than the tempo. We managed to get past the crowds, I must admit that the collective stares raised my concern like no other. And for once, I feel as if no mask would have offered me kinder attention from those around. We give the essence of elites who have turned a cold shoulder to the cries of those outside, on their way to celebrate yet another day. I wouldn't have blamed them had one of the protestors attacked us, but our short trek here feels safer than what awaits us behind this familiar door. I know if my identity happened to be revealed on our way here, they would have only celebrated my life and shielded me from danger. I must also admit that the stares tempted me to remove my mask, but I suppressed that urge.

We stand at the back end of the cabaret, Maddox looks around in fear. He worries that some authorities followed us. I do not fret, however, I've lingered in this alley and I've experienced enough of that same fear, before realizing that they do not scan this area. We are more safe here than we will be upon entering these doors. However, before we do so, we must interlock our fingers with the hope that these doors find themselves open. We once had it easy. Luis was one message away. We've lost that privilege, and even if we were to reach out to him, we will only be putting his life in danger. Big brother is always watching.

"No one is coming," Maddox frets, and I long since noticed that he does not want to step behind those doors.

"People sneak out of these doors all the time," Aria assures. "We'll just have to wait."

Maddox steps away and kneels down, making every attempt to control the pattern of his breath. He fails to do so, the fog from his breath only rushing into the air. He is panicking, and I fear this is the worst time to do so, still I do not want to invalidate his emotions. What fear he is portraying, lives inside of me. My tranquil demeanor is a facade for the sake of everyone else but me.

I kneel beside Maddox and can nearly see his heart beating out of his chest. I swiftly demand his attention, my hand rested on his shoulder offering sympathy. "You're ok," I assure. "You're safe."

He offers me his stare, his eyes as red as Aria's lipstick. We are similar in many ways. Even his fear mirrors the challenges I try hard to conceal. Still, what differentiates our similarities is what lies behind the fret in his eyes. He is scared to hold hands with death, his stare is enough to speak what his lack of breath allows him to. I long since let go of that fear, and what permits me to pay it no mind is the motive to continue for those around me. They deserve to wake up another day, and I fear my demise wouldn't offer me the promise that they are okay. While scolding me, Leander did note that if I were to die, there is no escape to the west.

"Once we get behind those doors," I say. "You do not have to go any further."

Slowly, he nods through in hesitation. I do not intend on pressuring him beyond his limitations, still I will not accept he stay outside. If he can manage to settle in the long hall behind these doors, I will be able to resume tonight's goal with the peace of mind that he is not exposed to the night moon. The moon only offers surveillance, his power is far from enough to shield Maddox from any danger.

"You will be our watchman," I offer him priority, because I know his honest fear will later torture him into believing his lack of worth. I have been in a similar position, and I do not wish such inner-conflict on him.

He offers another nod, except this time he finds the strength to steady the pace of his breath.

The door crashes open before us and makes a raucous bouncing off the wall beside it. A couple passes through, and I take a sigh of relief. Their lips are interlocked, leaving no room to breathe in their moment of passion. They pay no mind to the people around them and I assume they'd be happier in a room above all. I still sigh the moment I am exposed to their intimacy, only because we've managed to get our way in.

Aria rushes for the door, the lack of stability in her stilettos nearly adding an extension to our wait. She peaks in the hall, confirming our clear entry before giving us clearance.

I turn to Maddox, he collects himself as he rises back to his feet. I offer him further assurance, before the lot of us honor Aria's lead and follow behind.

The music inside is extremely loud, and this long hall only acts like a headset. We all share one final look before entering what feels like a gladiator's dungeon, and I only hope that Francis is an honest man. I just hope he is there. I rather he not show up and his intentions be left up in the air over him being present and leading us to our demise.

"Be sure to find us if you sense anything suspicious," Aria says. She hugs Maddox, and as she attempts to release, I could see his hesitation to let her go.

Aria turns to me, "If he's out, we have to play the part," she says, settling herself beneath my arm and leading our entry.

My heart nearly skips a beat, and I've now found a second purpose for this mask—it works to hide the blush in my cheeks. I am relieved, as that blush will only break Maddox, and our act is no more than what she assured it be. We have a role to play, and I will not let my feelings deem us more suspicious than we already might seem.

The music welcomed our entry before we even had the chance to step foot on these floors. I do admit, I did not miss the retraction that comes with every step we take. And the adrenaline that once came with seeing the flood of people celebrating as if no one is watching no longer lingers. Rather, my heartbeat matches the rhythm of the beat spewing out of the speakers.

"Stay close by," Liam demands. "Find me if you see him," he insisted as we swiftly part ways.

Aria and I garner another collection of stares on our way to the bar, except I know much of those looks honor her. I do not remember a day Aria has looked as beautiful as she does tonight. And perhaps I grin at the idea that the people around us are led to believe that these two masked beings go together.

We reach the bar, and if those around could see my face, they'd see my dropped reaction from seeing Luis. It is our first time seeing him in months. I almost want to hug him upon our approach—Aria's demeanor proving she feels the same. I took some time to reflect on what would those who knew us personally think about our sudden rise to the media. I do not seek their pride in us, nor do I expect their celebration. Luis, however, has never had a judgmental bone in his body and I pondered on whether or not his position forces him to have a certain opinion on us, one that does not align with the roars echoed outside this building. Ultimately, I do not expect he sees us any differently than he did our last encounter.

I pull out a seat for Aria at the center of the bar, yet I hesitate to take mine. The last time I embraced this seat, we raised a toast in honor of Steven. It was our final night with him, and the strain the memory puts on my heart makes me want to drop everything and find an answer on what truly happened to him. However, that time will come, and when it does I will assure his true death is exposed for all of Sudom to see. In these past grieving months, I've tried hard not to spend much time reflecting on what torture he inflicted upon his death. That only supplies more fuel to the grief I already have hardship in accepting.

"What can I get you folks?" Luis draws to question when he reaches us.

Aria and I look at each other, the hesitation washed over our glare. Quickly, Luis notices our demeanor. "Would you like more time?" he asks, his tone proving that Aria was honest when she had said she could not notice us beyond the masks.

I slowly shake my head, assuring him that we in fact are ready to order drinks.

"We'll have two Miami vices," I say, offering no alteration to my voice. I came here with every intention of concealing what identity lies behind this mask, but I had no interest, nor any need, to hide from Luis.

I doubt he recognized my voice through the blaring chaos, but our order did more than suffice to reveal our identity. Had it not, he would have never initiated a double take.

His eyes are very telling, and perhaps they admit to his awareness. His eyes subtly twitch before he begins to prepare our request. His speed, too, is very telling. He pours slower than usual—his mind clearly occupied.

I steadily watch the shift in his demeanor and fear I presumed a happier approach. However, he does not attempt to expose us. I never expected him to.

The moment he finishes our drinks, he places the glasses ahead of us. And the moment I reach for the glass, he fails to let go, his subtle pull demanding my eye contact. When I do offer it to him, he grabs a napkin and places it under the glass.

"Who let you rascals in?" he smiles through his favorite line.

I sigh in relief, still I do not offer him much emotion like Aria does. His silent collection of thoughts spoke before he did, and I fear he fights to put on a smile for our sake. And I do not intend to invalidate how he feels. However, I do not find it conducive to tonight's goal if I ponder any longer.

"How have you been?" Aria asks.

I take a large sip out my glass, and the moment I do, a collection of previous need for distractions rushes through my mind. My relationship with the firewater could have turned a foul corner, had we had more time to mingle. This drink is strong, and I soon realize neither I nor Aria should be drinking.

"Good," he mouths, offering a stare of compassion before admitting the truth. "I've been worried."

"We're fine," she says.

"Alive," he smiles, his relief proving that I could let go of my guard. However, a nearby Forceman calls for his attention, evidently intoxicated. It breaks our interaction short—which is just as well. Again, it becomes clear to me big brother is always watching, and while I do not believe those opposing eyes to be suspicious of us right this moment, I fear a future where the veil is lifted and they punish Luis for an interaction longer than it should be. I am glad to now open my eyes to what could hurt those around me, and for that I take one final sip, and place cash beneath my drink, leading Aria and myself away from the bar. He might not understand the gesture, but what I do is for his sake. I do not intend on returning to this bar tonight, still I walk away with the urge that our lives once more cross paths. Hopefully then, I can offer you the explanation the chaos of tonight and fear for your safety failed in allowing me to. But for now, I am happy to honor you with a smile from knowing we are alive and well.

Our shoulders brush with those we pass along the way, and despite the abundance of people, I have memorized Francis's face enough to be able to distinguish him in any crowd. His features are rather unique, and ingrained in my mind's photo memory.

Aria and I accept the dance the song offers us, however, we lack the energy to embrace it for what it is. No amount of distraction is enough for us to turn a blind eye to what greatest fear of ours is held with our ignorance. And until we have an answer, I do not anticipate our minds running on anything other than turmoil. We've been forced to take multiple steps back on what progress I assumed our sanity was taking, and perhaps it is fair to admit that we are currently losing our battle against Mason. And I do not see enough of a victory to take away the pain the lingering thoughts have since left on us.

"I don't see him," Aria whispers in my ear.

"Me neither," I hurt to admit.

Suddenly, a repetitive shrieking sound echoes through the crowds, and it garners everyone's attention—enough to silence what cheers and conversation once banded together just a second ago. The blaring bass and music comes to an abrupt halt, the echoes failing to return. It is a public service announcement, and before the large screens above display the bunker, my heart has already reached the ground and I lack any strength to control the shake in my hands.

Aria is frozen in place, her arms still resting around me, and I can feel her racing heartbeat from just the palm of her hands. She doesn't let go, rather she holds me tighter, pulling me closer to the beat of her already fragile heart. I almost want to cover her eyes, as if she is a child who needs protection from a foul movie scene. However, this is the scene we long awaited, and I hate that even my own eyes betray my sanity and glue their attention to the screen.

Once again, Justin stars in tonight's broadcast, and my eyes twitch at his same old grin. They walk through the bunker, once convenient to us, and the reason Aria and I are able to still wake up another day. The one and only reason we are able to stand here. Together, like it has always been.

My mask starts to become humid from the tears that seep down my face, and I no longer try to conceal the drops that fall off my chin. They'll find a home on the ground beneath me, and I will allow these immoral floors the privilege of my tears. Because I give up. And I want to surrender all I fight for, because they won.

Familiar faces are dead, and they parade their bodies on television for all the coast to see. It is much more torturous for us than anyone else, still I hate that those virgin eyes of the coast, too, are punished with such dread. I hope they are strong enough to turn a blind eye, because I no longer have that power. It feels like I have lost control of myself, and he who invades uses all his might to punish me.

I am surprised by the silence that remains. I do not anticipate those who remain within these walls oppose what is revealed. It is there people who raided the bunker, and they now carry the blood of those innocent people in their hands, and I honor this silence as a recognition of their own actions. And if it weren't for this mask, I can assure they would have finished the job at hand.

I can physically feel my heart strain the moment Elandra appears on the screen. She is lifeless. She'll never spend another day with Amir. She lived for Amir, and despite the pain she lived with, she always put on a smile for him. And he was always blind to it, and that is all that mattered, because what facade she tried so heavily to maintain was in honor of him. And I only hope that she knew how much he adored her for it. The early mornings, the tense evenings, and the late nights. They only benefited his well being, and this is no way for a soul so selfless to leave this earth. I can nearly still hear her voice, her plea for my defense of her dearest son. Perhaps I failed her, and if Amir is to appear next on this screen, I might as well be at fault for his death.

Next to appear are rows of patients. They lie lifeless on their beds, and I hate to imagine their last moments being consumed by those they chose to run away from. They sought a life much greater than what the coast had to offer. Because had they never fled their cities, they would have met a demise much sooner than they did. Still, they did not expect such an outcome, and I can feel the self-blame begin to once again impose on me. Many of these familiar faces despised their peace I ever so distrusted, however, I never challenged their animosity, rather I offered them space. Despite that, I still knew most, if not all, and I could hear Maddox once telling me to not become attached to the patients. There always lies the chance that they do not make it through treatment, and will one day die. Thus, I would only train myself to grieve much more when that time comes. I am glad I took his advice. But now, to be exposed to those blood stained sheets forces me to feel more pain the what should be humanly possible.

The moment the camera pans towards a familiar hall, Aria and I share a gasp alike, and I feel her hands grip my shoulders far stronger than before. This hall led towards the room Cynthia called her own. Much time was spent in her coma where she dreamt about a life where we once again shared our happiness, as the family we are. I snuffle and can almost smell the jade vines.

The camera continues, and there lies her door wide open. I take note of the brief shot of the broken glass decorating the floors below. The camera enters the room, and I feel Aria's hands drop, before I can accept what reality is being held in our faces. I cough, my body begs for the air I am unable to acquire. Cynthia has been killed. The woman who I long accepted as a second mother, her life decisions honoring me as much as Aria's, because she saw me as one of her own. My body shakes, and still I can not grasp a breath of air, perhaps I wait to wake up from this nightmare before I am able to do so. She is dead, and here her demise is celebrated on screen. Cynthia is dead. My dearest Cynthia is dead. My lips mouth an apology, I hope her spirit accepts my cry.

Finally, I gather the strength to look away. Still, my blurred vision would have stepped in for my ransom had I not. And through that blur, I get a glimpse of Aria, who is frozen in time—the only movement her body shapes are the fallen tears she, too, surrenders to the immoral floor below.

"There is still more to go," Justin's voice pierces through the ring in my ears.

I grab for Aria, still she is put in position. Her body refuses to accept the reality, and I fear I do not have what it takes to save her from this pain, because I myself need a savior.

I turn around to Liam, whose eyes cry for our sanity, but I fear we will no longer live a life where our sanity is obtained. It has taken from us, and the living vendetta has a clear victor.

I give Aria another look, before my eyes beg Liam to offer her what I am unable to. He nods, and I embrace him with my hand on his shoulder, before my legs rush for the exit on their own. If I stay another moment in these walls, my tears will flood the building allowing those around me a pool to swim in. I do not want to give them that pleasure.

I brush through shoulders, my subtle collisions fail to consider that my identity can be noticed. And perhaps I urge it is, as I hope to speak to Cynthia once more, offering her the conversation I failed to attain in my final moments in the bunker. I embraced her smile for all it was worth, and I fear that it was not enough to heal the pain that haunts my subtle neglect. I do not see a future where I will stop hating myself for failing to give her a goodbye. A farewell, enough to make her aware of how much I adore her. She is gone, and I will no longer be able to assure my appreciation for her. I despise the universe for allowing me a story far more somber than anyone could ever wish for.

As I near the exit, I crash into a dull shoulder, the collision enough to put a halt to my escape. I turn, unsure if I intend to apologize. However, my heart drops once more the moment I see the man we intended to meet tonight. Francis' broad shoulders suit his leather jacket, and he still uses the same glasses from his photo.

"Excuse me," he politely apologizes. However, I fail to respond. Rather, I slowly nod, and his eyes prove that he notices my distress. His eyebrows flutter, but he doesn't question me. Instead, he wishes me a good night before walking away. I do not stop him, and I fear I will later regret not doing so. However, I need to find refuge outside of these walls.

I rush down the hall, and Maddox jumps in fear when he notices what unease I carry.

"What happened in there?" he asks, however I walk straight past him, slamming through the doors I hope to never meet again.

He follows me in concern, as I drop to my knees. My screams synchronize with the shouts of the coast, my fears are proved: the people of Sudom too have been forced into watching the souls and bodies of those I once resided with.

I take off my mask, and my cries finally echo down the alley. My chest finally finds a grip of the air. The deep breath I take hurts much more than what it did to lose it.

Maddox stands back and is hesitant to approach me. His eyes cry for me, still he doesn't inquire any further than he did the first time. Rather, he offers me space, assuring he keeps a close eye on me. He is providing me safety, except I do not know how to assure him that I am okay if my loud cries are what puts an end to my painful life.

Distant crowds rush for the front of the cabaret, and their roars only grow closer. They no longer fight in my sole honor; they rebel for those innocent lives taken in the bunker. They have had enough, and I only fear what will prevail from their retaliation. And the moment gunshots enter to raging shouts, my concern is once again, unfortunately, proven right.

Soon, Aria punches through the doors, her force sending Maddox off balance. She falls to the ground, and her knees scrape against the cool pavement, before she throws her mask against the building as her cries match my previous shrieks. I hate what pain is inflicted on her, and I make every attempt to cancel out the cries she lets out. It is the worst tune I've ever been exposed to, and never have I been able to sit through Aria's cries. They hurt me, and I hate how futile I become when around them.

Maddox's face questions our pain, and his hands only shake in search for an answer. He is unsure what to do, and the moment Liam and Nasir follow out the doors, I can see a subtle wash of relief on his face to see our unity resume. However, I do not know what awaits when he is exposed to what we just saw.

"Brandon," Maddox calls for my quick attention, but I ignore his cry. I do not intend to for I know he simply wants an explanation. However, my body can not do anything other than shout into the night's chaos, and beg for an explanation of my own.

Footsteps that were once distant a second ago begin near my vicinity, not a step around me taken to prove it's a familiar beat. I sense Liam's sudden guard, the grapple of his weapon echoes as the footsteps only get closer. Nasir's sudden reaction mimics his, and I do not have what strength is necessary to offer them any more attention.

A few seconds pass before I look up. Ahead of us stand a pair of teenagers. The two of them stop the moment they see our faces. I do not react to their fear. Rather, I force myself to breathe through the pain inflicted in my chest.

They hesitate to approach us, however, they initiate a few steps closer towards our humiliation. And despite Liam and Nasir's precautionary grip of their weapons, we still offer them a safe space, one of them kneeling down before Aria and wiping the flowing tears off her face.

I finally manage to focus on the two young ones, and perhaps the chill that rushes down my spine is a result of their dynamic reflecting an earlier Aria and I. I want to further cry at the thought that the coast, too, stripped away the innocence of these two children. They should be home, enclosed in the only walls that can keep them safe. However, they rebel in the streets, honoring our name. And for that, I will always admire their favor for what life I have left.

The girl embraces Aria with a hug against her will. Aria's initial confusion turns to a recognition of her desperate need for consolation. Both the children's eyes are relieved to see us alive, and they are left speechless at our sight.

"Fight back," the girl finally says, her eyes meeting every single one of us. "For us," she begs before removing her pink beanie.

Slowly, I nod, still I look down at her reveal. I soon realize I am the only one to offer her any form of response. Perhaps the rest do not want to extend a promise they can't keep. We are only five, and I myself can't even visualize our victory. Still, I offer them a nod, because had I been in their shoes, I would much rather they lie and offer me a peace of mind.

Quickly, they continue their trek, and I beg they make it home safe. I would hate to see more lives taken in my name.

As we rise up to our feet, Maddox urges us to put on our masks once more. Footsteps once again emerge from the distance, except this time they echo through the gap beneath the door leading into the cabaret.

We rush for what little identity we have left, and put on the mask—fighting through the humidity that lingers within them.

Finally, everyone's faces are concealed, and when I believe to have fastened the last strand on my mask, it falls to the ground, proving Aria's previous assistance to be more valuable than I had thought it was. When the door opens for a final time, Francis comes out, his demeanor expecting to find us. Perhaps his observations did not fail him. My eyes intend to meet his, except his are busy fearing the weapons Liam and Nasir hold in their grasp. His quick hesitation forces our guard down, and his body language only proves his honesty we ever so doubted.

"I come in peace," he assures, his hands raised in innocence.

Slowly, he walks out, and Liam raises his gun when he begins to walk towards me. His face drops, and I am unsure whether he expected such allegations against the people he intended to meet.

"It's okay," I assure Liam, pleading he lower his weapon.

There is honesty behind Francis's eyes, and I do not want to burn the bridge that will lead us to safety.

"Brandon," I introduce myself, extending my hand.

He looks down. Perhaps he is still startled by Liam's aggressive reaction. However, I do not blame Liam. We fed our minds with the idea that Francis would be the one to raise a weapon against us first.

He looks at all of us, before accepting my hand. "Francis," he says, proving that we have managed to prevail our night's intention.

I sit on the balcony, staring at the moon who I once exposed all my thoughts to. His light casts a glow on my expression, and it reveals the distress that continues to decorate my face. The cold is striking, complementing the heat of my rosy cheeks. I believe I am catching a fever. My head is rather hot, and the strain in my throat reflects far more than just my cries into the night. However, I neglect what unease arouses and try to not pay it any attention.

I reflect on the young kids in the alley. They asked us to fight back, yet here we lie with all the will to give up. It hurts when you've lost purpose, and feel stuck in a timeline where all you do will only come back to laugh in your face, and drink the tears you lack control of. Tonight, the afterlife welcomed two mothers and an utterly disturbing amount of innocent souls. My mind is too consumed to observe every body, but I can attest to those I didn't see. Leander kept part of his promise—my parents were nowhere to be seen. Neither were Harrison, Nova, and Amir. They continue to live, and despite my righteous pondering, I need to find what strength is left to live for them. To fight back, because I refuse our next encounter to be at their demise. Perhaps I am being rather ambitious, but I do not want to accept a future where I am grieving any more of my loved ones. The pain hurts like no other, and while I do not wish this on my greatest enemy, that does not detest my will to kill him. I do not see enough people loving him to grieve his demise, and if there so happens to be just one, they deserve all the pain that comes with it. No human should adore a mind like Mason, to love a mind like so is to love a mind alike, and I will forever despise that kind.

Slowly, the door creaks, garnering what little attention I have left. Liam walks over to my corner with no words. Rather, he sits beside me offering his silent condolences. It is a shoulder similar to what I gave him back at the motel, except the hurt I carry is far worse. I am glad he was able to accommodate Francis inside—my head space is too far out of touch to once more paint out all of my past mistakes to a new face.

"I'm sorry," he finally says, after a few chimes in the wind.

I respond with half a smile, hoping my attempt says more than what I am able to.

Soon I pierce through the silence that once again emerged. "Treatment was low." I painfully admit. "Many of them were going to die anyway." The expression on his face is evidently perplexed, overpowered by confusion more than anything else. I do not blame him, but I no longer want to allow my pain an extension, and perhaps these words are not in the slightest convincing to even myself. "I'm not saying that I don't care," I continue. "I care so much more than you could imagine, and I wish I were not alive to experience this pain. But you've seen first hand how reflecting on the past affects me. And if I by any chance fantasize about a life where I grow old, I need to detract from what's going to kill me first than any being on this earth can."

He doesn't judge me nor invalidate my feelings. Instead, he solely listens. I know it seems impossible when those words come out of my mouth, but there comes a point in life where I have to accept what disaster I am inflicted with and hope that there is more to life where I no longer have to endure the pain of what it costs to live in this lifetime. I intend to remain hopeful, but that does not offer any achievement, nor did it offer any in the past. Still, I won't let go of the hope for later happiness, because It will come with honoring what the people of Sudom desire. Cynthia's murder hurts much more than any past homicide has, and if I will continue to live for her, I will only be content with the blood of Mason on my hands. So thick that I can paint my palms red.

I get up, and embrace the city once more. The crowds have diminished, I find relief in those shouting for us finally finding sleep. Still, I know they will return come morning. It is a fight that seemingly has no end.

"We need to kill him," I tell Liam. I do not offer a sense of permission in my tone, because I am not asking for any. Perhaps this is the first demand I have no doubts in initiating, and I can assure that I will not in any moment oppose what I request. He is the true disease lingering on this earth, and if his intentions are not stopped, I fear what more damage he will cause. It is no longer just about what he will do to me, there is a coast full of Brandons and Arias, Liams and Stevens, and I do not want them to give up on what a life they should be free to embrace. "We will go to the West, and get the help we need to do so."

Liam doesn't challenge my request, I am certain he agrees with my plea. Still, unlike me, he knows what dangers come with such a desire. However, if I am going to at any moment be murdered off this earth, it will be at the attempt of taking Mason out first. And if I am going to accept the title they paint me out to be, I will walk with my head held up high.

I offer Aria my presence, accepting the remaining seat beside her. I do not intend to push Maddox away, but he is kind enough to allow us time alone when I sit. Aria no more tears to cry; she's used all her body had to offer. I never prepared myself for how to console Aria if her mother were to die. That is only because no amount of readiness would have been enough to even get myself through the pain. I hate to continue to prove how useless I am when she needs me the most, but at least I continue to show her that I am here. And that there will never be a time when I abandon her. Especially not now, and if there is ever a moment where we are on the opposite ends of the earth, I will talk to the moon every night and beg him to watch over her.

"I'm so sorry, Aria," I finally say, and I hold back the tears that want to follow. It is far a greater challenge than I can accept, but I need to remain strong for her.

She stares at the wall ahead of us, and I take her silence to mean she accepts my consolation.

"I spoke to her that morning and told her everything," she finally admits, her words controlling the beat of my heart. Perhaps this is the first time I could envy Aria for having something I do not, a final moment with Cynthia. "She made me promise to take care of you."

Soon, I find myself staring at the wall along with her, and almost memorize the wooden pattern throughout. Cynthia's final wish entailed her concern for my safety, now here I lie in somber because I failed to save her. And despite the ache in hearing her final wish, it is not new to my ears. Since we were children, she's insisted Aria keep an eye on me. We are only a year apart, but that was enough for her to be given the chore of being my shield. While we spent our life together, our upbringings were still different. I lived a lot of my time by the stern manners of my parents—they did all to protect me from the coast. That is not to say Aria was not secure, Cynthia guarded her with her life. However, there was a level of leniency that allowed her to be prepared for what evil the world has to offer. Cynthia knew my innocence was always a bit more pure, and because of that she begged Aria to be not just my guide, but she who protects me from what danger lingers. It is a huge task, and perhaps I've long since rebelled against it, and insisted I be her savior. I can be sure, however, that Aria's intentions always lie in my defense, despite her continuous acceptance in allowing me the lead. We need each other, and what circumstances we are living in only call for the greater need of our junction.

"I'm not going to let him win," I assure Aria, and I stare in her eyes when I do, because I want her to accept this as a promise instead of just another desire of mine.

She rests her head on my shoulder, and I reminisce on the safety my shoulder has always given her. Here, she's cried many times, laughed more, and vigorously pondered on what life offers.

Soon Francis hesitates, but still he slowly approaches us. Again, Liam took the time to explain the circumstances, and to our surprise, he understood what terror we've gone through. I say he didn't expect his help to be requested for the sake of anything other than a final plea. And had it been such an easy request, I guarantee Harrison would have sought his refuge a long time ago. Still, I do not expect someone to be so generous without expecting something in return. And with the locale of Harrison being unknown, I can not attest to what exchange was agreed upon. However, I know what I am able to offer, the blood of he I can assure the West too despises.

We smile the moment he offers his condolences. It is kind of him, and I do admit I feel bad that he's come at such a moment. It does not benefit him, and the last time someone put their life on the line in my honor, a bunker of innocent people was punished for their courage.

"We thought we should go over what tomorrow looks like," Nasir says as he joins our circle.

"Tonight," I assure him, and despite everyone's hesitation, they do not challenge me. And if I were to be honest, I would not have allowed them to. "If we sit here and wait any longer, we are not guaranteed a morning journey."

Liam slowly closes the door behind him and walks into another impulsive decision of mine. Except this time I do not begin it with such uncertainty.

"I can make that happen, so long as I can confirm the radar from the port," Francis assures. "Once we get to the west, we will get you all settled, and figure out the next step."

"War," I say, my tone offering the same certainty.

Francis is slightly taken aback. However, I begin to reflect on whether or not his reaction holds any relief towards my words. Perhaps my suggestion is what he was hoping was an awoken topic.

He looks down, adjusting his glasses. "It's been in talks out West," he assures, proving my observations right.

It was a matter of time the West would retaliate and it is evident that we just so happen to expedite their urge to take over. They lost once, and I can give Reign and Mason praise for one thing, the Forcemen are not only trained to hurt their own people, but to rise in triumph come a day Sudom has to fight. I do not suggest ease, rather I offer what we can.

"We will do all we can to help you conquer Sudom," I assure. "But we have to agree that no innocent lives are to be punished."

Again, he looks down, except this time he smiles. It's enough to upset me, and while I try to not make notice of my frustration, Liam sees right through my facade.

"We know every Forcemen Base," Liam breaks the tension. "There is no need to retaliate against the cities."

"There has never been a war without hurting those who have no part in it," he explains, his tone rather careful to not upset us.

"Well that's because one has to first choose who they harm," Liam challenges.

"And what do we call the Forcemen who have your mindset?" He draws questions. "Hypocrisy should never be at the forefront of a war."

I look around, rather embarrassed by his confrontation. This feeling stems from the realization that he is far from wrong. If I remain stern on the idea that every Forceman is bad, then what makes us any good?

"Then we focus on the goal," I say. "I want Mason dead more than any person walking this coast, and if anyone gets in our way, then they will face the repercussions of it."

Finally, he offers me his genuine stare. Perhaps he's convinced. Still, he is a stranger to me, and I do not know him well enough to perceive his thoughts. Likewise, he does not know me outside of what we allowed him to be aware of. However, if I want us to relate on one thing, it's our hate for the man in charge of continuing the legacy of the most vicious being to walk this earth.

"I agree," he assures. "But it's a conversation with the West, not just me."

I look at Liam once more, because despite my abrupt lead, I must honor his consent before all. It is the only way I will resume what I sow. Our eyes quickly meet, because he already looks my way. He nods, as he was expecting me to seek his approval, and I am not upset by it.

We prepare ourselves to undergo our lives' greatest journey. What challenge I once thought was making it to the feeling grounds, has just been belittled by this venture. I do not know what lies on the post-war grounds of the West. Our ignorance to their new culture falls in the hands of those who detained it from us. Still, I trust what they offer above the crisis of Sudom. And perhaps it's the desperation that controls my perspective, but my options are on the ground that soaked up my tears.

I have a goal, and if I want to reunite with my parents once more, it can only be succeeded with the help of those who hold greater power than what I solely do. I can not draw a conclusion on whether or not the West will hold up a good fight, but had they not thought so, Francis would have long since opposed my suggestion to annihilate Mason. I am ready for what is to come. At least this time, Steven will not be the only guardian angel to watch over me.

For once, the night is rather quiet, and I do not put the latest news past the silence that lingers. They retaliate for hours to come, and what remains are bullet cases that decorate the floor, and the damage done to our people sits heavy. They assured their retaliation was not only heard, but imprinted on the capital. Buildings affected by their rage, and a lot full of cars bound to be impounded. And as a result, the people honor my name. I can not help but grin as we drive by. It only soothes all of what I spent the last months perceiving what they thought of me. We ride down these roads, the same roads that are marked in their rage. It is time I return their favor, and honor them for what hero they make me out to be.

Our journey has a destination of an abandoned airport once home to desired travels. Francis was able to utilize his radar to assure where to appropriately land, and to our benefit it so happens to be just a few cities up north. It makes our trek less of a burden, still the drive makes me ponder on what journey we've once taken to the bunker. And near those grounds are my parents. I wish I didn't sound so oblivious to the circumstances, if I were to plea we go look for them. However, I do understand that if that were to happen, we'd drive into the guns that wait to point at us. This ride is not a goodbye to Sudom. Rather, it's my promise to use what courage I ever so carry on my back, and fight for a better future. Perhaps we all have different perspectives on what this so-called future looks like, but I can assure that mine reunites with my parents, and because of that urge, this is no one-way trip.

Aria rests her head on the window, leaving her silhouette in the fog. Still, she doesn't sleep, and I fear all of the distress has officially taken that privilege away from her. I look at her fragile hands, she wears her mother's ring. I failed to even notice that she brought it with her the day we left the bunker. It is now officially the only thing she has left of her. And aside from the memories I can assure she will store forever, I do not see there ever coming a time where she takes off Cynthia's ring. It is something that will die with her, and I do not blame her newfound attachment to the jewel. The ring is to her what Steven's shirt is to me. The only physical thing we have to remember someone we still love, despite their infinite absence. We wear it when times are tough, and it works to ease what anxieties lie in our minds. I currently wear Steven's shirt with honor, the same way she flaunts the emerald piece.

I can not remember the last time me and her were genuinely happy, and I do not see it in the near future. When I reminisce on our early days as children, I could never look back and predict that those two innocent beings would be a product of the tragedies of the coast. Still, we have to learn to wear that with the same honor because it managed to shape us into the brave souls we are today. And had I now believed that I am the coward I once convinced myself I was, I would have been walking the grounds of the afterlife a long time ago.

The road to the airport does not offer much light outside of the car's beam and the moon's kiss. Still, we've managed to accept what path awaits our trek. The entry to the airport offers the same chills as the day of my initiation. It is the feeling awakened by following the unknown.

Francis spent much of our drive properly introducing himself. Our first encounter was rather alarming, and while our intention was never to mingle, it makes trusting him a much easier task. He works for the western government. His role revolves around being a second-in-command to the military's general. He doesn't have a family, so dedicating his life to the West was far easier of a decision had it been if he had a wife and children. Like Harrison made note of, he was a pilot in his early days, and with what remained in the west he was able to use his talents to lead the aerial branch of the military. He was shocked to see that Reign was able to get as far as he did. He was even more shocked to find out that Mason was the one to end him. He remembers them as the close friends they once were, and could not accept the idea that a betrayal so big was displayed to the eyes of Sudom. I do not blame his neglect towards the news, I still have trouble accepting it myself. Not because I do not agree with his death, rather because I'd expect it to be at the hands of someone other than Mason. And had I not seen the broadcast of his death, I would deem anyone who makes such claims a liar.

Francis gets out of the vehicle to open the gate who stands between us and the runway. The gate is rusty, and nearly stuck in place forcing him to use more strength had it been new. Or even used in the years that remained untouched. The airport is almost upsetting to the eye—the building is decorated in moss and the ivy wraps around it like chains to an inmate.

As the gate opens, the shriek of the wheels resonates into the ghost town that surrounds it. The echoes mimic the foregoing cries of the coast. Those shouts are rather marked in my brain. I can still hear them, and I can already see them visiting me in my rare sleep.

Nasir drives the vehicle into the open gates, following Francis who treks to the plane ahead. It is rather small, still enough to fit us and then some. It is evidently a military aircraft, the moon reflects off its silver exterior, and the side of the plane marks A-07 Bella. I don't draw it to question, but I am sure to make a mental note of it.

The moment we reach the aircraft, Francis opens the access door. Our car comes to a halt, the sun slowly begins to wish us a good morning, still we beat its sunrise. I exit the vehicle, offering grace for how far it has got us. Now our lives soon lie in the hands of the West, and I can not detest that I am relieved. The air is crisp and I approach the plane, placing my hand on its rib—the cold from its steel surface forces me to flinch.

Aria slowly approaches me, her reflection on the wing joining mine. Once more, she uses my shoulder as a head rest and I accept her embrace. Her eyes spell fear, and I do not blame her hesitation. We've made this land conventional, and to blindly dissociate from it offers a newfound strain of worry. I obtain that same concern, however, my facade for her sake offers a much greater fight than the butterflies that flutter in my stomach.

"Are you okay with this?" I whisper to her as an honest question, as I do not intend my motives to be a dictator.

"We have no other choice," she admits. "We can't let them win."

Our eyes meet through the reflection, hers begging for sleep. Behind the cry for sleep is a plea for peace. Still, I know what fury she has. If I were to be granted any wishes, the first would be her sanity. I know in doing so, my own life would become much easier. We are two minds alike, and the only competition we will ever be in is who will get the greater revenge against the coast who stripped so much away from us.

The plane's engine echoes down the runway, and we are quickly taken aback. It roars like a lion. It is courageous, and with every passing second, it accepts the orange from the sun's new early rise.

"Abandon the vehicle," Francis demands, claiming it no longer fits with us. Soon after, he assures us that we can all board the aircraft.

We hesitate as we are all visibly intimidated by the look of the plane—all except Liam who takes the lead. He looks back upon his board, extending me the same nod of assurance as before. He evidently knows when to offer such confidence, and I appreciate his vows. Had he not been as attentive as he is, I do not think I would be able to remain sane. Every courageous facade has an influencer behind it. I soon step in realizing that I am to Aria what Liam is to me. And if I do not make such a move, she will remain put until the moment I do so. And to my expectations, she follows, and the rest behind her.

"No assigned seats," Francis assures, as he adjusts the pilot's chair. "But I could use the eyes of a copilot."

Nasir operates the door beneath us, terminating what access to the outside we have left. His demeanor highlights his ease, and he offers Francis his assistance. I find relief in his offer, the bulk of controls that already surround us are overstimulating to my eyes.

Aria accepts one of the two seats that lie towards the front of the plane, my instincts tell me to take the seat beside her, but Maddox soon approaches the space before me, thus winning her innermost presence. I try not to make my frustration noticeable, his sudden interference was innocent, and I can't let the attachment between Aria and I get in between the reality of their relationship.

Towards the back of the plane, three seats remain. Liam smiles, embracing my awkward stance, before offering me one of the empty seats. Again, he is one to notice everything, and I appreciate him for saving me from this one sided interaction. Still, I ponder from embarrassment as I sit beside him.

The plane rumbles, and the shake vibrates through my body. Luckily, it helps keep me awake. Francis makes it clear he is doing safety checks prior to lift off, and instead of just making a tune from the sound of the engine, I watch the sun rise from what little access I have to a view of the front window. It cast's an orange line on the left side of my cheek, and I embrace its kiss.

"There is going to come a time when you look back and wish you hadn't spent so much time in awe of her," Liam says, mindful of his tone.

I look down, embarrassed. Not because he's noticed my attachment, but because he is right. But to suggest I not be so astounded by anything Aria does, is to propose I fall out of awe with my first love.

It is hard to admit that I still see much more of this life losing myself in her eyes. I've memorized them for their brown pattern, a touch of sun makes them mirror the gold of honey.

"I can't fall out of love, Liam," I admit. "It's my greatest weakness."

"Your only weakness is that you believe you have any. Save yourself from another heartbreak."

I look over, the sun highlights Aria's brunette strands. They flow below her shoulders, and despite her eyes facing away from me, I still manage to lose myself in a stare. Soon I study the floor, ashamed to know what my second wish would be.

Francis assures that we all have fastened our safety harnesses before revealing that we are ready to continue our journey.

The aircraft shakes some more as the wheel moves forward, approaching the sun ahead. I almost do not consider that this is my first time on an airplane, and the fret is far more intense had the circumstances been different.

I try to meet eyes with Maddox and Aria, but fail. I look over at Liam. He once more nods to assure me that it is okay. Perhaps he noticed that the shake in my hands is not a reflection of the turbulence, rather my panic within.

I smile with the intention to convince him that I am at ease. However, I can attest that that attempt will always fall flat when it comes to Liam. Perhaps my facade is just made of glass, but his eyes could pierce through a brick wall if deemed necessary. When I offer my makeshift grin, his body retracts the belt of the seat sending him far across the plane. My seat jolts, my head crashing with the steel above me. A sudden strike puts a halt to what journey we sought. My eyes shut against their will, coming to a sudden close to the collective cries that bounce off these wounded steel walls.

The flames that wrap the right wing only begin to grow. I can barely notice the light that it offers. I lack the consciousness to realize my surroundings, yet I manage to acknowledge the sunlight snapping through the dark smoke that fights its way into the middle aisle, the moment the emergency door is forced open.

My shirt is soaked. Steven's shirt, rather. I truly do hope he's the guardian angel that's been watching me throughout the time I've dedicated to honoring his name. The white stripes slowly begin to blend with the red and I quickly notice that the clothes drench is far because of my slow streaming tears. Or because of the excessive sweat that seeps through my pores from the fire that taunts us. I'm hurt. I am beyond hurt, I am close to locking arms with those who I grieve every single day. The collision forced the overhead cargo to fall on top of me, and whatever was dismantled from it pierced into my torso. It has forced me deeper into the corner, my confinement only taking away any final moment I can have with those around me. I do not know how long I've been stuck here, but each minute gets more painful, and each second feels closer to death than I've ever felt in my entire existence. I'm scared. It is okay to admit that I am scared because I am knocking on heaven's door. No ego presents itself when your vulnerability takes control of the wheel. I look around and try to see through the haze for any help that lies beyond.

"Help" I quietly whimper, because my body can not handle the pain that ignites from the stroke of my voice.

I attempt a second time, a third, and a fourth before my voice finally finds the strength to bounce off the walls.

No one answers. Not Maddox, nor Nasir. Not Liam, nor Aria. Not even Francis. And as my lifespan only shortens, I realize that I was meant to be the last person alive because the evil that continues to interrupt my life would only want me to grieve their death before I do my own. All I can see is clutter, and their lack of response is the answer to the question I do not want to confront right now. My parents will not only grieve the death of their only son, but those who offered him and them a safe space.

Deciding to confront the way my story ends, I attempt to push the pressure away from my torso and see their faces one last time. The pain spreads into my body so abruptly that my yell manages to emerge. A cry for help, yet it holds no purpose. It's only left to be a cry of regret, because had I never become a Forceman, I'd never be in this position. I'd likely be on the rooftop with Aria laughing at the idea of our next night out to The Globe, not readying myself to confront her demise that I ever so clearly expedited at the cost of my emotions. The only shame to uphold would be never meeting Liam, nor Steven, but that shame would be nonexistent as opposed to the one I hold now. They all share a new home, waiting for my arrival and I don't want to face the reality that I forced us to be roommates. I continue to push. If seeing those lifeless in this plane one last time means enduring the worst pain of my life, I only deserve it.

My sharp cries grow with each attempt and I come to the senses that despite my fear of giving up, it's the only realistic way to live my final moments of despair. It's over. They won. The people of Sudom will continue to shout my name, and I won't be here to respond. I was stupid enough to wear the cape they offered me, and now it slowly burns to ashes beside me.

I close my eyes, ignoring the pain. Ignoring the past and the idea of a future. Rather, I welcome the present, but find my lost childlike imagination to offer a sense of happiness. The same child who deemed gunshots as fireworks, is the only child capable of glamorizing this very moment. Soon enough, he allows me to pretend the sound of flames is a campfire. It's extra hot, but it's a cold day and it is needed to keep us warm. The us in question being among the many who I love. We smile and laugh—there is no surrounding worry to affect us. I even see Liam smile for the first time in a very long time, too long for anyone to accept. His eyes no longer carry the distress of before. He too felt the pressure of being a hero but it stemmed from within. I still wondered why our allies never praised him more than me. And while it's too late, I hope he knows he is my hero and I will always see him as more of an asset to the coast than I'd ever been.

"Brandon," he shouts, his tone emerging from the distance.

I smile and wave, before realizing that the younger version of myself might have guided me to our new home light years above the horizon.

"Brandon," he shouts a second time, except he seems to be closer despite the distance between us.

When his third announcement comes, I am welcomed by a shake of my body. And when I open my eyes I see the figure of Liam above me.

He's alive. Wounds bound to scar and decorate his face, but he's alive. And while still at the doorstep of death, I'm not yet dead.

A tear slowly streams down my face, as I hate to have to watch him worry over me. Or even see me in this very position, offering a coat of crimson paint to the navy fabric that makes up a large some of the plane's interior. I only wish my tears were enough to put out the fire that surrounds us.

He turns around and shouts. "He's here," he says, and my sight regains a bit of vision the moment Aria strolls towards us—an injured Maddox, Francis, and Nasir behind her. She holds her left arm in agony ,but like me, a stream of tears flows the moment our eyes lock. She kneels beside me and begs I pull through. I ignore her plea, however, as I don't want to make her another promise I can't keep. Rather, I look her in the eyes, "I don't want to die," I cry. She grabs my hand tighter than before, slowly shaking her head. And the pain in her eyes indicate that she, too, is far from making a promise bound to be broken.

Liam garners the rest of the guys to help release me, each of them pushing through their pain to help ease mine. They force the weight of the overhead up, separating the attached dull metal rod away from my torso. The pain is beyond sustainable that I fail to consider how hard I squeeze Aria's comforting hand through my shrieks. The rod had made itself at home, and its eviction came with the price of a pool of blood that follows. Liam unbuckles my seatbelt and drags me out from under the overhead, before the guys drop it back down to its sunken state.

"We need to apply pressure," Liam urges. He takes off his shirt and pushes on to my exposed wound with the cloth's body, then utilizes the long sleeves to fasten it around my waist. He ignores the pain in my voice, and I can tell this hurts him just as much as it does me.

"We have to get out of here," Nasir assures.

"He's hurt—" Aria cries.

"I can do it," I interrupt. "I'll be ok."

Liam looks terrified and asks if I'm sure. "I'm sure," I say. The terror in his face offers the option to stay here as long as we need. But rather than see it for what it offers, I accept it as the need to do what's best for everyone else and not just for me. I'd suggest they leave me, to which I can continue the journey my imagination was directing me towards, but I know what would be expected. They'd die beside me, before abandoning me.

I give Aria an assuring nod, before Liam and Maddox assist with my arise. There is a limp in my right foot, and I realize the pain in my torso overshadowed my injured ankle.

With the help of Liam, I limp my way towards the emergency exit. Each step becomes hotter, yet it's the only road to safety. "Cover your mouths," Liam suggests as the smoke seeks to raid our lungs. He helps me off the plane before lending a hand to the rest. And in the dawn of light, I notice that we are not alone. A twitch of some blue and red beams decide to join the illumination similar to our road stop. No clear picture is yet to be painted through the thick smoke, but we all know what awaits. However, we all choose to confront our fate whether it is close to its end.

A sense of chill embraces my skin with each step we steer away from the burning plane. The cold air offers a promising feeling, and I hate that it's going to be short lived.

After getting past the accumulation of smoke, Forcemen and police unify, awaiting us yards out. They all aim their weapons, however, no one is yet to shoot. Tons of them are lined up, this moment feeling no other than orchestrated. They are finally confronted with the most wanted beings on the coast. And had it not been for the one discrepancy, their search would have been prolonged with no sign of a finish line. They look at us and feel betrayed. They are angry. They want us dead, but still not one of them takes this vulnerable opportunity to murder us.

"On the ground, now!" one of them yells, shooting a bullet into the sunrise.

We oblige to their demands, my arm still around Liam who moves for the both of us. We slowly lay face down on the ground, before the large sum charge at us. And in this moment, I realize our differences. They all continue to wear that uniform and be sheep to he who makes their demands. I retaliated. We are not the same, and we never were.

Liam urges them to be careful with me as a knee is shoved onto my spine, forcing my torso to kiss the pavement while they put handcuffs on me.

"He's injured," he yells, before a kick to the chin forces him silent.

I look at an already cuffed Aria who is handled as someone who imposes a sinful threat, yet it is clear as day she couldn't be any more vulnerable than now.

To my surprise, we are alive. However, as we are chained and forced on to our feet, I begin to think if our escape from death was the blessing I painted it out to be, because the moment I am thrown into the van, a punch strikes my jaw, reviving the ringing in my ear, all colors drifting away into oblivion.

50

The clinging sounds of chains are dull, yet they compliment the beat of my heart. It is slow, but present, and the moment I rise from my slumber, it elevates. This room is dark and cold, but my evident lack of clothing only intensifies the discomfort. I've been stripped, and when I attempt my first movement, I realize that long chains coordinate with the undergarments I've been stranded in. They don't allow me much movement and I am unaware of how long I've been in here. My final memory of consciousness ties to the pain in my jaw that stripped any form of it away from me. My body is in pain, far more than I can endure. And every movement introduces a new ache. Slowly I begin to panic. I pull on to the chains, yet my body remains in the structure that no force can alter. I shout, my cries stale, yet enough to be alert. I continue to pull, quickly realizing that being chained is far a larger fear of mine that no other can contend. Not even the torture that I already sense awaits me.

My shouting continues with no sense of time, not even an ounce of the sun's schedule. My exhaustion is the only indicator of time. I squint, and if it wasn't clear enough, I reside alone. No Maddox or Liam or Francis. This time for certain. And I'm haunted by the thought of them wearing the same chains as I. But what taunts my sanity is the thought of my beloved Aria. She is not made for this. I wish I can sustain any pain her frail bones endure. However, no amount of pity can reflect all that I've put her through.

A pool of white light enlightens the room, my eyes disturbed by the sudden wave. This room is built of cinderblock, and I could thank the door across the room for the little air that flows through its slits. I wasn't aware of the camera above me that documents my despair. I am sure that whoever watches on the opposite end is enjoying my reality, because no eyes with feelings behind them would be a willing bystander of my truth. I can assume who watches, but allowing my rage to shine through will only fuel their pleasure.

Beside the door is a television, and a quick observation makes the outdated piece of technology seem familiar. It is the television that resided in the bunker. The television that little Amir helped fix beside Levi. My heart pangs at the sheer reminder of the young boy—hoping he is safe alongside my dearest parents and Nova. Perhaps allowing Leander to retrieve them on his own was my greatest surrender. I can't imagine the pain that certainty of them, too, being in the plane with us would have caused.

"Don't cry," I think to myself. I will not feed their pleasure. I've fed them enough, and I will no longer parent those who anticipate my tears. They are undeserving, and ignorant to the sin of greed.

Time passes before the door opens, offering more light to the already lit room. Alone walks Mason, I assume the metal jewelry that glues me in position draws no fret. Except he fails to realize that I was never someone to fret over. My intentions were always genuine. At no honorable moment did I ever desire to be a reflection of the monster he painted me out to be. The painting he continues to boost with lack of morals.

He walks in, and the smirk on his face proves that he's won. He is the new dictator, and perhaps I was the perfect excuse for his execution. I'll never get a thank you, and even if I did, I'd never accept it. And while it will always remain an internal thought, I will never deny that he's played an extremely smart game of chess.

"Where are they?" I question the moment the door behind him closes.

He giggles, and it is clear that he needs no explanation towards my concern.

"No greeting?" His smirk extends, making it harder to conceal the rage inside of me. "Or a thank you so kindly for the stitches."

I look down, only to realize my wound was stitched. To my surprise, it was done properly, but I know they only concealed my wound because they weren't the ones to draw it on me. My body has become a canvas for sacrifices—written in scars, painted in burns, and shaded in bruises with no room to dry. I am willing to accept the challenge that awaits, he who wove my canvas definitely considered my tough exterior, yet no certainty determines how much crimson dye I can take. A roulette of brushes are taking their turns on me, and one is bound to puncture.

"Please," I beg. "Where are they?"

My vulnerable plea is as far from pleasure as I will allow. He wants a pool of tears, I can see it behind his eyes that fail the emotion to produce some of their own. Still, I won't offer them to him, but please tell me where the people closest to me are.

"I have no intention to lie, Brandon." His posture is firm. "The boys are chained in their own room. What will happen? I can not say, because I am not sure. You guys have caused chaos. Far more than necessary." He continues. And as he continues to write all of my wrongs in my face, his words become distant despite his near vicinity. Not because I am neglecting to study his reveals, rather because the person who means the most to me is not a boy. And my eyes begin to boggle at the thought of her. Don't cry, I repeat internally.

"The girl," I cut off his speech with no remorse. "Where is Aria?"

I care for nothing he has to say. And if his next words deflect from what I just asked him, no miracle can keep these chains to the walls. Perhaps that likelihood is best, I can fulfill what desire I continue to have towards him. More than once Aria has been granted a reprieve from the shadows of death, and if he concluded her life's story, I rather she had died on the plane. If there is anything he should dictate, I promise her livelihood is far from the list.

"She is fine," he smiles. "Well taken care of, actually."

I offer eye contact, challenging his words, and for some odd reason I believe what he blurts. It is the tone of his voice. Still my eyes pierce through his, contending for a broader answer.

He steps back, surprised by my fierce. "I told you I have no intention to lie, Brandon."

He turns to the television before turning it on, the walls so stale that they fail to echo the sound of its rise. And the static settles before my heart drops at the sight of Aria reflected on the small screen. He was being honest; she is being taken care of. She sits on a couch, and I squint trying to make out her location. And soon they widen, my racing heart rattling the chains. Aria smiles at the camera, and I want to believe that it is the facade learned by her mother.

"Thank you for being willing to tell your story," says the interviewer. "I know it must be hard to be forced into such disgusting actions by someone you once loved."

I look down, accepting defeat once again as my tears skip my cheek and flow on to my exposed chest. And when I looked up, I notice Aria had looked down at the same time as me. Still, we are so alike, except I would have never accepted to paint a lie about her, in lieu of my life. No amount of desperation can draw me to do so. I stare at the screen hoping her eyes meet mine. My surroundings blur the moment they do, and I watch in hopes that she looks at the camera with the expectation that I am somehow watching on the other end. This brief moment mirrors a sheer reflection of our immediate arrival in the bunker. Our opposed stances drew uproar within those walls, our livelihood grasped in the palms of the few who acted to reassure our paced safety. However, distinct to our reminiscent fear—Aria is the sole prey. One who lies alone in a space filled with predators. Perhaps she is aware of what danger she has accepted to take part in. The love in my mind pleads to be her companion, but the ache in my heart cries in disperse. In betrayal, far from my list of expectations. And along the stinging center of my skull, I offer the tears to cry, not because I am inches away from one of life's harshest traumas, but because my soul denies the energy to draw beliefs to the words I will soon be harshly exposed to. Her lifelong plea insisted my receptivity, never did I foresee the moment she would be the virus inflicting my beloved trust she ever so spoke highly of.

As her shadow slowly blends into the background, my heart churns at our traumatic dissociation. Except this departure cuts deeper than the battle wounds imprinted on my skin. Each one signifying the journey I confronted largely in her honor. Because my love lies farther than the miles we inflicted in our escape. Than the stars we ever so gazed in admiration and desire for hope. Peace, if you will. However, my greatest flaw continues to laugh in my face, abandoning me in a pool of hopeless embarrassment. And despite our constant encounters, this will not be the final meeting with my flaw. Because ironically, my heart only has room for love. And no matter how many punctures it sustains, its exterior acts its purpose and masks any shame that lingers through the fragile windows, concealed to the extent where the moon fails to behave like a brother. Each guarded scar signifying a disguised lesson learned. And while it will carry minimal value, Aria is the purpose for a newfound wound, fighting to heal the moment I am forced to allow her wings to fly. Because I am in no place to dictate her flawed decisions. Nor was there any evident benefit to her past settlements. Perhaps we are equivalent in that sense, but I now refuse to forcefully act in that nature, because every placed puzzle piece raises questions towards our previous intimacy. I was blinded by her illusion, but It's only a matter of time before I attempt to rebel in honor of my newfound lenses, designed to put myself first. Even if that mirrors a crippled, cherished bond.

I spent much time in the garden, my eyes keen to see what sprouted from the ground. Never did I anticipate a Judas tree among us.

Mason smiles at my demise, and the moment I taste the salt of my tear, I spit in his face. I don't have the energy to embrace his embarrassment, but if he finds pleasure in my torture, I'll assure I am the initiator.

AKNOWLEDGEMENTS

I cannot believe that I finished yet another novel. I do admit, writing this was lowkey a lot more work! No, I did not escape to another country to finish my book, however, I do admit that I envy the old me who enjoyed the island!

I need to first and foremost take time to appreciate my supporters. From the friends to family to strangers who all gave my first novel a chance, I appreciate you seeing a debut author and picking up his book! It means so much more to me than you could ever believe.

My mother, Glenda. You spend every day trying to break me out of my shell and seek every moment to tell any passing person about my book. I always been shy, but you are the voice and confidence I need to keep going.

My best friend, Dari. You motivate me every day to keep going. From walking into bookstores with me to help me get my book on their shelves, to agreeing to, and hyping up any crazy idea I have next for my career. I genuinely appreciate you and can't wait to include you in every next acknowledgment in many books to come. You will be the first to assure that I keep releasing.

Another greatest friend of mine, Hillary. I swear you markets my book so much more than me and always do it with the biggest smile on your face. Continuously suggesting we do videos and photos. You are always one of the first to congratulate my craft and are so happy to share my craft with everyone you know. A huge shoutout to your mom!

My dearest friend, and definitely my arc reader, Liz. I garner such great feedback from you. You read every single thing I send you. You literally respond to every single chapter in all caps on how great of a writer I am and let me be the first to say that I cannot wait to be one of your biggest fans and readers. I hope you know that your craft is just as good.

My aunt, Elizabeth. You still listen to my weekly updates about my book and motivate me to keep going! The week is never fulfilled until I tell you all about what I've written, as well as what is next.

My character artist, Johnathan. Talent comes in many ways, and yours so happens to be in the art you create with anything from a pencil to a brush. I continue to be amazed by your craft. The moment my characters were designed, I saw exactly what I imagined in my head the moment I wrote Modus.

Chantel, I cannot wait till the day we finally are able to work together. The day I released Modus, you've been an honest supporter. I loved visiting your class, and your students are so well articulated and talented. It made me so proud to be a writer the moment I discussed my novel with them. I hope to see the day we discuss Judas, and I hope it answers all the questions you were all curious about.

My cousin Genesis, I love receiving the weekly videos with a new idea on my book. From designs, to manufactures, you always think about how I can better my craft. You are one of the first pair of eyes to see my book cover art, and I admire the genuine advice and motivation.

My nephew, Isaac. I do what I do for you! Everything I aspire to be is in honor of making you proud. We have our newest edition to the family, Isabella. This book will always mean so much, as you were born when I was in the early stages of writing it. I cannot wait till you are both old enough to read my novels, and I hope you notice the ways I always include my greatest admirations into my writing.

I'd like to thank more people. Delia, for answering all my medical questions that I definitely need for my stories. My aunt, Gretchen, for being the first person to ever purchase my novel and telling everyone how proud you are of your nephew. My brothers, Brayan and Braulio, for always supporting anything I do. My father, Braulio, for always being proud of his son. My grandma, Celeste, who tells every person on the phone to Dominican Republic about her grandson's novel.

Lastly, I want to offer another moment to thank every single person who read Modus and became a fan and supporter of my craft. I did not expect for my book to be loved by so many, and I genuinely appreciate every single person who's supported me from the start of my release. The social media comments, the discussions, the reviews--you all remind me why I love and am so lucky to have a writing career.

Thank you,

Brandon Castillo.

ABOUT THE AUTHOR

BRANDON CASTILLO is a Rhode Island native who holds a Bachelor of Arts. His love for creativity sparked at a young age and he soon began writing pieces of his own, including his first novel, Modus.

@Realbrandoncastillo

@Castillopressbooks

@3BrandonC

www.Brandoncastillobooks.com

JUDAS PLAYLIST

www.ingramcontent.com/pod-product-compliance
Lightning Source LLC
Chambersburg PA
CBHW010517100726
47903CB00009B/2783